TENGU CHILD
Stories by Kikuo Itaya

Translated by John Gardner & Nobuko Tsukui

Southern Illinois University Press
Carbondale and Edwardsville

Library of Congress Cataloging in Publication Data

Itaya, Kikuo, 1898–
  Tengu child.

  Short stories.
  Translation of: Tengu dōji.
  I. Title
PL830.T35T413   1983   895.6'35   82-5876
ISBN 0-8093-1081-3   AACR2

        83 84 85 86 87 5 4 3 2 1

CONTENTS

PREFACE

Kikuo Itaya was born on November 23, 1898, in Kanazawa City in Ishikawa Prefecture, on the western coast of Japan. When he was still a child, his family moved to Tokyo, where his father, Hazan Itaya, built a kiln and began his career in the art of ceramics. (In time Hazan Itaya would come to be known as the most important ceramist of modern Japan. He died in 1963.) In 1912, the year of Emperor Meiji's death, Kikuo Itaya entered Kaisei Gakuen, then called Tokyo Kaisei Chūgakkō, one of Tokyo's most prestigious private schools for boys. Mr. Itaya was, by his own account, a "lazy" student, not interested in school subjects; his math grade, he recalls, was the lowest in his class. But he was intensely interested in literature, art, and music and became an avid reader of the novels and short stories of such classic Japanese writers as Natsume Sōseki, Shimazaki Tōson, Shiga Naoya, Akutagawa Ryūnosuke, as well as works in translation by Henryk Sienkiewicz (especially his *Quo Vadis, Domine*), D. Sergeievich Merezhkovskii, Maeterlinck, and Ibsen. Sometime around his third year at Kaisei he was strongly drawn to Buddhism and read Buddhist theology—"without real understanding," he says, as he was then very young.

In his fifth and final year at Kaisei, while most of his classmates were busy preparing for entrance examinations for universities, Mr. Itaya devoted himself, at his father's strong urging, to ceramics. In 1918, the year after his graduation from Kaisei, he submitted several of his vases at the national contest. To his father's great satisfaction, not only were all of the young Itaya's pieces accepted, but one of them won a prize. Yet in the end Kikuo Itaya decided not to follow his father's path and entered Waseda University to study Japanese literature. He gives several reasons for his decision—his rebellion against his father, who had become much too famous; his reluctance always to be viewed as the master ceramist's son; his realization that his father's pursuit of classical aesthetic perfection and his own search for a plainer, simpler kind of beauty were completely at odds; and his conviction that, where ceramics were concerned, he would rather appreciate than create.

At the university, Itaya contracted a severe case of pulmonary tuberculosis and spent a year of solitary life of recuperation on the seashore of Tateyama in Chiba Prefecture. The period was for him an important turning point of his spiritual life. "During my illness," says Mr. Itaya, "I did not think much about death, perhaps because I had a stronger attachment to life than a healthy person would; but my interest in the lives of religious recluses deepened. I gave much thought to how one ought to live, and in the end I came to a conclusion that I should live a life of detachment or transcendence. That is, I decided that while living in the actual world of good and evil, I should live one step above the usual, in the region where I could judge or evaluate good and evil objectively, in a state of mind which allowed me to float over and around the world of good and evil like an airplane flying low but not so low as to get lost."

In 1923, recovered from his illness, Mr. Itaya graduated from Waseda University and began to teach Japanese at Kaisei Gakuen. He continued teaching there until March, 1977, when he retired. Though Mr. Itaya's main concern, throughout his 54 years of teaching, was the intellectual and spiritual welfare of his students, he never forgot his early devotion to the arts. The carefully polished and repolished stories in *Tengu Child*—the only fiction he has ever permitted to be published—are the proof; and recently he has admitted that he did not leave ceramics without a backward glance. Asked about his long life as a teacher, he remarked, "I am glad that I have been able to give my advice in one form or another to bright students; but if I could live my life again, I would not become a teacher. I would like to choose a profession in which I bear the sole responsibility for anything good or bad. If I could be sure of my health for a long life, I should pursue the family vocation of ceramics. Although I hesitate to speak of myself, I think I have an excellent sense of form and color, so that I would be suited for ceramics."

Tengu Child is a result of, among other things, the author's lifelong dedication to Buddhist thought and his love for classic Japanese literature. Mr. Itaya's interest in Buddhist ideas and principles forms both the emotion and the symbolism of his fiction. At one point, in fact, around 1925, he lived alone in a wintry mountain cottage practicing ascetic disciplines, as does his central character in "Two Priests." He has, as all his stories show, a Buddhist's fondness for reality's underside as well as for its grandeur. In an article on Itaya and his work, published in the nationally important Tokyo newspaper *Mainichi*, we are told, "In the area of his tree-surrounded house there were many abandoned cats and dogs. He could not leave them to die, so he took them in. . . . Worms, frogs, he's on the side of anything and everything that is weak." Like a proper Buddhist of the old tradition, he cannot kill roaches. Another newspaper, *Sankei*, quotes Itaya as saying, "I keep roaches," then adding with a laugh, "Of course I keep them loose. Nothing has stronger maternal love than a roach."

It may also be partly from his fascination with Buddhism that Mr. Itaya gets his interest in the supernatural, reflected in such stories as "The Fox Who Became a Wife"—a story of shape-shifting— and "The Message"—a tale involving the return of a ghost. Though his handling of religious and spiritualist ideas is always aesthetically restrained and seemingly noncommittal, sometimes even delicately comic (consider his treatment of chanting flies in "A Telescope"), his concern with the extraordinary is serious, even scholarly. He was for a time a member of Nihon Shinrei Kagaku Kyōkai—the Japanese Association of Science and Spiritualism. Not surprisingly, he was much admired among his students for his ghost stories.

In his "Postscript" to the original Japanese edition of the stories collected here, he writes at length of his debt to classical Japanese literature—a debt often visible in the *Tengu Child* stories, for instance in his explicit use of the *Tale of Genji* in such stories as "The Mystery of a Mountain Villa" and "The Camellia Mansion." He speaks of an increasing preference, as he grew older, for legendary literature of the kind to be found in the *Konjaku Monogatari*, a collection of ancient tales and legends, and ultimately for the simplest, most unadorned of ancient literature, found in the *Kokon Chomonshū*. That sublime simplicity is everywhere visible in these stories.

Mr. Itaya is a widower—his wife died in 1978—and has one son.

April 1982 John Gardner
Nokuko Tsukui

MEDITATIONAL FICTION
An Introduction to the Stories of Kikuo Itaya
By John Gardner

Most Japanese fiction known in the West, like most Western fiction from Homer to the present, is fundamentally "storytelling." From the *Tale of Genji* to the novels of Mishima and Kawabata, Japanese fiction ordinarily gives us, as does the Western fiction most of us know best, a causally related chain of events with a "beginning, middle, and end," as Aristotle would say; it "actualizes the potential which exists in character and situation." At its best such fiction claims to show us, more clearly than life ordinarily does, how and why things happen: shows us how a chain of events takes shape, the motives and values of the characters involved, the effects of physical inertia when characters seek to impose their will on the world—in short, it helps us to understand reality-as-process. As we read such fiction, we experience suspense mainly for two reasons. The first accounts only in superficial terms for why we read on. We feel we are getting somewhere; that is, we feel relatively confident (so long as we sense no deconstructive impulse, as in the fiction of Samuel Beckett) that we can trust the traditional contract, the author's age-old promise that he will follow the event-chain to its natural end, throwing in no irrelevant accidents of the kind so common in actual life—a telephone call at just the wrong moment, Napoleon's cavalry sinking through the ice and losing a battle that should have been won— those flukes that so often make real life and history seem just "one damned thing after another." The second main reason we experience suspense in fiction of this kind—the deeper, more philosophical reason—is that as we proceed through the story we feel we understand exactly what conflicting forces are at work, so that in watching events unfold, anticipating and worrying over the characters' choices, we grasp the moral significance of the progressive value-conflict. In short, fiction of the kind approved by Aristotle tends toward argument, teleology: As in logic or mathematics, the conclusion matters more than the process, so long as the process appears sound.

These familiar principles are not very helpful to a reader of the fiction of a Buddhist writer like Kikuo Itaya—as they are not finally very helpful to a reader of the Anglo-Saxon *Beowulf*. Like the *Beowulf*-poet, and like certain other Western medieval writers, Itaya tends to use storytelling as a facade: the deeper impulse of the fiction is what I shall call meditational—though it must be added at once that Buddhists and Christians do not meditate in the same ways or on the same things. As the only relatively well-known example of Western meditational fiction, *Beowulf* may be worth pausing over, though even *Beowulf* will in the end prove helpful only as a contrast.

Though we enjoy the *Beowulf* first for its plot (not strictly an Aristotelian plot, since the end is not causally related to the middle), the manuscript seems finally to have been designed as an object for religious meditation. The poem is a veritable thicket of Christian-Platonic verbal and imagistic symbolism: the meadhall Heorot recalls the Biblical "hart," identified in the Psalm, as here, with the religious, thirsting heart, but also emblematic of "the World"; meadhall feasting is identified with "the feast of life" and looks forward to the heavenly banquet; the poem's three monsters symbolize perversions of the Platonic tripartite soul; and so on. And recent scholarship has shown that, subtly hidden in the poem, awaiting discovery by the patiently diligent, there is mathematical symbolism as well—for example, in the line-count ratios between key words, we find instances of such mystically significant figures as the Pythagorean "Golden Section." No one hearing the poem read aloud could possibly catch all of the poem's symbolism, but a monk reading and rereading *Beowulf* in his cell might hope to catch much of it. Like the Bible and the poetry of Virgil, as these were understood in the Middle Ages, the literal narrative teases the mind toward higher things.

As we muse on the stories of Kikuo Itaya, lured in by the graceful surface—the apparently coherent but sometimes puzzling line of action—we gradually realize that here, too, nearly everything is symbolic. Yet neither the medieval symbolic method nor the more modern symbolic method to be found in such works as James Joyce's *Dubliners* and *Ulysses* can take us far—except by contrast—toward appreciation of the technique of a writer like Itaya. To get at the difference, let us look more closely at Western symbolic methods.

In Western fiction, symbolism is the writer's means of suggesting relationship between the particular and the general, the temporal and the eternal. The connection can be established in a variety of ways. One kind of symbolism connects the story of the moment with some abiding, culturally loaded myth. Beowulf, Melville's Bartleby, and Faulkner's Joe Christmas—literary "Christ figures"—are more or less lifelike human beings presented in such a way (by puns and action parallels, mainly) that as we read their stories we are reminded of the Christ story. Having noticed the parallels, we have an "angle" on the story; a perspective, or, better, a lever and a place to stand. A similar mythic method shapes Joyce's *Ulysses*, where a story set in modern Dublin parallels the story in Homer's *Odyssey*.

Another kind of symbolism encourages us to connect characters, settings, and events with abstract ideas or institutions, as when Edmund Spenser's Red-Cross Knight comes to represent the idea of holiness, and Lady Una, the One True Church. The "story" becomes an abstract argument cunningly translated, as if by one of Swift's projectors, into things physical.

Still another kind of symbolism, the kind derived from our observation of recurring psychological mechanisms, connects the individual's problems with archetypal or universally human hopes, needs, and fears. Thus one woman's fear of mice and mouse holes may connect with universal human anxieties about sex and death. Needless to say, this kind of symbolism (or any other kind) can appear in combination with other symbolic forms in a given literary work and is most likely to be effective if its relationship to the literal is not overbearing. Generally speaking, though one can point to exceptions, when an element in fiction seems present only for its symbolic import, the fiction is likely to seem to us thin, intellectual, frigid, even preachy.

All three forms of symbolism I've mentioned share a common assumption. We in the West habitually divide the world in Plato's way, between the abstract and concrete, ideal and actual. The Platonic form "Chair" is not the cracked and battered, man-made chair I sit in as I write this, though my chair may feebly imply the shadowy "real thing," the ideal chair in the mind of God. Judaic tradition, which to some extent influenced Greco-Roman thought and powerfully contributed to our own way of thinking, tends to make the split between actual and ideal irrevocable. The God of the Old Testament almost never works through men who, like the Jesus of the New Testament, are perfect embodiments (incarnations) of the divine nature; on the contrary, in the Old Testament, God works his will through visibly flawed mortals: Jacob the sneak and liar, Abraham the bargainer and sometime coward, Joseph the egotistical young braggart, Moses the stammerer.

The sort of dualism which produces Western symbolism is foreign to the Eastern way of thinking. For a Buddhist, every being and every event embodies, whether or not we're aware of it, the universe. Present time is not different from eternity but, like the tip of an iceberg, the segment of eternity visible from here where we are. To know and feel this oneness of things—or perhaps we should say, to *be* this oneness—is "enlightenment." What vibrates in the universe vibrates in each of us, the "unique principle" that is everywhere always. A man can resist, even dislike the signs of his oneness with everything, or he may be wholly or partly blind to it, but he cannot escape it. In Eastern symbolism the distinction between vehicle and tenor—the thing said and the thing meant, or the temporal instance and the eternal principle—is illusory. To see only the temporal instance (*this* character in *this* story or life-situation) is to be unenlightened. Whereas for the medieval Christian mind "this" world is false but carries intimations of the "other" eternal and true world, so that what we must achieve is *contemptus mundi*, a mild scorn for actuality and a love for the reality behind the mask, for the Buddhist mind this world is, properly understood, a small and precious piece of the whole. The purpose of Buddhist meditation, in whatever form, is to melt away the walls, the "egoist illusion"—dissolve the barrier that splits subject from object—and thus help to bring about enlightenment.

Eastern thought agrees, from India to China to Japan (insofar as traditional Eastern thought survives in those regions) that all the intellectual knowledge in the world cannot, in itself, bring about enlightenment. (Compare the German idealists' distinction, derived by

Schopenhauer from Eastern texts, between "knowledge" and "understanding.") Enlightenment is a simultaneously physical and spiritual experience, perhaps analogous to what Ezra Pound saw as the experience of a true poetic moment, the sense of sudden release from time and space. Whereas Western symbolism tells us *X is like Y*, Eastern symbolism tells us, in effect, *X is this end of Y*. Such ideas are not completely foreign to Western consciousness (we are, after all, one human race, trapped in one universal vulnerability and need). The focal character in the medieval English poem *Piers Plowman*, a character who comes to represent Everyman, is finally revealed to be not just *like* Christ but absolutely Christ himself. And we may recall that Plato, in contrast to disciples like Plotinus, shrewdly avoided admitting any gap between imminence and transcendence. Still, argument from a notion of oneness is not the usual way of Western symbolism. The "epiphany" in a James Joyce story is more intellectual than ontological, more a matter of discovered knowledge than an experience of pure *being*. The symbolism in a story by Kikuo Itaya may look, superficially, like our kind of symbolism—he makes use of all the symbolic methods I've mentioned—but it is no more the same thing than wings are to, respectively, a butterfly and a bird. The two are products of distinct evolutionary lines.

Since we are not Buddhists, one might ask, why should we read the stories of Itaya, a writer not widely read even in his native Japan? The easy and immediate answer is that they're beautiful. (Why should we look at ancient Celtic art, or Chartres Cathedral, or the great temples of Kyoto?) But that answer, though right in the end, does not quite make clear or give due weight to the point involved. Whatever subtle irony there may be in Keats' claim that beauty is truth and truth beauty, it may well be that beauty is indeed a door to enlightenment, or wholeness. One may or may not wish to accept the Eastern idea that all is one, but surely it is true, or at least worth considering as possibly true, that the individual's search for harmony with the universe (including the universe as represented by one's choleric neighbor or that neighbor's vicious dog) is a program at least as likely to prosper as is the egoistic struggle for dominance. Not all Eastern thought is splendid. The late Chairman Mao has the Guiness world record for genocide, and the cheapness of life in India, except for bovines, is notorious. Nonetheless, the West has no corner on the virtue market. The twin shrines of the West, technology and banking—increasingly powerful forces in Japan, as Itaya is well aware—split us off from our fellow human beings, perhaps from life itself. Buddhism at its noblest, perhaps most clearly expressed in the humble Shinto temple and the ascetic's hut, makes that tendency seem a sad and futile, perhaps ultimately comic, madness. Kikuo Itaya's stories violate many of our normal expectations as readers of fiction; yet if we let them have their way these fictional meditations can prove as persuasive and liberating, it seems to me, as the idealism of childhood.

I began these musings by talking about suspense as we experience it in fiction of the West. We are now in a position to consider the Eastern alternative, not that this alternative is common even in modern Japan, where the Aristotelian method of Mishima and Kawabata, to mention only the two modern Japanese writers best known in the West, has come to be standard.

Perhaps for us the chief strangeness of Eastern meditational fiction is its disorienting (or maybe re-Orienting) attitude toward suspense. Reading this fiction, we soon discover that we cannot count on the writer to follow out normal Aristotelian process: he may at any moment send his plot in some unexpected, seemingly irrational direction, tricking the reader in much the way a Zen master may betray his disciple, for the disciple's good. The writer-reader contract still obtains: the writer can be trusted; but the terms of fidelity have changed. Thus it frequently happens in an Itaya story that the central conflict we're intently watching turns suddenly to a harmony (as in "The Robber and the Flute," discussed below). Characters and actions we felt safe in judging as "bad" or "good" emerge in a surprising new light. Suspense in Western fiction has a moral and, as I've suggested, argumentative or "educational" dimension. It delights and instructs. Understanding the central conflict, knowing what value the main character pursues (love, wealth, justice, etc.) and what values he may have to sacrifice to attain that primary value, the reader anticipates and worries over the character's choices. If the character chooses nobly, we affirm the choice and feel something like the pleasure we would feel if we ourselves, or some friend, had made the choice; if he chooses badly, we feel vicarious embarrassment or shame. We experience the story's affirmation as, in effect, a learning event. Familiar as we are with this kind of fiction, we may find it disconcerting to discover at some point in a meditational fiction that the choices we've stewed over are aspects of a false dilemma. What kind of suspense can meditational fiction generate, then? What—besides elegant language and that delicacy of metaphor that seems the special province of the Orient—keeps the reader turning the pages?

Itaya stories stir the reader to suspense of two kinds. First, we feel the plot suspense familiar in Western fiction, a form of suspense that, in these stories, may at any moment—like some kindly, impish Oriental spirit—laugh and vanish, abandoning us to the holy grove where it has lured us. The plot suspense may be a trick (it is not always), but as we see in stories like "The Pilgrimage of the Curse" or "The Fox Who Became a Wife," it could not be more effective, while it lasts, if it were the author's deepest concern. In the beginning, at least, "The Pilgrimage of the Curse" has all the elements to make a highly suspenseful story in the West. The premise of the action is the old Japanese belief that if one pounds nails into a shrine's sacred tree at a certain time of night, uttering a curse as one does so, the curse will take effect—unless one is seen performing the ritual, in which case one must kill the witness, lest the curse fail or, worse, return on one's own head. Itaya makes of every element of this belief a wonderfully suspenseful dramatic situation. First we are led to sympathize with one of the two witnesses to the nailing ritual, young Shinta, as he flees for his life; then we are led to sympathize just as strongly with the woman driven by her husband's infidelity to invoking the curse, a woman whom Shinta finds attractive, however ambivalently so, a willful woman but also a gentle one, in that she spares young Shinta; and then we learn that (further complicating matters) the faithless husband against whom the curse has been invoked was the second witness who escaped, young Shinta's best friend. Whether the curse fails, lands on Shinta's friend, or returns to the invoker, the result will be tragic. What will happen?, we wonder, and anxiously read on—but about the curse and its effects we hear nothing more. Shinta begins to find elegantly prepared food left for him in his house; he travels to the east (country associated with religious pilgrimage, but he goes on business); he returns to find

Kyoto cramped and busy, his house surprisingly small; and in his house, in a patch of sunlight, he sees water trickling in a thin, trembling stream from a rock basin, and at precisely the point where the water and light meet, sees "a small branch of hydrangea, swaying to and fro almost imperceptibly." One feels baffled, disappointed, partly because in the Western tradition a story whose conclusion is withheld, or given only through elusive symbolism, almost always strikes us as arch, intellectual, self-conscious, ultimately mean-spirited.

"The Pilgrimage of the Curse" is not elusive because the writer wishes to seem cleverer than his neighbors, wishes to play the role of the Romantic bull who imposes on ordinary herd humanity the duty of following wherever he may lead. The story is meant to be elusive in the way the world is, or to put the same thing another way, meant to be elusive in the way enlightenment is. Baffled by the surface of things, we are teased into looking for what we know must be there, the inner orderliness, the coherent other end of the story's seemingly disparate metaphors. The suspenseful situation which leads us into the meditation—the "Western" suspense which in this story is soon to be abandoned—is *itself* metaphoric: it expresses the anxiety of individuation, subject cut off from object, temporal as opposed to eternal consciousness—in other words, the anxiety of the unenlightened man, the man who does not understand that he is one with the universe and therefore safe. It is difficult to speak of these things without seeming to talk gibberish, but the main point is simple, so simple that, as the Taoists say, "If a fool were to learn the truth, he would laugh aloud." Plot suspense is not irrelevant to meditational fiction, not *simply* a facade: The reader's entrapment in time—his anxiety over what will happen next—is both pleasurable (we love our blindness, our proudly egoistic small-mindedness) and illusory. At the end of the story the reader will see that (for reasons perhaps not clear) all is well. Plot suspense, like the surface of reality, is fascinating; we're tempted never to pass through it. But if we do, teased inward by our bafflement, we discover that all conflicts resolve themselves into a cosmic smile, and it is us. This wisdom, if I may call it that, is not something the story would persuade us to. Eastern meditational fiction is not interested in argument, persuasion. It assumes its metaphysical grounds, its essential paradox—that our ex-

Introduction

perience of separation between subject and object (seer and seen) is an illusion—and dramatizes the assumption.

The more important kind of suspense in Kikuo Itaya's stories has to do with understanding. One soon learns that in every story secret forces are moving, and that the visible surface of those forces may be misleading, prompting us to judgments we will regret. For a devout Buddhist, compassion, sympathy, peacefulness, humility, and pride-in-mastery are not so much virtues as desired states of being, and it is such virtues as these—such states of being—that the stories chiefly celebrate and instill. Once the reader has caught on to the meditational method, this distinctly Eastern kind of suspense can be highly effective. We learn to watch surfaces with a wary eye: We begin to distrust our admirations and feelings of antipathy. In "The Pilgrimage of the Curse" we gradually discover that our anxieties concerning particular people lead us *away* from what is important, the larger span that redeems (or expresses itself through) Time. Fussily translated the title might read, "The Pilgrimage of From One to Three A.M. [The Hours of the Curse]." How can the two darkest hours of night be a "pilgrimage?" How can Time be (since pilgrimage implies spatial movement) Space? And even if these strange things can be, how come the story treats months of time, not just two hours, and wanders off the point to a businessman's trip into pilgrim country and then home again? We notice, after a bit of pondering, that the female curse-sayer is at first dominating and Shinta dominated, and that then the curse-sayer is helpless, all but crushed, and young, weak Shinta determined to be strong, the most powerful of merchants. We notice that the curse-sayer is a large woman (implying strength and a certain unattractiveness) but has on her face a smudge that looks like a butterfly; that Shinta travels into holy country with the hope of becoming there the toughest, finest salesman in the business, and that in his search for the ideal woman, someone who is not too strong-willed (as the curse-sayer has told him she is, to her sorrow), he cannot tell whether or not any given woman is strong-willed; that in the land of pilgrims the one "vision" Shinta has is of the large woman with the butterfly smudge (a vision the Christian Middle Ages would call earthly); and that Shinta's ironic "pilgrimage" recapitulates the central contrasts set up in the two hours of the curse (activity vs. passivity; dominance vs. submission;

chase vs. flight, reversed when Shinta takes the "masculine" role; and so forth). At the end of the story, when the faithless husband has vanished from the face of the earth (on the level of plot, he presumably fears that his wife will kill him to save the curse), we understand or suspect that the food left in Shinta's house was left by the abandoned wife—is a courtship in progress?—and that Shinta, back home in the ancient capital, the city of temples, which he sees as grubby, crowded, and mercantile, has reached, without even knowing it, enlightenment. After noticing the tray of food (evidently the lady has been watching for him), Shinta sees *being* in several manifestations, from most substantial to least substantial—*rock*, *water*, and *vegetation* brought together in a single point of *light* . . . and not just any vegetation but the Japanese hydrangea, whose blossoms are said to move through the seven colors of the spectrum (another focal point of the eternal and temporal, since the colors of the spectrum never change, though hydrangeas come and go).

None of this "meaning" (from the Buddhist point of view it is misleading to call it that) directly answers the plot questions set up at the beginning of the story. But at last we understand that the power of the curse was an illusion. This is not at all to say that for Buddhists as for modern liberated Christians curses are empty superstition. Rather, it is to say that one same power operates in curses and blessings: both misapprehend one same *Is*-ness. Both the worst man and the best man, the strongest and the weakest, the worst fate and the best fate, express one same reality, the everywhere visible divine nature. In Western fiction, the fundamental principle of suspense is (in effect) when will the murderer be identified by the detective? In Eastern meditational fiction the question is, at what point will I shake off my misreadings and see truly? Great meditational fiction like Itaya's has secrets behind secrets behind secrets, all of them the same. On the first or second reading one may be baffled. On the third, if not before, one suddenly cries, "Ah ha!" On the fourth and thereafter one cries "Ah ha" to more and more details. By the tenth or fifteenth reading one begins to guess how bottomless the mystery is: on its deepest levels, meditational fiction is unplanned: intuitive: entranced. Needless to say, the Western expectation of learning more and more—seeing more and more deeply into the writer's philosophy—is frustrated. In a sense the writer of meditational fiction *has* no individual philosophy. He has, instead, the gift of a great designer of Oriental carpets, the ability to lead the meditative mind, by an astonishing variety of colors and forms, again and again to the same place. Or to put all this another way, the difference between *Beowulf* or *Ulysses*, on the one hand, and the fiction of Itaya, on the other, is that no matter how deeply one may penetrate *Beowulf* or *Ulysses*, the mysteries are still "intelligible," that is, rational. Even on the surface, Itaya's fiction is irrational, not so much antilogical as amused by logic; and the deeper one strikes, the more amused-by-logic (but by no means disorderly) things become.

The Western mind, generally speaking, feels restless when not learning (or imagining it is learning) something new. The Eastern mind, in its classical form, tends to be annoyed by what it views as trivial philosophical variation—the difference, for instance, between the thought of Kant and Schopenhauer. It is not, of course, that the Easterner is stupid and incapable of making fine distinctions. It's just that, from the older Eastern point of view, the Western mind moves more and more carefully and shrewdly in the wrong direction, out into the foliage, away from the trunk. Compare the situation of a young man in love with a young woman. His friends, who are not in love with her, tell him, with the best of intentions, that she's wonderful at balancing her checkbook, that she's a surprisingly good driver, for a woman, and that her chin is much like that of so-and-so the movie star. All of this, the lover knows, is true and indeed very interesting, but irrelevant to the case.

The opening story in Itaya's collected works serves as an excellent introduction to his method, as perhaps, given its placement, it was designed to do. In this story, "The Robber and the Flute," we meet a robber named Hyōzō, the finest, most brilliant robber in thirteenth-century Kyoto. With his ear to the wall, listening for their breathing, Hyōzō can figure out the location of every occupant of the house. Once he knows where all the people are, he moves in and steals grandly, then leaves by the one route no one would expect a robber to leave by, the central gate. He works by a shrewd principle, which is never to steal from the same house twice, and for that reason he moves out from the rich central city to poorer and poorer sections, so that, more and more, he must steal from his own class. One night as he is about to rob a small, rather shabby house, he is stopped in his tracks by flute music that comes flowing with the wind from the river. He feels drawn to the music, like a man possessed, and finds that it comes from an ancient-looking, rather humble estate. Hyōzō goes home, unnerved by the music, and for the next couple of nights feels unable to work. He feels obsessed by the music, goes timidly several times to the flute player's house, and at last decides to steal the flute to silence it. All this time Hyōzō has been unable to work, and each time he goes home—on those occasional nights when he's able to overcome his strange inertia and go out—his wife, who was once beautiful (before she learned he is a thief), stares at him angrily.

His chance to steal the flute comes when one night he sees the musician leave his house, a man who wears an aristocrat's *eboshi* hat; but when Hyōzō searches the house he finds, in the clutter of the musician's objects, no sign of the flute. He decides to pursue the flute player and attack him, and he heads along the river in the direction the musician must have taken. Beside the river he feels suddenly lost and empty, as if the wind were blowing through him. Then he hears the flute, experiences a queer disorientation like madness—the river and flute seem to play a duet, and then Hyōzō seems to hear other, perhaps ghostly musicians—and the robber, momentarily not himself, falls into the water. The flute player serenely helps him out, elaborately thanks him for having taught him to create a new musical sound (inspired by the splash), tells him that flute playing and stealing are much alike, then invites Hyōzō to become his student. Hyōzō agrees without a moment's hesitation and studies diligently. His wife once more becomes beautiful. At the time of the Moonlight Viewing Feast not long thereafter—a great festival at the Emperor's palace where the Emperor and all classes of people celebrate together—Hyōzō and his fellow disciples of the man in the *eboshi* hat, along with the teacher himself, play for the assembly. Afterward Hyōzō is proud of himself, but no one, the narrator hints, is more proud than the teacher. The story closes with the odd sentence: "For he was no other than Toyohara Tokinaga, the best-known flute player of the period."

No brief summary of an Itaya story can hope to be more than barely adequate, since every slightest detail in these stories is charged with meaning, but the summary here should be sufficient at least to suggest the general method of this fiction. Hyōzō and the flute player are not opposites, as we at first think—one a thief, one a great artist; one a poor man, one a great (though shabby-genteel) aristocrat. What they do, as the flute player says, is similar. Each "tunes in," so to speak, to the vibrations—the "breath"—of the universe, becomes one with the universe and makes use of that oneness for his own ends. Hyōzō, listening to breathing inside the house he means to rob, is comparable to the flute player as he listens to the river, becoming one with it for the purpose of playing its music. The flute music bothers and psychologically incapacitates Hyōzō—steals from him his will, his ego—by making him feel worthless, empty, "as if wind were blowing through him." The reason for this is never made explicit in the story, but we can guess it. Hyōzō's way of using the rhythm of the universe is selfish, shortsighted, moving him more and more into a realm of mere objects, away from the center of the city into areas dark, shabby, and (for a robber) unrewarding, the clutter of brute substance suggested in two images Hyōzō encounters in the house of the musician when the musician and his flute are not there. One image is the *nikai-zushi*, a two-shelf bookcase in which the bottom section is closed, the top open—an image of the universe as perceived by the unenlightened, part of it visible, part of it hidden. The other is the clutter of "pieces of paper on which someone had written things," an image of the physical, the pieces of paper, brought together with the intellectual or, more likely spiritual (since what an aristocratic flute player writes is likely to be poetry), the writings Hyōzō does not bother to read.

Hyōzō, in other words, steals from the universe without enhancing either the universe or himself. The beautiful woman he married without telling her his occupation—"stealing" her, in effect—he makes ugly: isolated and angry. When he once more becomes, as disciple to the flute player, a part of the universal hymn, she once more becomes beautiful. We may imagine at this point that the central difference between Hyōzō and the flute player is that Hyōzō is an egoist, the flute player a selfless servant of the beautiful. The gently comic irony of the story's final line corrects that impression. Withholding the name and fame of the musician until the end of the story, Itaya suggests the great pride in mastery that master musicians share with clever robbers. Borrowing the universal rhythm, the musician enhances the cosmos, the whole society, and—not least—himself.

It is of course significant that Itaya's stories are set, with immense care for historical accuracy, in medieval Japan, for the most part in Kyoto, the old capital, traditional center of both Japanese political order and Japanese religion. It is not in Itaya's gentle, humorous nature to criticize the ways of modern Japan—or anyone or anything else. He does not, like Kawabata, lament the passing of the old order, or like Mishima rage against the secularization and softening of will everywhere visible (he would say) in contemporary Japanese life. Yet Itaya's writings are not without social overtones. Without upbraiding or condemning what he sees around him, he offers Japanese readers an alternative, recalling for them what he sees as a wiser time, though that time too, he would be the first to admit, had its faults and limitations. His stories have a sweetness hardly to be matched elsewhere in Japanese fiction, though not uncommon in the poetry of that nation. The nostalgia of his fiction is never simpleminded: he asks Japanese readers to reexamine their cultural traditions, not throw them off too lightly. He admits that human beings have always had tendencies toward cruelty and narrow-mindedness; but in reinvigorating the old Buddhist worldview, the old style of manners, the old social consciousness, and above all, perhaps, the old asceticism, he offers an understanding of the modern world's troubles that all of us, Japanese and non-Japanese, might do well to ponder. Whether or not we feel an affinity for the religious and ontological assumptions behind these stories, we cannot help but be moved by their temperance, justice, delicacy, and humor. The lyrical simplicity is like the purest well-water, and the pervasive humor is so elegant, so subtle, and so entirely good-hearted that one wonders, at least while one is reading the stories, why anyone should choose to be comic in any other way.

Itaya's characters are wonderfully lifelike, given the oddly formal world in which they move—a world of grave and subtle courtships, fragile longings, and whispered, apologetic mysticism. If they are all to some extent comic, like self-important, troubled children viewed by a wise and loving grandmother, they are comic because their universe is comic, that is, ever-threatening but secretly serene. Itaya's fictive world can deal comfortably with the whole range of human emotion, though the terms are always muted, distanced by the medieval settings of the stories and the extreme stylistic simplicity of the narrative voice. It is a fictive world that can easily embrace both the sober-minded, harried medieval Japanese businessman or politician and the shape-shifting lady fox, the age-old magic of fairytale. We feel no shift of gears, no abrupt change in attitude or point of view. It is a world we experienced directly when we were children and now look for in vain except in stories like these, a world entirely symbolic and entirely literal, created not for thinking about but for meditating on in the special Oriental sense: a world to become one with, to experience, as the enlightened experience the surrounding reality the fictional world of Kikuo Itaya reflects.

TENGU CHILD

THE ROBBER AND
THE FLUTE

There was a robber whose name was Hyōzō.[1] Even at the height of the Heian period[2] there were always robbers, but in a sense he was one of the most notorious. In spite of all his robberies he had never been caught, nor had he hurt anyone. The experienced police department officers, called *hōben*,[3] could only wander about aimlessly, following his vanishing shadow or his footprints after a rainfall. He was agility itself. He had also mastered the psychology of the pursued and the pursuer and always got away.

From the appearance of an estate—the outer main gate and the surrounding walls of mud and plaster with their tiled roofs—he could generally guess the plan of the house, the location of goods, and the size of the household. If there was a dog on the premises, it would wag its tail at his approach.

When he stood outside the lattice windows or the sliding doors of the target house, Hyōzō could read the exact number of household members by their breathing as they slept. It was especially easy for him to sense out the movements of the men on night duty. Only when success was assured would he attack. Once inside a room, he could instantly detect the location of valuables. As soon as he secured them, he would slip away into the street, usually escaping through the main gate, taking the route the lord of the house least expected. He always acted alone. In truth, no one could keep up with him. This was no doubt another reason he had never been caught.

For many years he concentrated on robbing the aristocratic man-

1. Hyōzō—literally "soldier #3." (NT)

2. Heian period: During this period (794–1192) of the aristocratic reign, Japanese civilization was firmly established. Especially notable was the flourishing of literature and the other arts. (NT)

3. Ex-convicts who were hired by the police department—the *Kebiishi Chō*—after their release from prison and were especially assigned to arresting criminals. (NT)

sions of Kyoto's Fourth and Fifth Avenues. He had two reasons. For one thing, in a huge mansion with a large household, it was often surprisingly unclear who was responsible for what, and locking up the doors would be neglected. For another, a successful burglary of a stately mansion gave him immense satisfaction. This was perhaps a reflection of his innate rebelliousness.

Recently, however, his field of action had been reduced, for he made it a rule never to go back to the same place where he had once achieved his end. This was probably another important reason he had never been caught.

At any rate, necessity forced him to change his targets. He therefore decided to choose an area slightly to the north of the heart of the city, along the Kamo River. It was a mixed neighborhood of temples and modest homes, but with its good visibility and the river flowing through its center, it seemed an ideal place for his activity.

The result, however, was not so satisfactory. One reason was that the houses and gardens, being smaller, made it harder for Hyōzō to make his getaway. Another reason was psychological, and this one was an even greater hindrance. He discovered that the lives of the people who lived there were similar in some ways to the lives of his own people. This familiarity was most disconcerting.

As a result, he several times failed to clear fences, and repeatedly turned back when he had come half way, unwilling to go forward. Every day he would lie idle in his small house in the west section of the capital.

"If I continue to do this sort of thing, all my muscles and bones will be weakened," he would think, and he would finally decide to go out.

On one extremely sultry summer night, he walked for a long time. Though the road was still hot, the breeze from the Kamo River was cool as usual. He began to feel his nerves coming alert, stirring to the tips of his fingers and toes. He was now walking near Sanjō Gawara, an area occupied by modest homes. The arrangement of the main gates and the alignment of other buildings was informal here, not like the design of the aristocratic area. But his professional urge was not stirred by the sight of wooden-roofed houses with their lattice windows half open to let in the cool air, or by the relaxed figures of the inhabitants against the flickering candle light.

The Robber and the Flute

"Am I going to fail again tonight?"

With a feeling of mixed relief and vexation he was about to turn around, when suddenly all his nerves seemed to be concentrated in his ears. His feet stopped moving. The sound of a flute[4] came flowing with the breeze from the river. He was drawn toward the heart of the sound as if he were possessed.

Near the river bank lay an ancient-looking estate, with narrow boundary walls. The outer main gate was low and rather small, and only in front of the house, by the gate, were the walls of mud and plaster, with roofs of tile. The tiled roofs were covered with dirt studded with blooming pinks. On the other three sides of the house stood simple wooden fences. It was from within this house that the sound of the flute came out to him.

He stood still. The sound, like rolling river waves, penetrated him from the crown of his head to the tips of his toes, flowing deep, yet with minute precision, as if to change completely all the currents of his body.

He decided to turn back. When he reached the Sanjōbō Gate, his heart became calm. But here he hesitated again, possessed by a desire to listen to the flute. His unlined robe was soaked with sweat.

"How frustrating! Again tonight my willpower's been shattered! What an eerie sound! Tomorrow I'll go and investigate that house by daylight. Surely a strange house."

When he reached his home, he wagged his left hand limply at his wife, who came to greet him, and went directly to bed.

The next day was sunny and hot. He did not feel like going to inspect the house of the night before. Although it became a little cooler after sunset, he gave up his plan to go out.

Several days later he left his home and started to walk in the opposite direction from the flute player's house, but soon he was seized with a strong desire to go by it. After the rainfall, the night fog was thick. The sound of the flute was already flowing from the house. He stood still, waiting. At that moment, the sound ebbed and stopped. Then it started again. This repeated several times. Abruptly, the sliding screen door opened and he heard someone stepping out on the

---

4. The flute is a *shō*, used in playing *gagaku*, the ritualistic music of the Imperial court. The flute has seventeen bamboo pipes, two of which produce no sound. (NT)

wooden floor. The footsteps came upon him with the force of a shock. He moved hurriedly away from the sound.

When he arrived at his home in the west section of the capital, his wife's fierce eyes received the silent robber.

A few more days passed. This time he tried to walk toward the corner of Rokujō and Mate no kōji, but somehow the muscles of his legs felt awkward and toneless. The sound of the flute flowed back and forth between his ears so that it was impossible for him to concentrate his attention on his target.

"All right!" he thought. "Tonight instead of going anywhere else, I'll go listen to the flute. Then maybe from tomorrow on I'll feel better and my work will go more easily." Having reached this decision, he headed toward the house as eagerly as someone on his way to the Aoi Festival.[5] He went behind the house and peeped through an opening in the wooden fence. But he could not hear the flute.

"Funny," he thought. "Is he out?" He looked cautiously around the building. On the paper sliding-door of the hallway connecting the main quarters and the adjoining quarters stood the shadow-bust of a tall man wearing a ceremonial hat, an *eboshi*. The shadow-figure stood absolutely still. The robber, feeling as if ice and boiling water were pouring into him, turned frantically and ran. Though his sandal went flying from him, he kept running. Finally he reached home. The glint of his wife's dark, sharp eyes pierced his heart.

"You! What's *wrong* with you? Every day you come home looking pale as a shadow, like an abandoned child. Aren't you ashamed of yourself?" Even when she scolded, her voice was very beautiful.

Three years ago, his wife had been a fruit and vegetable woman by the Shijō Bridge. When he went past the bridge on his reconnoitering expeditions, she would call to him in her pretty voice. He would buy purple eggplants or yellow tangerines from her and idly look at them lying on the wooden floor of his cottage. Before he knew it, they were husband and wife. When his wife learned of his occupation, she cried bitterly. After that her character changed com-

5. The most important and the most elaborate festival of medieval Kyoto, held in the Fourth Month of the lunar calendar (now on the fifteenth of May), in commemoration of the two Shinto shrines—Kami Kamo and Shimo Kamo. The festival was attended by everyone—from the Emperor down to the humblest citizens. The people of medieval Kyoto were said to live for this annual festivity. (NT)

pletely. Now, hearing her voice, he could not suppress his anger. She sounded as if she had a knife hidden in her heart.

"This creature's coldness is exactly the same as that man's," he thought.

A fierce hostility toward the man in the *eboshi* hat flared up in his heart.

"All right! I'll sneak into that house when the master is out, steal the flute, and smash it for revenge." He realized that there was no other way to save himself and regretted that he had not understood this sooner. Strange to say, knowing that it would take several days to accomplish his revenge, he somehow felt more at ease, and his irritation disappeared.

He waited for two or three days before his willpower returned. Then he set out from his house. The night air was cool, the wind moving gently. The early autumn moon was bright. The black silhouette of the mountain range of Higashiyama, which had been a familiar sight to him, seemed tonight to be aiding him, stalking alongside him.

No sound of the flute came from the house as he approached it.

"Good. Maybe he is out."

He strained his ears.

Suddenly one of the main gate doors opened and the man with the *eboshi* hat appeared. The robber immediately hid himself. The tall man began to walk slowly toward the Kamo River. The robber's heart was overjoyed at the rapid arrival of his opportunity.

"Now is the time!"

The door of the main gate swung open easily since it was not bolted. The robber slipped inside and pushed with his body against the wooden door of the middle gate. It yielded easily. The entrance to the main quarters had been left open just the width of his body, allowing him in. Thus he entered the room like an invited guest. The room appeared to be the master's sitting room. On a bookcase, a *nikai-zushi*,[6] were piled various books. The flute was not there. The wooden floor was strewn with pieces of paper on which someone had written things. The flute was not there either. On one part of the dark wall, light from the lamp in the adjoining room flickered slightly. Swiftly the robber fled the main quarters.

6. A two-shelf bookcase in which the bottom section is closed, the top section open. (NT)

"Well, then, the master wearing the *eboshi* hat must have taken the flute away. Maybe he was invited to someone's house and took it with him."

When he encountered the wearer of the *eboshi* hat the robber intended to hurl himself at him, make him lose balance, and snatch the flute. Such had been this robber's favorite technique.

The robber eagerly pursued the man wearing the *eboshi* hat. The road along the river became more and more narrow, and there were hardly any houses. The moving light of water became visible. On the low embankment, willow trees stood regularly spaced above random growths of Japanese pampas grass. Swayed by the northwesterly wind, countless spikes of pampas grass brushed against small willow branches.

The man in the *eboshi* hat was nowhere to be seen. Disappointed, the robber knelt down at the end of the embankment and took a deep breath.

"Ah, what's the matter with me? What will become of me if I go on this way day after day? I'm tired of that look in my wife's eyes, too. But wait. It would be all over with me if I should get caught while my spirits are low."

Black Higashiyama began to look merciless.

"What's this? It's only a huge lump of earth! Absurd!"

All at once he was seized by loneliness. As he listened passively to the murmur of the stream, he became aware of a mysterious reverberation in the current. But then he realized that it had nothing to do with the problem facing him, and he felt a sudden emptiness, as if his body had opened up and the wind was blowing through.

That instant, the sound of a flute rose from behind a large spray of pampas grass. It came when he least expected it, and his heart's resistance to the flute slipped away. The sound of the flute, heard fitfully at first as the small waves beat the water plants on the shore, soon began to dominate the current with loud echoes over the surface of the water. As he held his breath, listening with strained ears, the duet of the flute and the Kamo River gradually changed, becoming the music of the flute alone, and at the same time he heard from somewhere the footsteps of musicians as they walked and played wind instruments and drums. He could not keep his hands and feet from itching for action.

He stood up unsteadily, but his body lost its center and jerked back in an exaggerated motion while his feet and legs pushed forward of their own accord. He splashed with a loud noise into the water. The moon on the waves shattered in an instant, so that his figure was now in sight, now hidden from view. He was already crawling up the bank when he came to himself.

A man in a black silk *eboshi* hat and a light purple-blue ceremonial hunting costume, smiling gently, extended his right hand over the water. In his left hand he held a flute. Hyōzō squatted down on the bank and panted. The man was clear-eyed and looked to be about fifty. He spoke kindly.

"I'm sorry to have frightened you. You are the one who has been listening to my flute these evenings, I believe? Some people, I'm afraid, come to listen in order to steal the secret of flute playing, but you don't seem to be one of those. Actually, I was pondering on the technique of flute playing. Soon the Moonlight Viewing Feast[7] will be held at the Imperial Palace." The voice of the man in the *eboshi* hat was calm and clear.

"On that night, the Waves of the Blue Sea dance will be performed. It is a beautiful dance in which the movements of the rolling sea waves are represented by the fluttering sleeves of the dancers' costumes. The flute may sound simple enough to an idle ear, but by such techniques as changing the way one breathes in and out and very slightly shifting the hand position, one can produce extremely subtle variations. Consequently, in the hope that it might not be impossible to express the heart of the river water as it flows, shattering the moonlight, I have been toiling night and day."

Listening to the grave confession of this tall man, Hyōzō felt that there was some affinity between his recent anguish and the other man's struggle, and in spite of himself, he listened respectfully.

The man continued, "Earlier, on this spot, I had been trying to attune the flute to the stream and had almost gotten the knack of it. Just then the sudden splash of the water enabled me to produce a sound never heard of before. If you had not fallen into the river, this

---

7. A festival in the court to enjoy the moonlight on the fifteenth day of the Eighth Month of the lunar calendar, attended by the Imperial family and the noblemen, highlighted by the musical performances of both the noblemen and the professional musicians. (NT)

exquisite sound would never have come forth. With all my heart I express my gratitude to you."

The gaunt cheekbones of the man in the *eboshi* hat were wet. His words took on increasing intensity. "I suspect that you are perhaps a renowned robber. The way of stealing and the way of music may have something in common. You seem not to realize it yourself, but from my observation you are better suited to be a musician than to be a robber. Listen. Wouldn't you like to become my disciple? Surely if you follow this profession, you will rise in the world." Hyōzō silently knelt down and bowed his head.

From that night on, the robber became a musician. His passion for the flute flared up at once. He soon got rid of his habit of casting a suspicious look around him. The look in his wife's eyes became gentle, and youthfulness returned to her voice.

Shortly afterward, a grand Feast of the Moonlight Viewing was held at the Imperial Palace. Hyōzō, joining other musicians behind the dancer, played the accompaniment. Needless to say, the flute performance of the man in the *eboshi* hat won the highest praise of the whole assembly.

Late that night when the master returned to his home in Sanjō Kyōgoku, he patted his disciple's shoulders fondly. "Your performance tonight was exceptional. I was not mistaken in my judgment." The eyes of the man in the *eboshi* hat gleamed with double satisfaction. For he was no other than Toyohara Tokinaga, the best-known flute player of the period.

TANABATA[1]

The sun was about to sink behind the rim of a dark grey evening cloud. The tired, hot air had become a soundless breeze. It was ten days after the first day of autumn.[2]

There was nothing particularly remarkable about the movements of the people coming and going in the streets of Kyoto, and yet one might detect in them an air of restlessness and dark shadows on the sides of their faces. Three months before this evening at midnight, late the Fourth Month of the lunar calendar, a fire had started near the corner of Higuchi and Tomi no kōji, south of Fifth Avenue, and by morning one-third of the city was reduced to ashes.

His honor Fujiwara Tsunefusa, Assistant Deputy Chief of the City Guard Unit and Deputy Chief of the Police Department, was continually busy with his combined duties. This evening, however, he was carrying a small encyclopedic dictionary of poetry in his pocket.[3]

---

1. The Festival of the Star Vega. *Tanabata* literally means "the evening of the seventh day of the Seventh Month" of the lunar calendar. According to the legend once a year on that evening, the star Altair (the Shepherd) and the star Vega (the Weaving Maiden) are allowed to see each other across the galaxy. According to ancient Chinese tradition, Shokujo or the Weaving Maiden, the daughter (sometimes granddaughter) of the Emperor of Heaven was an excellent weaver. At her father's command, she was always busy weaving her father's clothing, and for this reason she did not even have a lover. Pitying the daughter, the Emperor of Heaven married her to a shepherd lad, Kengyū, who came from across the galaxy. Intoxicated with their newly wed life, the Weaving Maiden stopped weaving. Her father became angry and separated the two, sending the shepherd back across the galaxy. In tears, the Maiden resumed her weaving. Her father saw her grief and allowed her to return to her husband once a year, on the night of the seventh day of the Seventh Month of the lunar calendar. But if it rained that night, the river water of the galaxy would swell and she could not cross. On such an occasion, the half moon would float in the downstream of the galaxy. But the jealous boatman of the moon would not come to the Weaving Maiden. As she would remain there in grief and sorrow, a flock of magpies would come flying from God knows where, build a bridge, and let the Maiden cross the river. (NT)

2. According to the lunar calendar (corresponding approximately to the middle of August of the solar calendar). As might be gathered from the title of the story, the date coincides with the Tanabata festival. (NT)

3. A kind of dictionary—entries include a list of poems using a given term, e.g., *Tanabata*. (NT)

His present location was the northeast part of the city of Kyoto, an area burned down by the great fire. The cleaning up of debris had recently been finished, for the most part, and commoners' homes and commercial shops were beginning to be rebuilt. Here and there huge temples with gigantic roofs stood naked, giving a bleak appearance to the area.

The Imperial Palace itself had fortunately escaped the fire, but sadly, the Sujakumon Gate[4] was no more to be seen. In the vast Imperial District many structures had been lost to the fire, including the Ōtenmon Gate, the Imperial Council Hall, and many other large and small offices of the Eight Ministries.[5] Indeed, it would be almost impossible to enumerate one by one the residences of the lords and other high-ranking courtiers which had been lost.

To Tsunefusa, the number one problem was that a group of prisoners had broken free of the Left-Hand Prison of the *Kebiishi Chō*[6] and had escaped. Day and night he felt the tremendous strain of trying to round up these escaped prisoners—and also trying to handle the annoyance of poverty-stricken men turning robbers—but of late the situation had much improved.

He was passing through Konoe Gawara on horseback, followed by two attendants on foot. This area was a quiet residential section, most of which had been fortunate enough to escape the great fire, not that there were no signs of damage. On one side of the road was a narrow stream, from which each house drew water. The water which was drawn off flowed through the front pond of each house and back to the stream.

It had been some time since he had last traveled on this road, now nearly deserted. That morning he had paid a visit to the Imperial Palace in his capacity as a responsible police officer. Now, in the evening, as a middle-rank nobleman, he was enjoying the scenery of the town. It was obvious from his ceremonial *eboshi* hat and pale-blue plaid hunting costume that he was not on the business of the police department.

He came to a gentle curve in the road. There, in full view, stood a

---

4. The Sujakumon Gate—the entrance to the Imperial District. (NT)
5. Eight departments of the central government, much like Great Britain's Ministries. (NT)
6. *Kebiishi Chō*—the police and prison system. (NT)

huge willow tree and, below it, a rock to sit upon. The current of the stream by the side of the road rushed around the curve, making small ripples and murmurs, then hurrying on.

He dismounted from the horse and handed the reins to one of his two attendants. He sent the other with a written message to the house which was his object. The messenger returned shortly. Unexpected joy immediately surfaced on Tsunefusa's face, and from the way he tried to hide it from his two attendants, it could be guessed what was in his mind. Tsunefusa ordered the two men to wait there and started to walk.

At the end of the street stood a house, one of the largest of its kind in the neighborhood. The outer walls of mud and plaster, apparently repainted not long since, stretched their cold sides straight into the gathering dusk. Inside the walls lay a garden, harmoniously arranged, with carefully trimmed trees rising above the walls. The walls of the house next door bent away irregularly, like a bow, making a clear view difficult. There was not a soul in sight, not a sound to be heard.

Suddenly he felt something like a sharp gust of wind rising behind him. A huge man stood close to his right side and gripped his wrist. At the same time the stranger's other arm reached Tsunefusa's left side across his back. Tsunefusa felt a short, hard object digging into his side.

"Tsunefusa, I'm here to take your life. I have been waiting for this night."

A cry of anger rings loudest in the ears of the man who utters it. Tsunefusa thought he had heard the voice before. He remembered that the man was a thief who had escaped from the prison of the *Kebiishi Chō* at the time of the fire near the corner of Higuchi and Tomi no kōji.

Tsunefusa could just see the man's face. He was about twenty-five or six; his cheek was pale and rather flat, his eyes narrow slits. Tsunefusa felt the power of the man's arms, but also the trembling of his fingertips. This gave Tsunefusa his first opportunity to recover a little of his willpower and resist. First, he tried to remember the man's name.

"You must be Gengo. What on earth *is* this?" The words spilled out of Tsunefusa's mouth, and instantly they made his heart more calm. His will to live churned below the layers of frozen feeling and at last, despite his fear of death, he rose partly to his senses.

"That shiny thing," he thought, "is a dagger with a shrimp sheath. How do I escape from the hands of this thief with a minimum of damage? If only I could find some quick way to get in touch with my men!"

But the dagger was frightening; his consciousness was muddled, and the dagger pointed at his side did not seem real to him.

Gengo's voice sounded in his ear. "When I was caught and tried at the *Kebiishi Chō* several years ago, you gave far more testimony than the case required. That's why I stayed locked in the bottom of the jail when my fellow convicts were released at the end of their terms and hired as *hōben*."[7] A groan of indignation burst from the thief's mouth.

"Indeed, was that so?" asked Tsunefusa. "I'm a busy man. I don't remember the details."

"None of your impudence!" snarled the robber. "I'm telling you the details. I broke in on Rokujō Shōnagon. When he was the provincial governor of Tōtōmi, he embezzled a huge amount of rice collected from the farmers and had the provincial official report to the capital that the crop had failed. Later, when Rokujō Shōnagon returned to Kyoto, he confiscated my home to expand his estate. To get even with him, I sneaked into his storehouse and set fire to the straw bags of rice. Is that so wrong?"

Tsunefusa was surprised. He remembered the name Rokujō Shōnagon, a relative on his mother's side.

"But arson is a grave offence. It has nothing to do with my forgetfulness."

In truth, Tsunefusa had been busy every day. Days such as today were practically nonexistent for him.

"You're quibbling!" snapped Gengo. "Listen, this is important. At the trial you said, 'This criminal's father obtained a position as a government clerk-accountant through the good offices of my grandfather, but he soon proved ungrateful. The son of such a man is clearly up to no good.' You can't deny that that was your statement."

---

7. Ex-convicts who were hired by the police department—the *Kebiishi Chō*—after their release from prison and were especially assigned to arresting criminals. (NT)

"Some such thing may have happened," Tsunefusa answered. "Yes, it did, in fact. But saying these things was my official duty."

The robber continued, "You spoke very ill of my father. But the fact is that through my great-grandfather's effort, your grandfather became the chief officer for household affairs of the family of Konoe, the *Kampaku*,[8] so that later, when his work met the approval of the great lord, your grandfather was able to rise to the position of *Kawachi no jō*.[9] Now we are even, aren't we?"

Unexpectedly this revelation stirred a faint nostalgic feeling in the depths of both men's hearts. But Tsunefusa shrewdly retorted, "I see that in the distant past our two families were in some strange way tied together. Isn't it rather cruel of you, knowing of such a bond, to want to murder me?"

The robber slightly nodded. Tsunefusa continued, "You want to take my life because you've realized that you have no chance in life yourself. Isn't that so?" Tsunefusa's professional consciousness had begun to revive and his tone of voice suddenly became stern. But at the same time he began to consider Gengo a "staunch fellow." As for Gengo, Tsunefusa's words seemed to have become painful shackles around his heart. The strength in his two arms suddenly waned. Tsunefusa's words abruptly took on kindness.

"If you will quietly return to the prison, I will recommend to the warden that he hire you as a *hōben*. What do you say to that?"

The tip of the dagger lowered toward the ground. "Down the road by the side of the stream," Tsunefusa said, "there are a willow tree and a rock like a seat, where two of my attendants are waiting. I swear not to call out for them. I'll expect you to return to the prison tomorrow and ask for me. Go now. Don't forget."

At that moment Tsunefusa felt as if a black storm were sweeping through his body, and he barely managed to keep his feet.

He ran to the house at the end of the street and knocked with all his strength on the door of the outer main gate. Since the message had been sent earlier, the door was opened at once. He could see, beyond the inner gate, the pond and part of the island in the middle of the pond. He hurried through the grounds between the pond and

---

8. *Kampaku* was the most powerful post of regent for an adult Emperor. (NT)
9. The third-highest-ranking official in the province of Kawachi. (NT)

the main building and ran up on the wooden porch of the connected west building.

The lord's daughter was already there, sitting at the doorway and following Tsunefusa's movements in the dusk with her eyes. Tsunefusa collapsed in front of her and firmly grasped her arms over her lined robe of pale reddish-purple.

"I'm saved! I'm saved! Water—please give me water!" He cried out loudly and took a deep breath.

The daughter's eyes opened wide, more in dismay than in surprise, but she got up quickly and, after removing its lid, brought him the water vessel[10] from the side of her dressing table. Tsunefusa leaned forward and emptied the bowl at a gulp.

Fear gave way to relief. He knew that he must have appeared terribly upset, and so, though he was suffering extreme fatigue, he told her briefly of the startling incident a few minutes before.

Her eyes opened even wider, and glistening tears ran down her cheeks. Her trembling hands rocked his shoulders back and forth.

"How terrifying! I'm so glad you're alive! No one but you, only you, could have escaped." She brought the words out one by one, breathlessly. Tsunefusa began to feel that the crisis he'd overcome was gradually becoming a thing of the past. On the daughter's white face a relaxed smile now appeared, and she stretched her hand to straighten the hair about her forehead. At last she said, "Look over there! The Tanabata festival! It's like a celebration of your life!" The place to which she pointed lay not far from the area he had just run past.

On the south side of the covered passageway connecting the dwelling of the lord with the west building, two large, four-legged stands were placed together, covering a few plants of autumn flowers. On top, centered on the two stands, lay a *koto*[11] with tuning bridges already in place. Next to the *koto* stood a lacquered wooden bowl filled with water, and to one side lay a paper mulberry leaf in which someone had stuck sewing needles with threads of five different colors.[12] Around these objects lay several unglazed white plates on

10. Water is used for the hair, hence the vessel is by the side of the dressing table. The vessel is a covered bowl, usually placed on a high stand. (NT)

11. A thirteen-string Japanese musical instrument. (NT)

12. At the Tanabata festival, threads were dedicated to the Weaving Maiden star by those praying for improved sewing skills. (NT)

which pears, peaches, and vegetables of the season, and even dried fish—breams and abalones—were piled in profusion.

On the four corners of the stands there were flower-patterned candles with their lovely little flickering flames. Even the scent of incense floating in the air seemed to flicker.

The two stepped down to the garden and peeped into the lacquered wooden bowl. On the dark silver mirror lay two faces.

"These are the real Shepherd and Weaving Maiden," she said softly.

"You are the Weaving Maiden incarnate."

The faces in the mirror continued to talk to each other in this way.

"I have received two treasures this evening," he said. "One is a new life."

"I have never seen you look more magnificent than you do tonight."

Again the two whispered to one another their similar feelings. Tsunefusa was like a man in a light trance. It seemed as if the *koto* were playing, the fruit rolling about, the breams and abalones swimming.

She spoke once more. "Looking at the pond and the island, I feel as if we were in the Sea God's palace."

Tsunefusa realized anew that her face would suit equally the Weaving Maiden or the princess in the palace of the Sea God.

The two went back to the room. Then, leaving Tsunefusa behind, she went to the main dwelling and soon returned. Her father, the former *chūnagon*,[13] and his lady, her mother, entered the daughter's room hurriedly and in some disarray, alarmed at their daughter's tale, but they quickly recovered their composure as they saw the young couple quite safe.

Tsunefusa told his story, with little embellishments. He enjoyed himself, talking, watching the parents' changing aspects.

The former *chūnagon* was a man who had quite abruptly become graceful as he grew older. He said, "We are impressed anew with your courage, Deputy Chief," and he quietly opened his eyes wide. The lady looked at Tsunefusa intently from the top of his *eboshi* hat to the knees of his *hakama*.[14]

---

13. The second-highest-ranking official below the ministers. (NT)
14. A divided skirt for man's formal wear. Here Tsunefusa is sitting back on his heels. (NT)

When the parents rose and left, maids came in in turn, lit several candles on high stands, and lined up the tables. The maiden devotedly served *sake* many times. Tsunefusa emptied the cup joyfully, peacefully gazing at the plants in the garden.

The night air was clear. Crickets sang behind the rocks by the pond. A part of the flow of the river of heaven was broken by the eves over the wooden porch, but countless stars seemed to exchange glances, looking down upon the two below.

The lord's daughter spoke. "A year ago today a rain cloud unfortunately spread over us, to our sorrow."

"Indeed, that was so," replied Tsunefusa. "It was a great sorrow to me. When you gave no poem in response to the one I'd presented, I left your main gate, and sat on the rock under that willow tree, alone and crestfallen, gazing at the dark stream."

Tsunefusa put his hand in the front pocket of his hunting costume and took out a piece of writing paper. On the clear-blue, flower-patterned Chinese paper was the precise calligraphy of the Sesonji school.[15]

"This time I've tried something like this. Please take a look."

She received the paper and unfolded it, and her two eyes eagerly perused the written words.

This night of devotion to the long thread of the Weaving Maiden,
Would that we too might as endlessly
Tie our bond.

She nodded with a smile, selected a narrow brush from the ink-stone case on the low table, and wrote on the paper with graceful strokes.

"How would this sound? To change 'Would that we too might as endlessly tie' to 'Behold, we two are as endlessly tying'?"

Tsunefusa felt intense emotions stirring within him, and tried to suppress them. As he gazed at the paper his emotions changed to pure ecstasy. He told himself, "The past is done with."

He recited the poem aloud two or three times. She joined him. Before they knew it, they were firmly holding each other's hands.

15. One of the most important schools of Japanese calligraphy, originated by Fujiwara Gyōzei (also called Yukinari, 972–1027), and considered the most influential school until the late fourteenth century. (NT)

Tsunefusa was happy. After he had eaten a hearty feast, he left through the main gate of the former *chūnagon*'s house. She had given him a firm promise for the time of their next meeting and joyfully saw him off. The chill of the breeze going through the front pocket of his hunting costume was sweet to him. Tsunefusa was gradually becoming once more an official of the police department. Already tomorrow's schedule was automatically arranging itself in his busy mind. The figures of his men rose up in his thought, waiting under the willow tree at the end of the street for their superior's return. He could not help hoping that Gengo would appear at the prison of the *Kebiishi Chō* the next day. What his heart was now whispering confirmed his earlier decision.

"Yes, it was because that man appeared here that I was able to attain my happiness tonight. Tomorrow I must get the warden's permission and by all means take care of his life in the future." He tried to find the spot where Gengo had thrust his dagger at him a few hours before, but the night was too dark for him to find any sign of the place.

When Tsunefusa had made this decision, he felt great fatigue sinking into his intoxicated body. At the same time, he felt expanding in his heart something he had never before tasted as an official.

The mysterious relationship with the thief Gengo, inherited from their ancestors, would henceforth be a chief subject of his concern. Meanwhile, he was confident in his newly established love. There was no fear for the future.

Tsunefusa paused and for a while looked up at the stars.

THE PILGRIMAGE OF
THE CURSE[1]

The summer night is strangely dark. Stars floating in the damp sky look as if they might fall.

From here the Yodo River is not visible. On the north side of the Yamazaki roadway along the river, surrounded by dense woods, is an area called the Rikyū Shrine. Straight beyond the stone gate stands the magnificent main temple. To its right stand the residences of the priests, and to the left and forward stand the middle temple and the small temple.[2]

That evening, on the premises of the shrine, candles were lit and voices could be heard only in the chief priest's residence. There, members of the oil merchants' guild of the Shrine were holding a trade meeting. Traveling merchants were filling their sales records for the past ten days and receiving new supplies. After the monetary transactions were concluded, the meeting turned into an informal *sake* drinking party. Then the merchants went home.

Shinta remained there with Kuraji.[3] As was his habit, Kuraji had drunk too much and had fallen sound asleep.

When Kuraji opened his eyes, it was about the middle of "*Ushi no toki*"—between two and three o'clock in the morning. The two men went outside. Just as they were passing under the stone gate, their feet froze to the ground.

1. The original title is "*Ushi no toki mairi.*" "*Mairi*" means "pilgrimage." "*Ushi no toki*" designates the two hours from one to three in the morning. There was a common belief that if one pounded nails with a curse into a shrine's sacred tree during these two hours, the curse would take effect. If anyone saw the person pounding the nails, he had to be killed by the one carrying out the rite, or the curse would take no effect. Worse, the curse might fall on the one who uttered it. (NT)

2. The Shinto shrine usually consists of three temples—the main temple and two auxiliary temples, middle and small—each enshrining different but related deities. (NT)

3. The name Shinta is made up of the units *shin* (new) and *ta* (large, excessive, thick); the name can give the impression of youth and vigor. Kuraji contains the units *kura* (storage) and *ji* (the number *two*). The number *two*, in Buddhist writing, can suggest vagueness, lack of definition, doubleness. (NT)

"Konk, konk. . . ."

It was the sound of something small and hard squeakily hitting something large and hard. The sound echoed and reechoed. The two men twisted their necks toward the noise.

On the left side of the main temple stood a pitch dark, towering Japanese cypress, the sacred tree of the shrine. In front of the tree was a whitish human figure. The upper half of the body showed small movements. Over its head, two or three candlelike things flickered. The two men groaned simultaneously.

"A woman!"

"Pilgrimage of the curse!"

The middle of Kuraji's forehead twitched spasmodically. He threw down the oil barrels slung over his shoulder by a pole and strap, turned nimbly around, and dashed into the darkness of the woods. Shinta, too, put down the back-pole on which he was carrying his barrels and, kicking the stepping stones, headed directly to the main roadway, then continued to run south toward the harbor. This area was crowded with crude buildings—shops, tea houses, warehouses, stables, and sheds for ship equipment—jumbled together side by side. The long street ended abruptly, blocked by water.

But the street led to a small pier, and to the left of the pier three freightboats were moored, carriers of perilla oil from the west, the same cargo Shinta and Kuraji had been helping to haul to the warehouse on the premises of the shrine.[4]

Shinta entered between the sides of the boats and kept his head as low as possible. The cold of the full-tide-depth water pierced him from the soles of his feet to his upper thighs, and at once his mind calmed itself. He looked fearfully in the direction from which he had come. Time passed.

"Well, am I safe?" he wondered.

But things did not turn out as he wished. Under the slanting roofs a tall whitish figure rose up and grew larger. The flickering lights that had been above its head were no longer there. It was evident that the white shadow was pursuing Shinta.

He who sees the pilgrimage of the curse shall be killed.

The memory of these words, heard years before, returned sharply

---

4. This shrine is said to have had an oil refinery on the premises. (NT)

to Shinta's mind. Unless the woman killed the man who had seen her, the curse would return to her, they said.

Quietly, as if crawling over the water's surface, Shinta went around the far end of the boats and came ashore again. As he pulled at his foot, sunk to the ankle in the clay at the bottom of the river, he accidentally made a splashing noise.

The woman saw him. His heart thudded and he jumped in the opposite direction, like a wild rabbit hit by the wind of a flying arrow.[5]

Now the river bank was sandy and thick with reeds. The middle of the stream embraced several long, narrow shoals, no ripples visible on the dimly lit surface of the water. The stream from the northeast, squeezing itself between the shoals, had to be the River Emmeiji, although it was not clearly visible. Then he noticed the murmur of another small stream which seemed to join the river at that point. Along this stream a narrow path led through the rice fields.

Without thinking, Shinta chose this path and kept on running. The way became narrower, and here and there reed-covered wasteland cut into the rice fields. In all the area, no human figure was in sight.

"Surely this path leads eventually to the main roadway," Shinta thought. "I'll hide somewhere until daybreak." Though still running, he had recovered his calm. He came to a place where a narrow road crossed his path, and made out an earthen bridge a little farther ahead. Under the bridge it was pitch-dark. He quickly squeezed himself into the darkness. As his head became logy with the smell of mud and decayed grass, he began to feel a sense of security.

"At last I am safe."

Without thinking, he poked his head out on one side of the earthen bridge. It was a mistake. What a shock! The woman was right in front of the bridge. She had taken an extremely narrow road to the south of the crossroad—something Shinta had never dreamed of.

Shinta clung to the bottom of a bridge post. At the same time the

5. In the original, the arrow is a *kaburaya*, that is, an arrow with a turnip-shaped head. This special kind of arrow makes a noise while flying. (NT)

woman's head appeared under the bridge floor, upside-down, with her hair spilling straight down, two eyes full of hatred directly in front of him. Shinta felt his head sinking into his body.

"Come out! I'm going to kill you! Quick! Quick!" shouted the woman.

"Forgive me, please, please! I didn't mean to watch you!" That was all Shinta could manage to bring out.

"Anyone who saw has to die. If I let him live, the nail will lose its power."

"I know. But someone else also saw."

The woman's utter dismay was at once revealed in her voice.

"Are you telling me the truth? What's happened to this someone else?"

"He took off right away. And I had the lousy luck to be the only one chased."

The thorn in the woman's voice was broken.

"Come up. I won't try to kill you any more. Ah, I'm ruined! I'm ruined!"

Shinta crawled up and squatted on the path in the rice fields. The woman sat down next to him. Since the woman was sitting very close to him, he repeated his words. "Please forgive me! Please!"

"What a catastrophe! Ai . . . Ai. . . ." Loudly the woman poured out her cries. As Shinta listened to the sound, almost unrecognizable as a woman's voice, and watched her writhing, he felt a boundless pity for her. The woman spoke.

"One whole year I've been thinking and thinking about tonight— and now it comes to this! Nothing's left for me but to die. I want to die! I want to die!"

Shinta could see that she meant it. Now he noticed a small, narrow, metallic thing tucked into the left side of her slender sash. It could only be a razor.

"Do you really have to die right away? You're impetuous. Until just this minute you've been saying you're going to kill *me*."

"That's true. I hate my husband and that woman, but I missed my chance of killing them."

"Is that so. Is your husband as bad as that? What's his name?"

"My husband's name is Kuraji—but the one I really hate is the woman."

"Kuraji? I'm Shinta. Kuraji's like a brother to me. He's my closest friend and partner. *He's* the one who ran away earlier!"

"What! My husband? Oh, what a disaster!"

It looked as if the woman were fainting. She cried in a thin, low voice until she began to gasp for breath. Shinta struggled to defend his friend.

"Kuraji may have done some wrong to you, but he's kind to everyone else. He's popular with all his customers. That's why he needs money—and why he drinks. It's the dandified trade of peddling oil to female customers that's to blame. Besides, you do seem to have a rather strong will."

"That may be true. I have been a little too strong-willed. I was the one to recommend oil peddling to Kuraji!"

"Is that so? Things are tangled in this world, aren't they. Being a bachelor and still young, I don't understand a lot of things, but it's almost frightening to think of the future."

"So you're a bachelor! No wonder you still have some tenderness. Come to think of it, my husband has occasionally mentioned your name. Surely you have someone you love."

"Not me! I'm too poor to be in love. I've been thinking, I wonder if Kuraji ran away because he realized it was you hammering the nail."

"Probably. Every day I've been saying I'll put a death-curse on that woman. Tonight I thought it was so late that Kuraji would no longer be at the shrine. That was my mistake."

A slight warmth came into the air, and the starlight grew dim. Koga Road, running eastward across the reed-covered marsh, was not visible. The huge black rise of Mt. Otoko, beyond the river, began to glow with subtle colors.

Shinta stole a glance at the woman. The upside-down tripod fastened to the top of her head[6] was much tilted. It must have been candles that caused the flickering light he had seen at the shrine, but there were none left on the tripod now. The woman had apparently painted her face black in order to look terrifying, but tears had left her face comically spotted.

"Maybe you should wash your face," said Shinta.

6. One was supposed to wear on one's head an upside-down tripod with lit candles on it in the pilgrimage of the curse. (NT)

When the woman realized what had happened, she removed the tripod, splashed her cheeks with water from the rice fields, and straightened her hair. Then she took off her white robe and folded it up. Underneath, she had on a simple dress.

Shinta said, "Let's go. I'll take you home."

"That would be kind of you. My house is to the southwest of the shrine."

Shinta walked in front, and the woman followed him, carrying the tripod tucked inside the folded white robe. The feel of dawn spread in the air. Shinta could distinctly count each leaf of the reeds which grew tall as a man on the east side of the path through the rice fields. On the west side of the path rice plants grew, but their green color was still pale, and in height they only reached the ankles of the two.

A river boat came from upstream. Was it perhaps delivering its cargo to a Yamazaki freighter? Someone on the boat waved in this direction. He began to feel refreshed, and the thought floated into his mind that perhaps he might travel in the Eastern region.[7]

"Shinta, what are you going to do now?"

The woman's voice had become gentle, and the two continued their unhurried walk.

"Yes, I'll go to the chief priest of the shrine and get a travel permit to pass through the checking station of Fuwa[8] and go to the Eastern region. I want to get new customers there."

"That sounds good. Make the best of it now while you're young. But I hear that the eastern women have strong wills, so you'd better not go near them. Besides, you're a bachelor."

"Yes, I'll be careful. Everything will be all right. I'm not popular with women. I'm too honest, I guess."

"Women love honest men. Anyway, be careful."

For the first time Shinta looked attentively at the woman. She was wearing an unlined, pale-blue dress with flower patterns. The small narrow thing tucked into the left side of her slender sash was, as he

7. As in "Tengu Child," the Eastern region, largely unexplored at the time in which the story is set, may symbolize the unknown, the poetic. (NT)

8. One of the three most famous barriers, or checking stations, of ancient Japan. One had to pass through the Fuwa station in order to go to the Eastern region from Kyoto, or to enter Kyoto coming from the east. (NT)

had guessed, a razor wrapped in a red silk cloth. She was a large woman with a round face light of complexion. Her brows were rather thick, but in her eyes and lips you could still see a young girl. The black paint on her cheeks was washed away, but a small spot remained, shaped like a butterfly.

"Aren't you glad you didn't commit a murder last night?" Shinta spoke with strong emotion, and the woman laughed softly for the first time. Shinta laughed too.

"If I had run away with Kuraji, you might have murdered both of us. It might have served Kuraji right, but for me it would have been a most unlucky accident."

"I know. I'm sorry that it was you that had to suffer."

"It was rather fortunate for you that Kuraji got away."

The woman laughed, carefree and loud. Shinta, too, laughed lightheartedly, and looked at the woman, then down at himself. His short linen *hakama*[9] was smeared with mud from his desperate attempt at escape last night. It looked as if the dye in the cloth had changed. His *eboshi* hat was gone.

"Shinta you're a fast runner. I suppose maybe in some things women can't beat men." Again the woman laughed.

Finally they came to the main roadway. They saw retreating figures of travelers and their packhorses heading west.

The oil barrels Shinta had carried on the pole over his shoulder were still lying by the side of the stone gate. Kuraji's were upside-down and empty.

Shinta took up his pole with its cargo and started to walk away. He said to the woman, "Even though they're empty, the barrels are necessary for business. You'd better take them with you."

The woman followed Shinta to the edge of the town. Mt. Tennō with its thick black woods overwhelmed everything around it. Kuraji's wooden-roofed cottage looked terribly shabby. Thin eggplants leaned against the bamboo fences hung with large bamboo tubes used as oil containers, drying and beginning to crack. The woman suddenly began to walk more quickly and entered the cottage. Shinta followed her. She took out Kuraji's short *hakama* and gave it to Shinta to replace the muddy ones he wore. Then Shinta came outside. It was now broad daylight.

9. A divided skirt for men's formal wear. Here, Shinta is wearing a shorter, less formal kind. (NT)

"Now, take good care of your health. Stay away from strong-willed women."

"I will. And you, try not to quarrel with your husband."

"I will. Good-bye."

The woman put her cheek against the opening of the door curtain, her eyes sparkling.

Shinta returned to his house at the far end of Kyōgoku. Suddenly overcome with exhaustion, he lay on his back on the wooden floor and let out a long breath. He couldn't tell whether last night's events were more Kuraji's affair or his own. It was at once terrifying and absurd. But also he felt pity for the woman.

For the next four or five days Shinta went about his business in Ide and Sumiyama and earned money.

Every time he encountered female customers, he remembered the words of that large woman. "This may be a strong-willed woman. I must be cautious. . . ." But he could never tell whether his customers were strong-willed or not.

One day he went out to a district called Kosobe. In the afternoon he was caught in an unseasonably cold rain, and was exhausted when he returned home. Next to the oil barrels in his house there was a small wooden tray. On the tray he found two or three small dishes of food meant to be served with *sake*.

Ten days later he went to another trade meeting at the shrine. Kuraji was not there. The other men laughed.

"What's happened to Kuraji? You must know. Has he switched to a new wife?"

"How would I know? Really, honestly."

The men laughed, amused by Shinta's desperate defensiveness. Shinta received the new supply of oil and had a travel permit issued at the chief priest's.

"Are you taking a trip, Shinta? Good luck! Don't follow in Kuraji's footsteps," said Shinta's fellow merchants.

"Don't worry," answered Shinta. "I'm not popular with women."

When he'd responded to his fellow men's encouragement, Shinta in some mysterious way felt his confidence rise.

The next day Shinta started his journey to the east. It was an exceedingly hot morning; steam rose from the road, which was wet from a rainfall in the night. Mt. Daimonji and Mt. Nyoi were veiled in white mist.

As he stepped toward the crimson-gold sun, he felt as if the big world were waiting for him with its gate wide open. He walked in high spirits.

But at the checking station of Fuwa, he was disappointed to find a surprisingly small, wooden-roofed cottage. Moreover, the checking station officials were few and they were all old. When he showed his permit and paid the fees, they bowed to him. Shinta now became somewhat emboldened. He continued his journey, proceeding to Tarui, Aohaka and Akasaka. He did not find these eastern regions significantly different. The scenery was rough, the appearance of the local inhabitants was humble, and their language sounded harsh, but the tone was much like that of Kyoto.

On the bank of the River Ibi, Shinta put down his cargo and rested. The high noon sun glared. As he watched the unhurried, side-to-side movement of the water, he began to feel a little lonesome.

"What a faraway place I've come to!"

He recalled the incident that night along the River Yodo and half-imagined he saw the woman with the black, butterfly-shaped spot on her cheek leaning against the bridge pole in front of him.

"I was nearly killed that time!" thought Shinta.

The large woman's burst of laughter at dawn on that path through the rice fields came back into his ears.

"She's a woman of strong will. She may have taken up the trade herself in Kuraji's place, to compete with me. I mustn't be beaten!"

Probably because he made this resolution, Shinta became quite a good businessman. His precautions against strong women diminished.

He was able to finish selling his merchandise sooner than expected, and decided to return home. He was in high spirits, and he did not feel very tired. He was simply happy.

When he crossed the Sanjō Bridge, he could not believe his own eyes for a moment.

"Are the streets of Kyoto so cramped and busy? Well, anyway, I'm glad I'm back."

When Shinta reached his home in Kyōgoku, he was surprised again. The house seemed much too small. As his eyes adjusted to the darkness in the room, he noticed something.

As before, he saw small dishes on a small wooden tray. But this

time there were more dishes. Under a small skylight window on the
west side of the cottage was a cistern made from a hollow natural
rock. The water trickling down from the gutter overflowed the rock
and pierced the light from outside. At that spot, leaning against the
rock, was a small branch of hydrangea,[10] swaying to and fro almost
imperceptibly.

10. The hydrangea blossom is said to change its colors seven times, from white to purple,
and so on, to light red. (NT)

TENGU CHILD

Every morning, with the first light of dawn, travelers' feet stir in the Awadaguchi—the Millet Field Gate—of Kyoto. Leaving the gate and its village behind them, the travelers climb the steep slope of the Hinooka Pass and reach the checking station of Ōsaka. There, on the station's hilltop, as they look down at Lake Biwa through the clearing mist, their resolve to make the journey is confirmed. Then they hurry on to their various destinations.

In the village of Awadaguchi there are beautiful temples and noblemen's mansions, also the shop of a famous sword maker. But the village has smaller houses as well, their roofs lined up like open umbrellas lying side by side. These, huddled together, are the simple homes of craftsmen, peddlers, and manual laborers.

The village serves as a kind of doorway[1] for the capital city of Kyoto. Travelers who come all the way from the Eastern region to see Kyoto must pass through Awadaguchi before they can cross the Great Bridge of Sanjō and, with their hearts dancing, set foot on the capital's famous main street, Sujaku Ōji. And similarly one must pass through Awadaguchi before he can set out on a poetic pilgrimage to the Eastern region, to visit places celebrated in poems— places where he can let his spirit and body swim outstretched in the vast heaven and earth of the Musashino territory.

When the Kyoto autumn is halfway along, fine days follow one after another. Mountains change color according to the hour and the nature of the sunlight—now deep yellow, now reddish brown. But before one knows it, winter stealthily moves in on the shadow of the mountains and with its moist breath fades the colors of the trees and darkens the town.

There was in Awadaguchi a boy with the strange name of *Tengu Dōji*, or "Bird-creature child."[2] He was about six years old. He was

---

1. Literally, official checkpoint for those entering and leaving—*sekisho* in Japanese. (NT)
2. The original title, and the boy's name, is *Tengu Dōji*. The *Tengu* is a legendary creature, derived from the Sanskrit *Garuda*, an imaginary bird, one of the eight guardians of the Bud-

always climbing up into treetops, gazing at the unmoving mountains or the moving people. In his neighborhood there wasn't a single tree which didn't carry the marks of the child's fingernails, but his small figure was most frequently seen in a persimmon tree by the side of his house, for not only was this a huge tree but also it had convenient branches for him to sit on.

The child's home was a small shop which sold travelers' canes and straw sandals for both men and horses. The child's father, a carpenter, sometimes worked at a construction site, when he was called there by the master carpenter, but more often than not he stayed home. The child's mother had her hair always tied up in a knot and wore a short, plain dress and a narrow, rope-like belt. Her face emotionless, she looked after the child and the father or tended the shop.

Not only the child's father and mother but all who lived in this neighborhood were people who had forgotten themselves. The reason the child stayed up in trees was that there was no child in any home who would be friends with him. And no pleasant seat was reserved for children in the company of the tired grownups; that was another reason. Moreover, he did not like to see his father pursued by the stern eyes of the master carpenter, and he hated the look on his mother's face as she watched the dazzling dresses of the wives and daughters of government officials, passing in front of the shop on their way to assignments in the Eastern region.

The night of the full moon passed without incident. A few more days went by. Then, one sunny morning, five or six villagers gathered in front of the child's house, talking in their usual loud voices. The carpenter, the child's father, held a round stone about the size of a large *kemari* ball.[3]

"What a strange stone! It's got beautiful blue moss on it."

"It has a fine shape—like Mt. Hiei."

"There's a beautiful crack in the middle—straight as can be!"

"It's got a kind of halo coming out of it!"

Suddenly the carpenter's face lit up in a smile. "I found it myself,"

---

dhist law. In Japanese folk legend, a *Tengu* is represented by a goblin with a human body, a red face, a long nose and wings, who lives in a remote mountain, carries a feather fan, and is able to fly and to perform miracles. (In modern Japanese slang a *tengu* can be a boastful person.) (NT)

3. *Kemari*—a game somewhat like soccer, commonly played by the nobility. (NT)

he said. "This morning when I stuck my neck out through the door curtain to see what the weather was like, here was this honorable stone. I almost kicked it!"

The neighbors decided that the carpenter should keep the stone until he could ask a priest or a *shugenja* monk about its origin.[4] Then they went back to their houses.

During their skimpy meal, the child's father repeated the neighbors' conversation instead of moving his chopsticks. His eyes glowed. The mother, too, looked unusually happy. The child kept his head down, biting his lip hard. He'd been behind the grown-ups and didn't need to hear it twice. But he kept himself from getting up.

While the boy's father was at the doorway counting his tools in their box, suddenly from the west came the sound of a trumpet shell ringing and echoing through the air. The carpenter's family and all the same faces that had gathered earlier came out to the street and together greeted a sturdy, middle-aged *shugenja* monk who came walking toward them with erect bearing and a measured step.

The monk had a small hood over long hair combed straight back. He wore a monk's coat, carried a monk's pannier on his back, and held an octagonal whitewood cane in his hand. His feet were neatly clasped in good footwear. Apparently he was on his way to the place of ascetic disciplines.

The people stood in a row, headed by the carpenter. The carpenter held up the stone reverentially in both hands, went down on both knees to the monk, head bowed low behind the stone, then stepped forward and briefly explained the incident of that morning. In his excitement the carpenter faltered several times. The *shugenja*, showing signs of deep emotion, looked now at the carpenter, now at the stone. The other grown-ups looked up at the *shugenja* apprehensively, then down at the stone.

In a stern, deliberate tone the *shugenja* identified himself.

"I," he said, "am a long-time resident of the Bujōji Temple on the remote mountain of Kurama. At the beginning of the season of ascetic disciplines this year I was unfortunately not able to lead my fel-

---

4. *Shugenja*—a follower of *Shugendō*, a religious sect blending Shintoism, Buddhism, Taoism, and Primitive Mountain-worship. Followers of this sect practice religious asceticism, self-mortification, incantation and prayer, and believe in the efficacy of magic. (NT)

low ascetic devotees up into the mountains because I had to attend
to some business. Consequently, at this time I have left my temple
gate in order to seclude myself in the temple of Zaōdō of Yoshino,
where I am resolved to read the opening and closing parts of *Dai
Hannya Kyō* scripture for thirty-seven days. What you have here is
no ordinary stone. This is a sacred treasure called a *Tengu* stone,
which the great noble *Tengu* living high up in Mt. Kurama lets fall
occasionally. Look at it carefully! The stone has a beautiful crack in
the middle, which was made by the claw of the noble *Tengu*. You
could not find such a magnificent stone however you might look. It
is a true blessing."

The eloquence of the *shugenja* overwhelmed those around him.

"He who possesses this stone will receive great good fortune. Also
if you worship this *Tengu* stone with true devotion, all diseases you
have will be instantly cured. Well now. I will make magical signs
with my fingers so that the stone may acquire an additional magic
efficacy."

The *shugenja* monk put down his pannier, straightened himself
up, rubbed the beads hanging from his neck, and smoothly recited
an incantation. The carpenter and the rest fixed their eyes on the
mouth and fingertips of the *shugenja*, half entranced by the flow of
his magnificent voice. Faces of travelers joined the others. The voice
of the *shugenja* stopped.

"That'll do," he said. "When I have completed my reading of
scripture and climbed back down the mountain, I will stop here
again and perform a further religious rite for you. Anyway, you must
build a shrine, no matter how small, as a sanctuary for the noble
stone."

"Thank you very much," said the carpenter soberly. "I'll begin
right away."

A middle-aged woman stepped forward, clasped her hands and
bowed. "Noble monk, I have been troubled with headaches for
many years. Please help me."

The *shugenja*, muttering something, stroked the woman's forehead several times with his beads. The woman blinked her eyes,
and cried, "Oh, I am cured! I am cured! Thank god, thank god!"

An old man with a bamboo cane came forward, trembling, and
complained of a heaviness in the hip. The *shugenja* took the stone
from the carpenter and stroked the old man with it several times

from the neck down to the hip. The old man closed one eye and submitted. "Ooh, ooh. My spine feels warm. I'm most obliged." The old man threw aside his cane and stretched his back. People flew to their homes and soon returned with gifts. The *shugenja* opened the lid of his pannier, which was filled in no time with copper coins, rice, peas, salt, and other good things. The monk put the pannier on his back. His octagonal whitewood cane struck the ground forcefully, and the sound of the trumpet shell reverberated like the command of the great *Tengu*.

The carpenter and the rest watched in tears as the figure of the *shugenja*, as if flying up into the sky, gradually grew smaller annd smaller until it disappeared from view.

The neighbors talked the matter over and at last chose, as the site of the shrine, the lot next to the persimmon tree by the side of the carpenter's house. The carpenter quickly completed the shrine. The shrine was a small one, slightly larger than an ordinary family altar. The stone was placed in the center and the candle was lit. The neighbors clapped their hands loudly.

The carpenter felt extremely happy. No wonder, for he rose to the rank of a priest at one bound. His wife's happiness was even greater. Not only was she now reborn as the wife of a priest, or as a priestess, but she was also getting prime-rate benefits with no work. Every morning when she opened the door of the shrine to clean it, she would find on the narrow floor washed rice, rice cakes, or at times even copper coins—one day one thing, another day another. The carpenter and his wife began to talk about their future.

"I will probably have to learn how to recite sacred prayers and how to perform the purification ritual. I will also need a ceremonial *eboshi* hat and a pair of *hakama*,"[5] said the carpenter.

"That's so," replied his wife. "Why don't you try to learn a little at a time? We would have to bring up our son so that he could succeed you."

"Yes, yes, that's so. And you, you ought to keep yourself clean and tidy like a priestess. I'll buy you a pair of red *hakama* soon."

The talk of the carpenter and his wife grew more and more se-

5. A divided skirt worn mainly by men for formal occasions, but also worn by some women (e.g., Shinto priestesses) performing special ceremonies. (NT)

rious. But their son grew less and less cheerful every day. His face became expressionless, and he began to avoid having meals with his parents. One after another he changed the trees he climbed.

His mother was the first to begin to worry. She was fearful lest their present happiness should suddenly alter and they should be hurt by some unexpected misfortune.

One day when the father was not at home, the mother talked to her son. Her voice was hoarse, her breath and words mixed together. The son kept his mouth shut. The mother questioned persistently and began to cry. The son also cried and at last started to talk. It was utterly beyond imagination. After sobbing for a long time and wiping his nose, the son said something like the following:

"The stone in the shrine is not a gift from the great *Tengu*. It is one of the many stones placed on top of the shingles of our roof. The other day, when I was up in the top of the persimmon tree, looking toward Mt. Hiei, a bunch of armed monk soldiers came by.[6] The ones in the lead looked especially ferocious. They were waving their huge, glittering halberds over their heads and shouting with loud voices. The tip of the blade of one halberd struck the eaves of our house with great force, and one of the stones on the roof fell off to the ground. When I climbed down from the tree to come inside the house, I moved the stone to the side of the door so that nobody would step on it."

After confessing thus, the boy again sobbed bitterly. "I thought many times of telling you all this honestly, but I was afraid it would ruin the happiness of our home."

The mother was stunned, her dream shattered into pieces. She remembered that she herself had heard the warlike shouts of the mountain monk soldiers and had crouched as small as she could make herself on the dirt floor of the kitchen.

In the evening, the carpenter returned from work. The child could not bear to see his father's sorrowful look as he spoke in a low voice, face to face with his mother. The carpenter, trying to shift the whole blame to his son, repeatedly questioned the child in a trembling, incoherent voice. The child answered desperately, "If the truth about this stone were known, how awful for the people who come to pray every day!"

6. Large temples and monasteries maintained armed monk soldiers as security forces. Often the monk soldiers were ex-convicts or fugitives from the law. (NT)

"Well, what then?" said the father.

Even the child could clearly see his father's futile effort to cling to his dignity. The boy said, "Right away, everybody will say to you, 'Carpenter, you deceived us!' Oh, I really didn't want to tell the truth!"

Again the child cried bitterly. The carpenter brought out a ladder and went up to the eaves. Sure enough, there was a deep cut at the edge of the eaves, and a roof stone was missing.

The three sat in silence for a long while. From time to time tears would begin falling, one after another, from the eyes of the mother and the son. With vacant eyes, the father was imagining the retreating back of a priest leaving the shrine.

The following day and from that day on, the child stayed in an especially high branch of the persimmon tree. Down below, he saw his father duck into the house hurriedly through the door curtain, his body no longer forceful, his small *eboshi* hat bent forward.

Every evening the parents repeated their consultation in low voices. On the sixth day, the father left without his carpenter's tools. When he returned, the child was high in the persimmon tree as usual, watching the red leaves glowing in the setting sun along the slope of Mt. Hinooka. The father called out to the child, "Oi, come on down! Good news!"

He looked unusually cheerful. The child obeyed. The mother was also called at the same time, and she stuck her face out of the kitchen while drying her hands.

"Today I went to pay a visit to the holy priest of Tawara about the noble stone," said the carpenter.

This holy priest had shown kindness to the carpenter in the past when he had worked on repairing the main building of Tawara's Zenjōji Temple. Recently the holy priest had handed over the temple to his disciple and built himself a hermitage in the valley of the Uji River. With great force the carpenter repeated the words of the priest.

"Stop worrying about this business and tell the whole truth. You may put the stone back in its place on the roof where it was before. When you find a mistake, you should fix it at once. The great *Tengu* would not be angry over such a thing. By the way, your son's a fine boy. He meets the Buddha's wishes. If he should want to become my disciple, I'd be happy to train him."

The priest's words were serene, as might be expected from a hermit. The carpenter was buoyant. He imagined the figure of a young high priest in a crimson robe and a seven-striped golden cope, his shaved bluish head shining. The stiff face of the carpenter's wife became completely relaxed.

"It's a splendid thing to be the archbishop of Mt. Hiei," said the carpenter. "Tens of thousands of priests and monk soldiers are his followers. Not even the *Kampaku*[7] is a match for him. How I'd like to show you, once in your life, the Grand Religious Ceremony of March. I saw it when I was working on Mt. Hiei. Incredible!"

At once the carpenter's son objected. "I don't want to be the archbishop. I wouldn't be able to climb in the trees."

"What about someone like the holy priest of Tawara, then?" asked the carpenter. The son shook his head. "I like him, but I don't want to live in a house smaller than ours. Besides, I hate such a low place as the river bank."

Emboldened by the holy priest's words, the carpenter postponed his effort to persuade his son and went around to his neighbors' homes to tell them the truth. It took a long time to make them understand. They reacted in different ways: some were angry, some enraged, some disappointed, some saddened; some smiled a grim smile, while others burst into laughter. The carpenter, meanwhile, became more and more eloquent.

"It's all that *shugenja*'s fault! Since he called the stone the *Tengu* stone, I was hoodwinked. I wasted my lumber and labor, and you wasted rice and rice cakes."

In the end, the carpenter escaped all blame by shifting it to the *shugenja*. Some wanted to hit the monk, some to yell at him, some to tease him, and some to snub him on his return. In short, they felt helpless anger at their inability to do anything at all.

"The *shugenja* said he would stop here on his way from Mt. Yoshino. When he comes, let us all laugh at him together." Such was the grown-ups' conclusion. Things had not gone as badly as the carpenter had feared they might; the feelings of the village grown-ups were easily soothed. The *Tengu* stone was reduced to a roof stone. The woman's headache and the old man's crooked hip, which once

---

7. The most powerful post of regent for an adult Emperor. (NT)

had been cured, returned. Worst of all for the carpenter and his wife, the shrine lay empty and their dream that they were priest and priestess of the shrine ended, leaving them with a sense of desolation.

A few days passed. Autumn was nearing its close. The frame of mind of those who had been fanatic believers in the *Tengu* stone had returned almost to normal, when one morning, through a heavy mist, the sound of a trumpet shell was heard trembling and trailing off in the air.

The carpenter was the first to rush out into the street, but he immediately went back inside. It was the same *shugenja* monk. He looked even more magnificent, perhaps because of his recent ascetic disciplines. The carpenter pressed his face against the short door curtain. His wife and son hid behind him. In the surrounding houses the people were crouched in the same posture; only the legs of a few men were visible beneath the short door curtains. No one uttered a sound.

The trumpet shell boomed two or three times. No one came out. The *shugenja* was now in front of the carpenter's house. One of the monk's eyes glistened. A strange shadow drifted across the side of his face.

"Ha, ha, ha!"

"Hoo, hoo, hoo!"

At the sound of their disrespectful laughter, the monk's spirit seemed to shrink inward for an instant, but he did not lose his erect bearing as he walked on, his figure gradually receding in the distance. The grown-ups went out to the street and roared with laughter. They had never been happier. For the first time, the weak had been able to assert themselves against a seemingly immovable authority.

The child, standing behind the grown-ups, watched the monk's diminishing figure fade into the distance like a white moth. He felt great pity for the monk at his unexpected reversal of fortune.

"I feel sorry for him," said the boy.

The mother nodded sadly.

The mist lifted and the sun began to shine. The street stirred with people. Travelers paid no attention to the empty shrine.

The incident of the *Tengu* stone shook the lives of the commoners' district for only a short time and then was gone. Nothing in particular was gained, though perhaps it could be said that after this incident the hearts of the people seemed more united, somewhat warmer.

The child's mind, however, was swinging and swaying in a complex thought. The grown-up world seemed to him empty, ridiculous, and shameful. He was weary of having to live in such a twisted world.

He spent every day up in the persimmon tree. He climbed to the very top and would not come down even after the stars began to twinkle. If a woman passed under his feet, the boy would pluck one of the few persimmons remaining on the branches and throw it down.

"Oh! A *Tengu* stone is falling!" the woman would cry out, and she would run away off-balance as if she were dancing. The child would smile a desolate smile. Such was his hopeless protest against grown-ups.

At times the late autumn rain of Kitayama was mixed with fine snow flakes; soon the wind blowing down Mt. Hiei began to batter the townsfolk fiercely. Before anyone realized it, the top of Mt. Hira behind the town became snow white. Not a single leaf remained on the persimmon tree. The black shadow of the child among the higher branches stood out, unearthly, against the hard, evening sky.

Such days went by one after another, emptily, and the New Year had almost arrived, when unexpectedly a great fear descended upon the people. Rumors floated about that the monk soldiers of Sakamoto, at the foot of Mt. Hiei, would soon attack the capital, and that the warriors of the Taira family were preparing for the attack with bows and arrows.

Earlier, the monk soldiers of Sakamoto had supported those of *Tōdō*—the East Tower of Mt. Hiei—and presented a direct petition to the Imperial Court. When their demand was not met, the Sakamoto and Tōdō monks had gathered together a large army and were said to be in a rage to achieve their end by force. It would not be easy for them to meet the ferocious arrows of horsemen by merely waving long halberds and swords.

The carpenter and his neighbors talked about the matter in front of the former shrine of the *Tengu* stone. Their voices became louder and louder.

"Awadaguchi is the doorway to Kyoto."

"We have beautiful temples and noblemen's mansions."

"Have the wild monk soldiers no fear of Buddha?"

"However it may be, it will be a terrible thing, having them riot in front of our homes."

"We will be spared, though, if they go around by the slope of Kirara, the way they did last year."

"How horrible if people's arms and legs should be thrown into our houses!"

"It would be great fun if the monks' heads should fall, instead of a *Tengu* stone." So someone tried to joke, but everybody's face became as stiff as a stone Buddha's.

"Why should the archbishop of Hiei look on in silence? Perhaps the scripture has lost its efficacy. Ah, unreliable, unreliable!"

Oblivious to such concerns, the child remained, as usual, at the top of the persimmon tree.

A TELESCOPE

"You should hurry to worship the new great Buddha. It's tremendous!"

"Is it really? Then I'll postpone my business in Tatsuta and go see the Buddha right away!"

Such greetings were exchanged daily among the travelers passing each other in the vicinity of Narazaka and Utahime. In Narazaka, the hum and bustle never ceased. In the past it had been a lonely village nestled in the folds of the hills, but now small tea shops and restaurants stood in rows to attract customers—pilgrims to the temple.

The difficult task of reconstructing the Hall of the Great Buddha in the Tōdaiji Temple had been carried out without interruption with the backing of the Imperial Court, the Buddhist temples and Shinto shrines, Buddhists of various regions, and, in addition, the strong support of the newly formed Shogunate government.[1] Now, fourteen years after the burning of the Tōdaiji Temple by the troops of the Taira family, the celebration of the completed reconstruction was to be held in just a few days. The repair work on the Great Buddha and the rebuilding of the Hall housing it, as well as the Nandaimon Gate, were finished. Today, lumber for the covered passageway and for smaller accessory buildings, as well as paving stone and stone for the foundation and facing were being hauled in. The number of artisans, laborers, oxen and horses required for the work was immense.

The time was glorious spring. When the woods and meadows of the mountains encircling Buddha's city—Mt. Wakakusa, Mt. Mi-

---

1. Headed by the *Shogun*, or generalissimo (Minamoto Yoritomo was the first one to assume the title, in 1192), the shogunate government established in Kamakura, in the Eastern region, theoretically represented only the military authority of the Emperor, but in practice it controlled all of Japan, while the Emperor (who remained in Kyoto) stood merely as a figurehead. (NT)

kasa, and Mt. Takamado—all stretched themselves, carefree, a breath of radiant green, why was it that the faces of the townsfolk were dry and dark?

For these people, homes and furniture destroyed by the fire were the chief concern, and also they were growing weary of the impersonal yet complicated and conflicting interests vexing the relationships of the diverse workers called for the reconstruction of the Great Buddha's Hall, both the innumerable common laborers brought in from various regions of Japan and the skilled artisans, some of whom were foreigners.

Be that as it may, after a long absence, the huge temple now once again towered above the people. The enormous precipice-like roofs seemed to avalanche down from the gigantic ridgepoles to be caught by long, Chinese-style horizontal beams. Numerous square chocks of wood were locked between the beams like the fists of a demon. Little wonder that the townspeople should bow their heads for no obvious reason, willing to pay respect to Buddha before the vast power shown forth by this monstrous structure.

The day was like a day in summer. With sunrise, long lines of men and black oxen laden with stones began to move along the Kiso Road. Several oxen formed a team, yoked to one another by thick rope, moving heavy boulders on rollers made of logs.

When the oxen reached the Narazaka slope, they were briefly unyoked to rest before starting the long climb. Sweat dripping around their unblinking eyes, the docile beasts made a rush for the water-troughs by the side of the road and dipped in their heads. Herders gave the oxen the fresh grass which had been cut before dawn, and one of the oxen licked salt from a man's hand. This ox, dull amber-colored, must have been especially weak. At that moment one could read mournful resentment in the eyes of the oxen nearby.

Now there happened to be a fly on one of the oxen. He was planning to gain safe entrance to the temple by riding on an ox passing by in the early dawn, and so to proceed to sightseeing. Feeling thirsty, the fly began to drink water at the corner of the watertrough. Suddenly, with a loud noise, a wave broke over him. At that moment the fly, caught up by the wave, was dashed against the nostrils of the sick ox who had licked the salt. The fly cried out frantically, "No, no! I won't be drowned! I won't stand for it!"

He was already climbing up the nose of the sick ox when he came to himself. Crawling between his two eyes and then between his two ears, the fly was finally able to sit on the ox's right horn. The fly was happy.

"Well, well, I'm safe!"

Presently, the black oxen began to move again, gathering the last of their strength. The men, too, pushed themselves forward. Climbing up the tortuous, rutted road to the top and turning east on the road connecting the Saidaiji Temple and the Hokkeji Temple, they could expect to see the Tegaimon Gate at the end.

The sick ox seemed especially wracked by pain. His loose belly swayed, and his four legs trembled jerkily. Slaver dribbled ceaselessly from his mouth; his eyes, staring down his nose, never moved. Behind him the oxen and men formed a long line up the sloping road, and the herders' whips flashed, making a continual dull racket.

"Why should these oxen have to suffer so?" muttered the fly on the ox's horn. "It makes me feel guilty, having such an easy time." The fly became remorseful, taking advantage of the poor, sick ox.

When at last, having climbed to the top of the hill, the ox reached the site of the burned-down Kairyōōji Temple, the fly noticed a large bamboo tree whose branches stretched over the mud walls. As he jumped onto the bamboo tree, the fly blurted out with spontaneous concern, "My dear, sick ox, take care!" Before too long, the thin figure of the amber-colored ox became woven in with the line of the black oxen.

Presently twenty or more packhorses came by in a row. Each carried on its back four straw sacks of charcoal. The horses looked lively, perhaps because their load was fairly light. The fly flew off the bamboo branch and landed on one of the straw sacks. Thus the fly entered the premises of the temple through the Tegaimon Gate.

He was shocked by the heat created by the crowd, but when he looked up at the newly built Hall of the Great Buddha, he was breathless.

"What a colossal thing these human beings have made!" thought the fly. "Even Buddha himself could never have succeeded at such a task!"

Quite indifferent to the fly's excitement, the horses came around the rear side of the Hall of the Great Buddha. Since it was a little away from the center, there were only a few people. However, the place was cluttered with large piles of sand and clay and straw sacks containing charcoal and minerals. Here stood both the forge and foundry, where the hardware for the building was being made.

The charcoal sacks were unloaded in front of the forge. Each time two or three sacks of charcoal were emptied into the furnace, the black charcoal would turn instantly to a glowing red mass of fire, and the hot air would burst out in gusts from the blower.

Several muscular arms dripping greasy sweat moved frantically in the flame. The air from the blower shot up into the sky like a whirlwind. The fly, who had carelessly perched on the edge of the furnace, was sucked up into this whirlwind. The fly let his wings and legs relax. This was a completely unexpected turn of events.

"Good lord! Am I being apprenticed to En no gyōja?"[2] said the fly to himself. The breath from the blower now blended with a gentle breeze in the sky. As he lightly floated in the soft wind, the fly was luckily able to land on a ridge tile of the huge roofs of the new Hall of the Great Buddha.

What a surprise! Except when he was there on some urgent business, the fly was not accustomed to wandering high in the air, so the rooftop became for him a wonderful observatory. The angle from which he looked down upon the lower world was wider and deeper than any he had ever achieved before. It gave the fly great pleasure that, by sheer luck, a small creature like him could step firmly on his six thin legs over the roof of the Hall of the Great Buddha, which had been completed by the collective strength and wisdom of not just tens but hundreds of thousands of people.

The fly looked around, turning his head in all four directions. The endless undulation of the mountains surrounding the plains of Yamato—especially, running from west to south, the peaks of Ikoma, Kazuragi, Kongō, and Yoshino, with their massive, reclining forms and outstretched, gigantic arms and legs under the clear, sharp sun—gave an impression of wonderful strength.

2. A famous religious figure in the late seventh century and the founder of the religious sect, *Shugendō*, which is a blending of Shintoism, Buddhism, Taoism, and Primitive Mountain-worship. Followers of this sect practice religious asceticism, self-mortification, incantation and prayer, and believe in the efficacy of magic. (NT)

Next the fly looked down upon the temple premises. Except for the temple itself, everything was in motion—animals carrying building materials, men unloading them, other men carrying them to their appointed places. It was strange, comical, even somewhat pitiful that all the men looked about the same size as he was, a mere fly.

He then looked down on the quietest corner, the southeast, where a colorful curtain enclosed a small area, and, inside, a large group of young girls was moving. Their long sleeves of red, white, green, purple, and yellow flowed forward and backward like a large wave. A strange sound moving with the wave—now slow, now fast, now loud, now soft, reverberating in the air—rose up toward him. They were doubtless rehearsing the heavenly maidens' dance and the Chinese-style religious masque to be performed at the celebration of the completed rebuilding.

The fly, rolling his lustrous, amber-colored eyes, looked all around, up and down, down and up, unhurriedly.

The fly's curiosity gradually changed to skepticism. "Why would human beings want to make such a monstrosity? Is there really any need for it?" One had to answer one's own questions. "The Hall was probably rebuilt to bring back happiness to earth. I don't know, though. Did people really have happy lives before the Great Buddha's Hall burned down?"

To the fly, this seemed an immensely reasonable question. At the same time he wondered if perhaps he wasn't becoming unduly argumentative. For a while he sat in deep meditation, thinking nothing at all. Suddenly a cheerful voice sounded in his ears.

"Good heavens, it's you! I never thought I'd see you in a place like this!"

The fly started. A huge dragonfly was sitting right next to him. The dragonfly had a wonderfully sturdy look. His four wings were spread out, reflecting the sunlight. The yellow lateral stripes on his body were like the stripes on a master athlete's shirt. The dragonfly freely moved his huge silver-colored eyes, never ceasing to watch the stir of the world below.

He said, "My territory is high in the air, while yours is low on the ground. Isn't it rather unusual for you to be here today? What in the world has happened to you?"

As the fly briefly explained the events of the morning, the dragonfly listened with intense interest, sometimes surprised, sometimes laughing aloud.

"Ha, ha! It's not a bad idea to look at the world from a different location now and then. You and I may have considerably different points of view. Tell me, what's the most serious thought that's struck you since you first arrived here?"

When the fly spoke of the question that had come to his mind a few moments before—his question about whether the temple was really needed—the dragonfly nodded repeatedly, emphasizing his agreement with his large eyes.

"You, too, feel that way?" he exclaimed. "And you've just arrived! You should congratulate yourself on your quick perception."

"Then do you, my dear dragonfly, have the same opinion as I do?"

"Very nearly, yes. But since I live here and look down upon the world every day, I can express myself with more confidence than you."

The dragonfly's self-esteem was contagious, and the fly began to feel quite happy.

"For example," said the dragonfly, "look at this roof-tile we're now stepping on: there are more than a hundred thousand just like it. Also, I'm told there are at least two thousand huge logs under these tiles. The logs were cut in the faraway Western region—so I hear—brought in across the sea on floats.

"I understand it was enormously difficult to plate the Great Buddha inside this building with gold. The gold had to be collected from the provinces, which had only a meagre supply. But apparently some places have more gold than others. They say a large quantity was dug and collected from the mountains of Mutsu.

"On the day of the completion ceremony, the great *Shogun* of the Eastern region[3] is supposed to take a seat right down there"—he pointed—"attended by tens of thousands of warriors.

"One thousand priests are scheduled to participate in the sutra-chanting ritual to celebrate the opening of the eyes of the newly made Buddha."[4]

The fly rolled his eyes repeatedly and said, "How awesome! It al-

---

3. See footnote 1 to the shogunate government. (NT)
4. This ritual signifies the investing of a newly made image with sacred qualities. (NT)

most makes me faint just to hear about these things! You are indeed a person of great knowledge!"

The dragonfly's words became more heated. "But consider! Consider! It all started when some scallywag threw a torch into the Great Buddha's Hall."

The fly, fascinated, nodded again and again, saying, "Exactly! You're quite right!"

"And yet, after some fourteen years of toil," the dragonfly continued, "the Hall has been rebuilt! And what's happened in the world in the meantime? You know as well as I! The bloody fights between the Minamoto family and the Taira family have continued on and on, causing the deaths of innumerable human beings, horses, and cattle. Then year after year the crops have failed, and numerous people have died of that too. In addition to all this, many men, cattle, and horses have been dragged from the various provinces to build the Great Buddha's Hall, and they're suffering horribly day after day. I can't help questioning whether the Great Buddha's image gives any real happiness to living creatures. It might be quite another matter, of course, if this newly built Hall of the Buddha could never be struck by fire, as it was before."

The fly was greatly impressed by the dragonfly's discernment and eloquence. "Exactly!" he said. "You are exactly right! Look around you, and you'll see ruins from the fire everywhere. And still more difficulties remain to be surmounted before the whole thing can be finished. The more the work expands, the more the minuses!"

"My dear fly, you put it very well! I've been thinking recently, just what is it that makes a great man?"

"Good point," said the fly. "But I suppose even among human beings it's not impossible to find some who are seriously pondering these problems. I don't know. I wonder."

While the two were engrossed in their conversation, the sun came directly above them. The reflection of heat from the roof-tiles was so strong that their feet hurt. Below, artisans were taking their lunch and rest break; cattle and horses were hiding their heads in the feeding troughs.

It appeared that a quarrel had broken out among the groups of artisans. More people joined both sides, and their movements became violent. Several men became motionless, scattered here and there on the ground. A man on horseback rushed in, swinging a long pole and screaming loudly. Gradually the movements of the people became subdued. Everyone went back to his original place, and the motionless bodies were carried off.

In utter indignation, the dragonfly cried in his loud peeping voice, "How atrocious! To commit murders while working for Buddha!"

The fly agreed completely. "Yes indeed!" he said. "But listen, going back to our earlier topic, have you decided what kind of person you consider to be the greatest?"

"Ah, that's the ultimate problem," said the dragonfly. "The conclusion is simple. In brief, like Chōgen the holy priest, he would be a man who thinks only of Buddha and does not waste his own or others' time and labor."

"I agree," said the fly. "But does any such man actually exist?"

"My four wings can generate tremendous speed. Whenever I hear a rumor of a man who might possibly fit the description, I fly directly to the place where he lives and have a look for myself. In truth, I've been disappointed all too often." The dragonfly looked proudly at the far mountain range.

"Oh, how I envy you! Tell me more precisely your standards for selection," said the fly.

"In brief, one who does not get involved in trivia. One who cherishes our world. Actually, Chōgen the holy priest may seem admirable, but in his love for Buddha's image, he is crushing the world under his feet."

"Indeed. I too want to go where you have been and have a look myself."

"Yes, yes. That's the only way. I must say, the ascetic of Mt. Kongō and the holy priest of Ryōmon are the only people I consider great. There's a rumor that the beggar saint of Narazaka is great. Narazaka isn't far, but since I prefer high places, I am not inclined to go to a low region."

"Hmm!" said the fly. "Listen, many thanks! I've heard of the ascetic of Mt. Kongō. He's quite famous. I'm afraid I don't know about the other two, off hand. But since I know the way to Mt. Kongō, I'll set out immediately. I'm very glad I chanced to meet you!"

"Good-bye. Let me hear your impressions later."

"By all means! Farewell, my dear dragonfly."

In an instant, with a buzz, the fly danced up like an acorn tossed in the air. The dragonfly's big eyes caught a flying dot, but it disappeared at once.

The fly continued to beat the air with his wings, heading in a southwest direction. High mountains created rigid walls from north to south and divided the plains in two—Yamato and Kawachi. In the north was Mt. Kazuragi. The prominent peak to the south was Mt. Kongō. Its eastern slope, densely covered with gigantic beeches, was extremely steep, but its western slope was gentle and trailed off toward the sea of Naniwa, a number of low mountains scattered in between. The roof-tiles of a large temple at the summit glared in the sun.

"Ah, that must be the Tenjōrinji Temple; the ascetic is probably somewhere near," thought the fly. Readjusting his wings, he made a rapid descent. To the east of the temple was a rocky ledge. Sheer precipices dominated the surrounding scenery. There was an inexplicable ghastliness in the sight; it seemed as if the swaying, flickering trees were becoming invisible flames.

On the rocky ledge the fly saw an ascetic, apparently middle-aged and rather short in stature, with several young disciples. The ascetic stood holding an octagonal, white-wood cane in his hand. His disciples sat properly, with crossed legs, chanting the Sanskrit scripture of prayer for the protection of the guardian spirit of the mountain, practicing magical signs with their fingers. The ascetic's voice, rebounding from the pointed edges of rocks and reverberating among the trees, had overwhelming power. If a disciple's voice failed, the octagonal cane struck him mercilessly on the shoulder.

As the fly continued to watch, circling above them, the disciples began to practice the art of breathing control. The ascetic groped with his hand, examining the lower abdomen of each disciple. From time to time, the cane poked their navels. Some fell backward, unable to get up. Some opened their mouths, letting their breath out willy-nilly.

The fly became bored and flew up higher. He began to fly toward the east. In effect he was going upstream along the River Yoshino. The high peaks of Mt. Yoshino and Mt. Ōmine on the south side, and of Mt. Ōdaigahara on the east, dominated the spaces of sky under the cloud.

A Telescope

On the north was a moderately high, isolated mountain. He saw what looked like a hanging white silk thread fluttering in the wind along the wooded slope; it had to be the Ryōmon Falls. There was an old temple on the summit, a small hermitage nearby.

"That must be the Ryōmon Temple," said the fly to himself. "The holy priest must live over there. Lord, was I ever disappointed with that ascetic of Mt. Kongō! From the looks of him, he was a demon incarnate. But I have a strong hunch that the holy priest here is a good one."

The fly descended, aiming toward the hermitage, and, landing on the branch of a cedar tree by the side of the place, looked inside. An old priest was sitting there. He had a gentle face. The cottage was small but tidy. Apparently he was preparing his meal. In a small pan over the fire, something was cooking. The priest blew busily at the fire with his cheeks puffed up and sometimes tasted the food. The bedding was neatly folded and piled along the wall.

The fly kicked at the branch and floated up into the air. This time he saw Mt. Yoshino in the south, and flew due north. The cherry blossoms were in full bloom on the mountain. It looked as if white clouds had fallen and been scattered all over the slopes. It was a beautiful sight.

"I must say, I have some doubts about the holy priest of Ryōmon. Should a hermit eat sweet food and sleep in soft bedding? He's no different from a layman. I wonder if the dragonfly's vision isn't distorted because he always looks at the world from too high a place."

As the fly was thinking along these lines, the ornamental ridge-end-tile of the gigantic roofs of the Tōdaiji Temple came in sight. The fly blurted out, "What an enormous building! Is Chōgen, the holy priest, the greatest after all? What would the dragonfly say if I told him what I saw today?"

Between the low mountains to the northwest of the Tōdaiji Temple, a single road appeared, its winding ascent clear as day. The number of men, cattle, and horses in motion was considerably less than it had been this morning.

"That must be the Narazaka slope. This morning I was nearly killed there. Maybe I should try to find the beggar saint the dragonfly told me about."

The fly lowered his altitude in a headlong dive and flew just above the roofs of the people's houses. Burnt ruins of houses, still unrepaired, stood along the edge of the road. Near the bottom of the slope lay a vacant lot with a few trees. Small flowers of various colors were blooming. He saw rows of gravemounds, almost none of them old.

"This may be a graveyard for those who died of wounds or illnesses while carrying the lumber and stones to the Tōdaiji Temple. I wonder if there are graves for cattle and horses. If that sick ox I was on this morning should die, I wish he could be buried here," the fly thought.

Looking at the gravemounds more carefully, he found that they were all of the same size and were kept with great care. A little apart from the rest was a new, large gravemound, around which the ground was especially clean. Beside the mound stood a number of white-wood dedication sticks.[5] These were also new. Strangely enough, only this mound was pitch-black and shining.

As he came closer and looked at it carefully, he was astounded— astonished beyond words. The pitch-black surface was nothing less than flies like himself, and there were tens of thousands of them!

The fly landed on one of the dedication sticks and rested his wings. Reading the letters written on the stick, he was shocked again, or rather, dismayed. The beggar saint had died seven days before.

The fly immediately jumped down to the ground and squeezed himself in among his kinsmen. He had been wondering what that sound was, reverberating in the air, like the moan of a cold wintry wind. Now he knew. It was the unison chanting of the Buddhist scripture by his relatives. An old fly with large, cloudy, motionless eyes struggled close to him and asked, "Where are you from? I'm glad that you came to pay tribute to the beggar saint on the seventh-day ritual of his death."[6] The young fly replied, "I'm ashamed to confess that I didn't know about the beggar saint. Only this morning did I learn of his greatness, which is why I'm here. I can't tell you how sorry I am!"

The old fly told the young one about the saint. He had not only

5. These wooden sticks, sometimes in more elaborate shapes, are placed beside a grave for the repose of a deceased person's soul. (NT)

6. An important religious rite performed on the seventh day after death, counting the day of a person's death as the first. (NT)

buried the corpses of the men and beasts that died while working for
the reconstruction of the Great Buddha's Hall, he had also taken the
sick and wounded to the aid stations and helped to give them medi-
cal treatment and nursing. Also, for many years, he had given the
flies leftover rice. The young fly noticed, behind the gravemounds,
several simple, straw-thatched cottages whose sides were covered
with straw mats. The old fly wept bitter tears and said, "The saint
died of exhaustion. Yet not a single representative has been sent
from the Tōdaiji Temple."

Only the sick and the wounded had made the grave, placed their
offerings, or recited the scripture. Today, the sick and the wounded
had performed the seventh-day ritual in the morning, and after
chanting the scripture, had returned to their cottages to rest. In the
afternoon, the flies took their turn. So the young fly was told.

The young fly's heart was filled with emotion. The back of his
neck twitched and tightened. His eyes became warm and watery. As
he remained among his kinsmen and chanted the scripture, the irritation he had felt since morning was assuaged and he began to feel
almost ecstatic.

When the young fly lifted his head, the sun was near the horizon.
Still, not one of the flies would stir from its place. The young fly,
however, thought he had better tell the dragonfly before dark what
had happened that day. Above all, he wanted to let the dragonfly
know of the beggar saint's death as soon as possible. He closed his
eyes for a moment and flew straight up.

Traveling only a short distance, the fly landed on top of the Great
Buddha's Hall. To his great regret, however, the dragonfly was nowhere to be seen. Since it was late, he had perhaps already gone to
bed.

The fly flew back to the gravemounds of the Narazaka slope. Now
he noticed something that had escaped him before. He said in a surprised tone, "Look at that! The watertrough in which I was nearly
drowned this morning stands right next to the grave of the beggar
saint!"

Now his surprise grew great indeed. Pale golden light was rising
from the gravemound of the saint. Oblique rays of the setting sun
shone in the golden light. The beauty and sublimity of the scene
were beyond description.

A Telescope

The fly flew into the light and joined his kinsmen. The sun went down. The golden light now shone with an increasing aura of holiness in the evening darkness. The unison chanting of the scripture by the flies rose higher and higher into the night.

THE FOX WHO BECAME
A WIFE

In the West Section of Kyoto not a sound was heard. In the sticky black evening air only clouds moved. Grey shadows hid the moon from time to time as they drifted eastward, continually changing shape. It looked as if light-brown sand had been blown over the tree stumps and withered water plants, but it was merely what was left of the powdery snow that had fallen a few days before.

There were no houses in this immediate neighborhood. On the wet land, which looked as if it had been flooded recently, stood only a few barns, their roofs clustered together. Behind the woods in the distance, the five-story Buddhist pagoda rose up prominently, its nine-ring steeple and the flame-shaped ornament at the top a central point in the barren landscape, creating a mysterious harmony.

A tall man came walking. Takesada, a soldier in the Right Division of the Imperial Guards,[1] seemed to have nothing to do with the midnight scene. Today, on the eighteenth day of the First Month, at the archery contest held on the archery grounds of the Imperial Palace, he had shown the greatest skill of any archer, and had received praise from the *Kampaku*,[2] ministers, lords, and other high-ranking courtiers. After being awarded numerous prizes, he had been treated to a hearty feast at the home of the *Taishō*, or commander in chief of the Right Division of the Imperial Guards. Now Takesada was on his way home.

He had received the highest honor available to a man of his rank and status. The commander in chief was most encouraging and had said to him, "Takesada, your performance today was brilliant. You are the treasure of the Right Division. We are counting on you for next year, too."

1. The officers responsible for the protection of the Emperor and his family and of the Imperial Palace. The Guards were made up of 300 to 500 soldiers in two Divisions, the Right and the Left. (NT)

2. The *Kampaku* was the most powerful post of regent for an adult Emperor. (NT)

The way was now open for promotion to the rank of officer. The effect of *sake*, with the taste of power mixed in, can be strong. The pale-blue official costume he was wearing began to seem to him the dignified black wisteria-patterned costume of a much higher-ranking official; his ornamental ear-cover was transformed to the silver star visor of a general's helmet.

In his exuberance, Takesada kicked a big lump of snow at the shoulder of the road. The lump bounced sideways and changed its shape. It was a white fox. Polite and well-mannered, the fox sat still with its tail lowered and looked up at Takesada intently. Takesada's right hand did not reach toward the flat quiver[3] on his back; the lacquered wicker bow under his left arm remained where it was. The encounter was totally unexpected.

"You are a fox. What are you doing here at this hour?" he asked, quickly regaining his calm. The fox's meek behavior helped him in this.

The fox answered, "I have been waiting for you. I came from the northwest. I waited for you because I was extremely eager to meet the most magnificent man in the world."

The fox's voice was thin but clear. It seemed not so much to come from the fox's mouth as to exude naturally from its body. The fox sat still in one spot, with its front legs straight, and continued to look up at Takesada.

"Surely you must know," said Takesada, "that if I should change my posture and move my right hand just a little, your life would be whistled away." Takesada was tempted to show off his newly-acquired authority to one so weak.

"Yes," replied the fox. "I also know that your arrows are not sharp-pointed but rounded and that your bow is small and can only be drawn rather feebly."

Takesada saw that he had lost ground. He now realized that the fox possessed something more than high office or weapons.

"True," said Takesada, "perhaps these arrows can't kill you. You must have come out knowing that fact well. What a creature you are! If you have such wonderful supernatural power, why should you have anything to do with human beings?"

---

3. A flat quiver is used for ceremonial purpose as contrasted with a round quiver, which is used for actual battles. (NT)

Unexpectedly, the fox showed pleasure. "For a long time I have wanted to hear someone say what you have just said, but no one has done so. You are the first person to speak these words. I am most delighted."

To Takesada this was a surprising reply, and he asked, "What do you mean? I don't understand you."

"Since we foxes possess supernatural power, we are looked up to by other animals, but we are no match for human beings. The human being's power to live is far superior to our supernatural power. Consequently, someone like you who has exercised that power to the full is, from our point of view, higher than the gods."

"So that's it!" said Takesada. "Now I understand you! Then why do you deceive human beings who are higher than the gods? Why do you possess them?[4] It's inexcusable."

"We know that it is wrong. But it is our hopeless frivolity that makes us wish to conquer—if only for the moment—human beings who have something greater than supernatural power."

The fox's words were touching, and it seemed to the man that the effect of the *sake* was wearing off. He began to feel a touch of affection for the fox.

"Now I'm going home," he said. "By the way, I have with me a package of food that the commander in chief gave me as a gift." The man took out a small paper package from his front pocket and threw it to the fox. The fox caught the package in its mouth and got up. Its white figure soon blended in with the withered grass all around.

"If I get something good to eat again, I'll give it to you. Wait until then," Takesada called. He shook the arrows once in the quiver on his back and as he began to walk away, he looked over his shoulder two or three times. He forgot that he had been talking to a fox. The moon, three days past the full, hung low over the way to his house.

Next morning, when Takesada paid a courtesy visit to the waiting room of the Right Division's commander in chief at the Immeimon Gate of the Imperial Palace, he found himself immensely popular. His superiors, from the *shōshō*[5] down, including lower-ranking officials

---

4. In Japanese folktales, foxes are capable of demonically possessing human beings. (NT)

5. The third-highest-ranking official in the Imperial Guards, the *Taishō* (commanders in chief of the Right and the Left Divisions respectively) being the highest ranking. (NT)

such as the *shōgen* and *fushō*, seemed to respect his accomplishment.

"At last my real ability is going to speak for itself," Takesada told himself with conviction. His sense of satisfaction brimmed over as if to run like a soothing hand over even his hands and feet. He was jubilant.

"How lucky you are! Keep up your strength for next year, too!" said a fellow soldier who had seldom spoken to him before. With a half-smile, he patted Takesada on the shoulder from behind. The man had been unsuccessful at the archery contest the day before, and he seemed to mean the opposite of what he said. Perhaps his words represented the feelings of most of Takesada's fellow soldiers.

Takesada felt defiant. "I won't be defeated! I'll win again next year by all means!"

But the next moment he recalled the arduous training of the past year. Though he was fond of it, he had stopped drinking *sake*. He had reduced his sleeping hours. He had spent less on his food so that he could buy torchlights for his practice at night. Unless he repeated the hardships of the past year, the honor he had earned would vanish into thin air. For the first time he realized that the high peak and the deep gorge were side by side.

After agonizing a long time over his situation, Takesada talked to Hisakiyo, his closest friend. Because they were the same age and both unmarried, they had in the past discussed everything with each other. Hisakiyo sympathized with Takesada. Hisakiyo was not a particularly good archer and had not participated in the contest of the previous day.

"It's not easy to be in your situation," said Hisakiyo. "But if the Right Division should lose such a skilled archer as you, I'm afraid we would be scorned by the Left Division. I hate to say so, but I want you to perform just as well next year. All of us in the Right Division would be delighted. I promise to help you as much as I can. Why don't we drink *sake* together tonight? It's been a long time."

They emptied their *sake* cups many times at Hisakiyo's small house. Takesada knew well the rivalry between the Right and the Left Division. Right now, however, the fox had become more important to him. He packed the leftover food to take away with him and went out into the night air. His heated cheeks felt the chill all the more keenly.

"Was it about here?" murmured Takesada and looked at the roadside. The fox was already sitting there with its legs close together.

"Here you are," said Takesada. "You must have known of my coming through your supernatural power. In fact, I, too, thought you would be here, and so I brought this for you." Takesada gave the small package to the fox. The fox bowed politely, and started to walk side by side with Takesada.

"I have grown fond of you," said Takesada. "Are you not afraid of me?"

The fox, still carrying the package in its mouth, shook its head.

"But I suspect your fellow foxes must not much like your associating with a human being," said Takesada.

The fox shook its head more vigorously, and managed to bring out, "They don't speak ill of me. If we disparage our fellow foxes, our supernatural power diminishes. That is a law with us."

Takesada parted with the fox and came back to his unlit room. He found the wooden floor hard and uncomfortable.

At Hisakiyo's suggestion, it was arranged that when Takesada was not on night duty, he would leave the guard station of the Right Division near the Impumon Gate and would go to Hisakiyo's house. Hisakiyo, who knew the limits of his own skill, was eager to see his dreams fulfilled in his friend.

Behind Hisakiyo's house was a forest of shrubbery. Hisakiyo had neighborhood children gather dry branches to use for torchlights so that Takesada could practice at night.

Takesada pulled the bowstring taut and twanged it. He repeated this two or three times and smiled with satisfaction.

"My left hand pushes the bow forward, and my right hand draws the bowstring backward. At the moment when the two forces reach equilibrium, the fingers involuntarily let the arrow go and the target reverberates. Can you understand this feeling?" asked Takesada.

Hisakiyo, a good-natured man, had until now worshipped Takesada's skill. Tonight, however, Hisakiyo could not help feeling a budding sense of inferiority toward a senior officer. But he concealed this feeling in faint smiles and bade his friend farewell in a casual manner, saying, "Takesada, your eyes are as sharp as ever. I'm pleased."

Invariably the fox waited every night. Each time, Takesada brought something or other as a gift for the fox, taking special pains to hide his gifts from Hisakiyo. As Takesada walked with the fox, his mental strain, his physical fatigue, even his uncertainty about next year were dispelled. To his great wonder, he never met a human soul along the way.

"Where is your home? Do you live by yourself?" asked Takesada.

"My dwelling is in the bamboo grove behind the Nison'in Temple in Sagano," replied the fox. "It is our rule not to mention our families. So please don't ask."

Takesada scanned the dark, frozen sky toward the northwest, in the direction of Sagano. He began to feel sorry for the fox, wondering how the animal could live in such a place.

"Don't you sometimes feel like living in the house of a human being?" Takesada asked. "A night such as this must be hard on you. I, too, have become extremely tired of living by myself." The fox shot a quick glance at Takesada and recoiled. "I'm not lying," said Takesada. "But your present appearance won't do. I want you to change into a woman. Then I'll shoot at the bull's-eye again next year to please you." Because of his burning, fierce determination, Takesada now hit the bull's-eye with his words. The fox, as if intoxicated at the offer of happiness, made a strange hesitation and then, suddenly jumping up in the air, at once disappeared. Like a swift arrow Takesada's hot look followed the fox's invisible path.

Again the next day, Takesada went to Hisakiyo's house. As Takesada was leaving, Hisakiyo spoke to him, looking rather serious. "Takesada, haven't you lost some of your skill lately? When you stare at the mark, your eyes aren't as bright as before. Also, you seem to miss somewhat more often."

Something in Hisakiyo's words went to Takesada's heart. "No, I'm all right," he answered. "It's not that I'm becoming arrogant because I'm now your superior. I'm determined to win next year." Takesada was all too conscious of the new difference in their ranks.

"Good, if that is so," said Hisakiyo. "Maybe I was becoming over-anxious. As far as we're concerned, there's no difference between the head soldier and the plain soldier. We've been friends for a long time."

The two men talked, over *sake*. As they emptied more *sake* cups, they became more keenly aware of the thin, cold wind blowing against their chests, even though the branches of the shrubs in the forest had begun to show white, mist-like buds, waiting for a warm breeze. It was near the day of the vernal equinox.

For the next few days, Takesada was in continual distress because he did not meet the fox. One evening he practiced till late before returning home. As he opened the door, a half-formed word broke loudly from his mouth. Then he cried:

"You're here!"

A young woman was sitting with her back to the candlelight. In the small kitchen there was a small new *sake* bottle and several small plates. Takesada understood everything in an instant. The woman smiled quietly and bowed. She wore a very becoming dress of pale purple-red with a bushclover pattern.

"I'm surprised!" said Takesada. "So it is you. I'm glad you came. Why didn't you come sooner?"

"I wish I could have," replied the fox. "But some preparation was necessary before I could change my appearance. I'll serve you from this evening on. Please continue your favor towards me."

Her voice was clearer and expressed more emotion than before. He was ecstatic. He realized clearly that his goals now were not just honor and power. He regretted that he had not understood this sooner, but it was a happy regret.

"I will make you happy," said the man. "I'm determined to win the archery contest again next year."

"I am most grateful to you," said the woman. "But please do not reveal my true nature to anyone at all. If the truth became known, everything would be over. Please don't forget!"

The woman's solemn voice made Takesada's determination firm. But he was bewildered, for he did not feel confident that he would be able to offer Hisakiyo a convincing explanation. At last he found the following rather evasive excuse: "My older brother who lives near the corner of Seventh Avenue and Muromachi Street brought me a daughter from a distant relative."

Next day, at the guard station, Takesada told Hisakiyo exactly that. For an instant Hisakiyo shifted his eyes unpleasantly, but soon his face showed his usual good-natured smile. "Oh, good! Good!" said Hisakiyo. "Now you can concentrate better on your practice."

The woman served Takesada devotedly. Takesada, for his part, loved the woman. She prepared *sake* for him when he came home tired. He was happiest while he held the *sake* cup. Nothing made *sake* more tasty than imagining the loud sound of hitting the bull's-eye against a background of the cheering voices of his many fans at next year's contest.

When he was at the guard station, Takesada began to speak less and less to his colleagues. He looked like a shadow when he came out of the Impumon Gate.

"Takesada is odd lately. He mutters things and smiles to himself. And he's pale. Is he possessed by something?" a soldier asked.

"If you become too popular, you might end up just like him," said another.

The respect his colleagues had shown Takesada now changed to contempt. In the end, Hisakiyo and Takesada had a quarrel. Perhaps knowing the feelings shared by his fellow soldiers, Hisakiyo was emboldened to say, "Listen, Takesada. You've changed since you took a wife. First of all, why is it that you've never invited me to your home? Besides, as you surely know, your arrows act as if they've quarreled with the mark. They no longer make that clear sound of hitting the bull's-eye. I'm worried about next year. Please be honest with me. Maybe I'm to blame."

Hisakiyo spoke pleadingly, but Takesada dismissed the matter with a laugh, and said, "That's not true. Perhaps my arrows have missed the mark sometimes. But that's because I've been drinking too much *sake*. I'll restrain myself. I'll take two or three days off from practice and cool my head."

That evening, Takesada went home directly from the guard station. On the way, when he was alone, it came to him clearly that his secret was ruining him. By his own effort he could never remove that residue of not yet fermented feeling stuck in the depths of his heart. His anguish was great.

The woman was glad to see Takesada return so early. But suddenly he yelled at her—something he had never done before. "*Sake*! Go and buy *sake* quickly! Hurry!"

Looking full of woe, the woman said, "I'm sorry, but I've found it difficult to go to the *sake* shop recently."

"What?" cried Takesada. "You've gone to the shop many times before. If you speak such nonsense, I'll miss the mark on purpose next year."

The woman stood with downcast eyes, then quietly went out, pushing aside the door curtain. She soon returned with *sake* but did not speak. When the man had drunk all the *sake* he wanted, he lay down on the same spot. His snoring sounded strangely mournful.

Again next day, Takesada sent for *sake* and drank. He did not go to the guard station. The following day was the same. The woman was utterly perplexed, but she went out noiselessly, came in noiselessly, and served the *sake* in silence.

In the mind of Takesada, too, many contradictory thoughts floated up and sank again. He tried to fix his heart to its proper place, but it was by no means as easy as raising the target in the archery ground. He took another holiday from his duty at the guard station and had the woman buy more *sake*. Sitting beside Takesada, the small *sake* bottle in her hand, the woman pleaded, sighing:

"I have been truly happy since I changed into human form. But the trouble is, my supernatural power has waned a little. The harder I try to be a completely human wife, the more difficult it becomes. I feel as if everything I do is ruined, time after time. According to our law, those who defy the supernatural power will be severely punished."

"Why should you attempt the impossible—to become completely human?" growled Takesada. "You know that I know the truth."

The woman wiped her tears repeatedly and said, "I was mistaken. Nothing can be done about the difference between a human being and a fox. I wish I had understood much sooner. I am most grateful to you for loving me so much, a mere fox. Please accept my sincere apology."

Takesada knew only too well that it was impossible now to turn back. "Why do you say such a faint-hearted thing?" he demanded. "If you don't stop, the man you love will be ruined. But I would not let you go! Have I ever once turned my face to a human woman? I would *never* let you go!"

The woman went on crying, her voice low. Takesada's *sake* cup was left on the wooden floor.

After a time, the woman smiled faintly, went into the adjoining room, and closed the sliding door. Takesada lay where he was. He was anxious to hide himself in a dream, abandoning everything. The rain which had started earlier now became noisy. Even though it was spring and the cherry blossoms had already fallen, the evening brought a marrow-reaching chill.

Hisakiyo, being a good-natured man, was genuinely concerned about Takesada. He thought that there had to be something seriously wrong for such a healthy man to be absent from the guard station for days at a time. Besides, Hisakiyo could no longer stand the malicious gossip of his fellow soldiers. "I wonder if Takesada took offense at my advice," he brooded. "I'll buy some *sake* and get him to talk. He must have plenty on his mind."

On his way from the guard station, Hisakiyo decided to go to Takesada's house that very night. He stopped at a nearby *sake* shop. At the sight of Hisakiyo, the shopkeeper, who had been washing small *sake* bottles at the well, jumped at him.

"Hello, sir!" said the shopkeeper. "You came at just the right time. I've been anxious to see you and talk to you."

As the shopkeeper began to speak, his wife became excited and went to the back of the shop, with her sleeves turned up over her elbows. She soon reappeared, holding something in her hand. The shopkeeper's story was most shocking.

"Takesada's wife is a fox! We were admiring Takesada for finding such a gentle and beautiful woman. Since he won the contest and took a wife, he's been drinking heavily, so that he must have run out of money. His wife would come, humbly and apologetically, buy some *sake* and leave. Later, we looked at the money she had paid us, and all we found was these."

The shopkeeper turned to his wife, who stretched her hand straight toward Hisakiyo. Three or four pebbles fell through her fingers.

Hisakiyo groaned. The destruction of his long friendship with Takesada lay before his eyes. Now there was only one thing left to do. He would have to grieve his friend and the woman. He gathered up his courage, took the pebbles, and left the shop.

When Hisakiyo peeped through the lattice window of Takesada's house, Takesada was drinking *sake* by the dim light of a candle. Takesada was at a loss for words when he saw his friend entering the house. He sat up straight at the sight of Hisakiyo's deliberately calm smile. Hisakiyo quietly put the pebbles in front of Takesada.

Just then the woman came in with a small *sake* bottle in her hand. She forced a smile and was beginning to greet Hisakiyo when, at the same instant, she caught sight of the pebbles.

The woman jumped up high in the air, and her body stretched out flat. The *sake* bottle hit a post and splashed all over. Even before the woman's body fell on the wooden floor, it had changed to a white fox. The fox looked back at Takesada once or twice, and then, switching its tail, vanished into the darkness outside.

Takesada, without uttering a word, drew the long sword placed by his knees and slashed it sideways. Thwunk, rang the sound, neither sharp nor dull. As luck would have it, the point of the sword hit the hilt of the long sword worn by Hisakiyo, and bouncing back, tore the left sleeve of his soldier's uniform and cut off the tip of his little finger. The fingertip flew, along with blood.

"Help! A murderer!" cried Hisakiyo, and tumbling to his feet, ran out of the house. Takesada stood up straight. His long sword made the wind dance over his head and Takesada's wits whirled. He began to run after the fox.

"Halloo!" he called out. "I'm going to the back of the Nison'in Temple. Wait for me there!"

Takesada was suddenly shut out of the human world. Or rather, he had shut himself out of the human world.

"Halloo! A murderer! Quick! Quick!" cried a few people in the neighborhood who had heard Hisakiyo scream, and they ran toward the road, which was patrolled by officials of the police department, the *Kebiishi Chō*. Soon several policemen came running. They signalled to one another by swinging their torchlights above them from side to side.

"Which way did he go?"

"He ran after a fox toward the Nison'in Temple," cried the neighbors.

A group of policemen and neighbors chased the criminal. The pale-faced Hisakiyo was among them. The moon, nearing the full, was screened by clouds. The shadow of the shrubbery which Takesada had just passed at a dead run was the place where the fox had waited for him the first time.

If it had been daylight, Takesada could have seen the soft, light-green chickweed spreading out with its numerous, small white flowers. But of course he was not concerned with that. His two feet desperately kicked through the soft ground of the marsh and the stumps of the pampas grass.

"Halloo!" cried Takesada. "Change me to a fox with your supernatural power, I beg you! Please!"

Hearing Takesada's voice, the policemen considerably shortened the distance between him and themselves. Takesada cried between gasps, "Halloo! I beg you! Please turn me into a fox! Please!"

Two or three flickering flames of the torchlights, drawing an irregular arc in the air, closed in upon him. Takesada continued to cry out into the darkness.

"Halloo! I beg you! Please!"

THE MYSTERY OF A
MOUNTAIN VILLA

Chief Councillor Lord Motohiro woke up shortly before noon. He crawled out of his sleeved coverlet and sat at his doorway to look at the front garden. Its trees and rocks, the sight of which was so familiar to him, seemed today to have an added grace.

Last night he had won a great victory at the poetry contest, held under the August moon on the estate of the *Kampaku.*[1] His competitor was a well-known poet, though not a man of high office.

When the official reader read the Chief Councillor's poem, Lord Motohiro felt as if a masterpiece of a previous era were being recited and involuntarily straightened his posture.

This was the lord's poem:

THE WANING MOON OVER THE RIVER

In the dead of night, in the swift current,
The waves of the Uji River reflect
The fluttering image of the moon in the darkling sky.

Needless to say, the theme, as well as the strict poetic form, was assigned to the competing poets. Many poems of this period were written on assigned themes. Under such constricting circumstances, unsuccessful poems were likely to be mere wordgames, but successful ones could become famous. And Lord Motohiro's poem was successful.

The judge explained the reason for the Chief Councillor's victory as follows:

"At the beginning, a similar phrase is used twice: 'In the dead of

1. *Kampaku*: the powerful post of regent for an adult Emperor. August: the most celebrated time for viewing the moon. The moon can be taken, in Buddhist thought, as symbolic of the religious man's "way," or the law of Buddha. (NT)

night, in the swift current'—expressing a sense of wonder. This technique gives the poem force and rhythm. It also achieves freshness."

The other participants agreed. The *Kampaku* himself nodded enthusiastically and, smiling at the Lord, said:

"The judge is absolutely right! It is a good poem. It would be wonderful to own a place where one could have such a view all to oneself at this time of the year!"

The Chief Councillor was delighted by his unexpected victory. But in truth, the poem had not been very difficult to write.

The poetry contest of that evening ended after fifty poems were presented. Then the feast began. It was after midnight when the guests departed from the *Kampaku*'s estate.

In the midnight streets, Lord Motohiro's ox-drawn carriage[2] moved along as if it were swimming in the bright moonlight. Intoxicated with excellent *sake* and high compliments, in a state of dreamy ecstasy, he surrendered both his mind and body to the motion of the carriage. He was awakened by the sound of the opening of the outer gate of his mansion. When he entered the main building, which was his dwelling, he was overcome by exhaustion and slept soundly for hours.

Now Lord Motohiro, seated at the doorway overlooking the garden, called one of his maidservants. She helped him change from his nightgown to a pale-blue robe, or *nōshi*,[3] and assisted him in arranging his hair. After a very late breakfast, he went back to the mat on which he had been sitting earlier and continued to muse on the *Kampaku*'s words of the night before. They helped him realize anew his talent as a poet.

The *Kampaku* owned, in addition to his estate and another residence in Kyoto, mountain villas in Kanjuji, Kitano, and Atago[4]—all magnificent villas—but he did not have any in Uji.[5] Lord Motohiro, for his part, owned two mansions in Kyoto. One of them, at the corner of Sanjō Avenue and Takakura Street,[6] he had inherited from his father and used now as his residence. It was not on very expensive

---

2. Reserved exclusively for noblemen and high-ranking officials. (NT)
3. An ordinary costume worn by all ranks of noblemen. (NT)
4. Suburbs of Kyoto, the capital city. (NT)
5. A town further beyond suburban Kyoto. (NT)
6. This district contained the estates of many famous noblemen. (NT)

grounds, but it was relatively new and comfortable. The other, inherited from his mother's side of the family, was occupied by his oldest son, Nobuhiro. Its buildings were older.

Since Lord Motohiro had attained high rank and had more time to spare now, it was only natural that he should wish to own a fine place in the mountains. In his five or six fiefs, there were houses for the caretakers to live in, but none of these could be called a mountain villa.

He had two reasons for wanting a villa.

In recent years, the traffic of horses and vehicles to and from the East had increased tremendously, and his residence was right on the main road. The situation was now so bad that he could no longer content himself by saying that his house was conveniently located. This was a major reason.

But there was another reason, much closer to his heart.

Among his ancestors there had been two or three men of taste and poetic talent whose poems had been selected for the anthologies compiled by Imperial order. And so it was natural that, each succeeding year, Motohiro should become more and more eager to live in a quiet mountain villa upon his retirement, to become the best poet in his family line, and to have his name placed in the Imperial anthologies. He began the process of buying a mountain villa.

There were several villas for sale, but none came close to his ideal. There was one in Saga, but it was said that the neighborhood was unsafe. There was also one in Nishiyama. It had elaborate buildings, but the wind was said to blow so hard against them that its owner had left it vacant. Thus Lord Motohiro had been spending unsettled, restless days; and then, last night, he had unexpectedly won his victory at the poetry contest.

The lord was becoming sleepy again when Atsuhiro, the chief officer for Motohiro's household affairs, came to him. Actually it was in anticipation of Atsuhiro's return that the Chief Councillor had remained at the doorway. He had sent Atsuhiro to Daigo and Hino the day before. Atsuhiro looked cheerful, and, probably because he had traveled on horseback, he did not even look tired. He approached his lord and bowed. A young servant accompanying Atsuhiro also bowed.

"My lord, we have come upon something tremendous," said

Atsuhiro. The Chief Councillor's knee almost slid off the doorway in his excitement.

"Thank you for your trouble," he said. "I can guess the news by the color of your face."

Atsuhiro gave his report. The day before, as he could not find any satisfactory villa, he had finally gone as far as Uji.

"There I thought to myself, if I don't find something here, I'll have to go home empty-handed. So I hurried out to look at two or three, and as luck would have it, I turned up something wonderful."

As soon as the lord heard the place-name Uji, a kind of dream came over him: it was as if river waves, overflowing from the rice paper on which his poem had been written, were cascading into the garden pond in front of him, sending a delicate spray up to his face.

"Where is the villa?" he asked. "What is the arrangement of the rooms? How are the trees placed? It seems that my presentiment has come true!"

Atsuhiro smiled quietly. "The villa is just this side of the Uji Bridge, a little way downstream. As you go west along the river, you come to a narrow path going northeast, winding among maple trees and Judas trees. At the end of this path stands the villa. There's no other villa in the vicinity, and the place is absolutely quiet. I understand that the Mimuroto Temple is due east beyond the river. Further on, beyond the temple, a shapely mountain rises up—Mt. Kisen. I was told that in a little while it will be beautiful with the leaves on its trees turning red."

The servant who sat behind Atsuhiro raised his head and frequently chimed in with Atsuhiro's remarks. Perceiving the intent expression in his lord's eyes, Atsuhiro became even more enthusiastic.

"The owner of this villa was the late Prince Shikibukyō.[7] As you know, my lord, the father of Prince Shikibukyō was an excellent poet. The villa is not very large, but it makes a clever use of the land and the rooms are very well laid out. The buildings are about ten years old. There's a caretaker living in the servants' quarters. He tells me he started serving the prince when he was young, and he

---

7. *Shikibukyō* is the title of the head of the Ministry of Shikibu, in charge of the rituals, ceremonies, and the civil service. Normally, this official was chosen from the Imperial family or the relatives of the Imperial family and was often called by his official title. (NT)

praised the prince very highly. As I listened to the caretaker, I became so satisfied that I even accepted the invitation to stay overnight."

Now the villa was becoming more real for Lord Motohiro, less dreamlike, and the lord became calmer.

"Is that so?" he said. "I can't thank you enough for your trouble. It was good that you talked over the matter while staying overnight. Did the caretaker say he could give up the villa immediately?"

"Yes," replied Atsuhiro. "He said that the late prince would have been pleased to see the villa sold to the Chief Councillor. I understand that the late prince's family all live in Kyoto and that they entrust everything concerning the villa to the old caretaker."

Atsuhiro's report satisfied the lord completely. He envisioned how it would be when he was the owner of that villa.

"Perhaps the spirit of the great poet-priest Kisen might wave his hand from Mt. Kisen behind the main building of the villa," he thought. "Every tree, every blade of grass, every stone along the river must be permeated with the joy and sorrow of the characters in 'The Ten Books of Uji.'[8] How often must the author, Lady Murasaki, have walked around the site of the villa when she was working on her tale!

"The breezes among the trees may still be carrying her sighs. A loose strand or two from her woven rush sandals may have woven themselves into the tree stumps. All of these things will be mine!"

The lord's mind was made up.

"Atsuhiro, I want you to go tomorrow and complete the purchase. Please convey my gratitude to the caretaker," he commanded firmly.

"I will leave at once, my lord. But you've decided this very quickly. . . ."

"Yes. It is an ideal villa. I don't think it necessary for me to go there myself to inspect it."

As soon as he realized that the lord had entrusted everything to him, Atsuhiro became uneasy. The lord noticed the man's nervousness.

"To be truthful, my lord," said Atsuhiro, "there was one thing more I should have told you. But as I got involved in my report, I made the mistake of putting it off until now."

---

8. The last ten "books" or chapters of *The Tale of Genji* by Lady Murasaki (c. 978–?), in which Kaoru, the son of Prince Genji, is the central character, and Uji is the setting. (NT)

"Is there something wrong? You must not hide anything," said the lord.

At Atsuhiro's signal, the young servant immediately excused himself. What Atsuhiro said after straightening his garments was something the lord had by no means anticipated.

"When the old caretaker saw that I was perfectly pleased with the villa," said Atsuhiro, "he looked uncomfortable and began to talk in a suddenly lowered voice. 'This villa is flawless in every respect, but there is one thing people dislike about it,' he said. I made a random guess and asked bluntly, 'Is it some evil spirit?' The caretaker's face became glum, with his eyes set, but soon he forced a smile and scratched his head. He was a good deal less eager to talk now, and after a while I retired to a corner of the building[9] next to the main building. But I couldn't sleep, though Kishichi, my young attendant, had already started to snore.

"I went to the summerhouse over the fountain[10] and for a while I watched the moon reflected on the pond. Suddenly, with a splash, a big *kappa*[11] stuck his head out of the water. Imagine, my lord, how astonished I was! The *kappa* held a carp between his teeth and ate the fish while it was still flapping. I couldn't stand the *kappa*'s fierce eyes. I jumped up and ran frantically toward the main building, and there another surprise met me. A young princess was walking all by herself along the covered passageway toward the summerhouse. She went by me as if she were flowing. Out of breath and hardly able to keep myself from falling over backward, I tumbled into my room. I had no strength left to wake up Kishichi. I put my forehead against the wooden floor, curled my toes up tight, and waited for dawn. What a frightening experience!"

Atsuhiro could not stop trembling. The lord forced a bitter smile

9. Connected to the main building by a covered passageway. (NT)

10. A small structure (called *izumidono* in Japanese) built over the fountain or pond in the garden of the estate and connected by a covered passageway to the building (sometimes identified as the east building) where Atsuhiro had retired to sleep. The summerhouse was used for enjoying the evening coolness in summer and for viewing the moon. (NT)

11. An imaginary amphibious animal with a scale-covered body of a small child, the webbed hands and feet of a frog, the face of a tiger with a beak, and the head with thin hair. In the center of the head is a hollow that holds a small amount of water. As long as water remains in his hollow, the *kappa* is said to be powerful and to drag other animals into the water to suck their blood. (NT)

and said, "Atsuhiro, you might have been kind enough to tell me all this sooner! What happened next?"

Atsuhiro had expected to receive a severe scolding, but now he continued to speak, much relieved.

"I'll tell you gladly. In the morning, when the caretaker came to greet me, I told him about the *kappa* and asked, 'Was that your hobgoblin?' The old man, with a serious, tearful smile, replied, 'It's not really a *kappa*, it's my grandson. He's a little crazy.' It was too absurd for me to get angry.

"Next, when I told him about the princess out there all by herself, the caretaker said decisively, 'She's genuine.' I was doubly amazed. According to the caretaker's story, the princess was the only daughter of Prince Shikibukyō. She used to go to the summerhouse on moonlit nights. She died several years ago and the prince her father was deeply grieved."

Atsuhiro took a deep breath, like a man who has just unloaded a heavy burden. The lord found himself, quite unexpectedly, standing at the crossroads. It was as if while he'd lost himself in admiration of a superb view, a precipice had begun to crumble under his feet. Under normal circumstances, he would reprimand Atsuhiro, then blame the caretaker, and in the end, terminate the negotiation.

However, the lord did not follow that course. Now that he knew that strange and sad phantoms were mysteriously concealed in the beautiful villa which retained the fragrance of "The Ten Books of Uji," he would not give it up at any cost. The revelation of the mystery did not diminish but on the contrary added to the value of the estate. So the solution of the problem was simple. He would hire a guard to watch the *kappa*, and as for the summerhouse, he could build himself another one a short distance away and let the ghost come and go as she pleased.

But before actually making the final decision to buy the villa, the lord needed to consider the matter seriously from all possible angles. He temporarily withdrew his order that Atsuhiro leave the next day. Finally, on the fifth day, he came to the following conclusion:

"There is a bond ordained by fate between myself and the villa. As poets, the father of Prince Shikibukyō and my grandfather Michitsugu must have been acquainted with each other. The spirits of the prince and my grandfather would welcome me to this villa.

"My long career at Court has seemed brilliant, but it has been merely a routine affair in a succession of power struggles. Besides, in recent times, the formidable pressure from the Eastern region, though concealing its fangs, has penetrated the Imperial Palace. The truth is that the members of the Court who've been absorbed in its ceremonial affairs and rituals, generation after generation, are now completely at a loss, as if carried off their feet. To involve myself in such a whirlpool of struggle would mean a dreary future for me. For what have I been called the 'Chief Councillor of Wisdom' if not for this decision today?"

He sat quietly at his writing table, opened his inkstone case, and started to write. It was a letter addressed to the *Kampaku*, informing him of his resignation as Chief Councillor and of his decision to name his oldest son Nobuhiro as the successor of his fiefs and estate.

The *Kampaku*, who was the Chief Councillor's superior, acquaintance, and rival, would welcome the news. It seemed a pity to resign at his age, but the lord gave up his position with serenity of mind.

A few days later, after the cleaning of his former residence, the ex-Chief Councillor moved to the mountain villa, or rather to the stately mansion, in Uji. His oldest son moved into the residence at the corner of Sanjō Avenue and Takakura Street. The older estate, inherited from the lord's mother's side, was left vacant for his private use. Atsuhiro and other retainers and several maidservants followed their lord.

As the lord gradually became settled there, the new villa in Uji pleased him even more than he had expected. As Atsuhiro had reported, every possible care had been taken in the design of the rooms, the planting of the trees in the front garden, the arrangement of the water drawn into the pond, and the position of the rocks on the island in the middle of the pond. In addition, the sound of the Uji River, sometimes whispering to him, sometimes calling to him, sometimes laughing, was always at his side.

When he had written his poem about the waves of the Uji River for the poetry contest some days ago, the lord had never dreamed that he would soon be the owner of such a place. Now he was almost ready to believe that Prince Shikibukyō had prepared this villa so that the ex-Chief Councillor might put the finishing touches on his poetic mastery.

The lord allowed the old caretaker and his grandson the *kappa* to live in the servants' quarters as before. Usually the *kappa* was very docile and worked hard.

After moving to the residence at the corner of Sanjō and Takakura in Kyoto, the lord's oldest son wrote to his father as follows:

"I would like to make a children's playground in front of the east building. And I would like to borrow your *kappa* for a while to help in the work."

The lord was a little sorry to hear that a part of the scenery of his former residence, which he had loved for a long time, would suddenly disappear, but it was no longer a great loss to him. He loaned the *kappa* with good grace.

The old caretaker unlocked his heart completely, as if he had been a life-long retainer of the lord, and told him some very personal matters.

"My grandson lost his parents when he was very young. I did not know how to handle his unusual physical strength, but the late prince graciously arranged that my grandson be given to the Mii Temple as a temple page. There he did a terrible thing." The caretaker's story started in this way.

"Apparently, for a strong boy like him," continued the old man, "getting only two meals a day, consisting only of rice-gruel, was unbearable. One evening, under the shade of some trees at Lake Biwa, my grandson built a fire and was cooking a carp which he had caught in its sleep. Some wild monk soldiers,[12] who were returning from a drinking bout in the town of Ōtsu, saw the child."

The lord knit his brows, moved his knees forward, and said, "Too bad! Too bad! Then what happened?"

"They behaved rudely, beating and kicking the child. One of them, I was told, hit the child on the head with the handle of his long sword. After that, the child was insane, and he was sent back to me as useless. He was indeed a problem."

"Can this be?" cried the lord. "How outrageous! Now I am beginning to understand what Atsuhiro told me."

The old man's face took on a darker look. "I'll overcome my scruples and tell you everything," he said. "I woke up one night to find

12. Large temples and monasteries maintained armed monk soldiers as security forces. Often the monk soldiers were ex-convicts or fugitives from the law. (NT)

my grandson missing from my side. I went outdoors. The moon was beautiful. Then, to my surprise, I saw my grandson under the summerhouse, with his head rising out of the water."

The lord reacted sharply. "Was it there that you saw the princess?"

"Yes, Sire. At that moment my grandson's eyes looked as if they would burst into flames. Soon the princess disappeared, and my grandson swam back. I had taken care of the princess when she was young, and to see her now, in such a form. . . ." The old man put his hands over his eyes.

"After that I watched my grandson and found that he always swam out there on moonlit nights. While the princess was still alive, my grandson always accompanied her carriage, whenever she went to Kyoto. Perhaps because of that, he became deeply attached to her."

The lord, as he listened to this remarkable tale, felt as if his youth were rushing back to him, making his blood surge up and tumble. At any rate, he was deeply pleased to know that the origin of the mysterious story of the villa now belonged to him.

Autumn was almost gone. The murmuring sound of the stream flowing into the front garden was clearly distinguishable from the reverberation of the river a little distance off. One morning, after the searing blasts of late autumn, the lord noticed that the bush clovers, *ominaeshi*, *karukaya*, and other autumn flowers had lost their blossoms, and their leaves had withered. In particular, the deep-blue color of the ray-like petals which still remained on a solitary gentian caught the lord's eye.

Mt. Kisen with its scarlet-tinged trees which had given him so much pleasure, now exposed its dark-gray and pale-yellow peak to the cold air and waited quietly for the approaching winter. Painting in his mind pictures of the mountaintops soon to be radiant with pure white snow, the lord cast wandering glances around him, meditated, and sometimes jotted something down in his bound notebook. It seemed that gradually a distance was growing between himself and the *kaishi* paper on which he wrote his poetry.

The lord came to have a strong desire to pray to the spirit of Lady Murasaki, author of *The Tale of Genji*. From the storeroom of his estate in Kyoto, he brought the entire fifty-four books of *The Tale of Genji*, treasured by his mother, and set them out prominently on the bookcase in his new residence. They were beautifully bound volumes.

First he read the book "The Bridge Maiden," then "The Fern-Shoots." As he progressed from "The Eastern House" to "Ukifune," the color and design of the book covers changed and the elaboration of the plot increased. The characters of these books—Prince Niou, Kaoru, Ōgimi, Naka-no-kimi, and Ukifune—became alive for the lord; or rather, he became one of the characters himself. The trees around the villa became a part of the illustrated tale. It was an experience simultaneously pleasurable, sorrowful, and transitory.

It was late at night. The lord was tired, having read through two bound volumes. Since he was unable to sleep, he opened the lattice window of the main building half-way and looked at the pond. The late-risen crescent moon was sometimes in sight, sometimes hidden from view behind the trees. Already an early frost was on the ground. The mist hanging over the water was particularly thick around the summerhouse. The lord felt his body stiffen and stood motionless. Only his eyes moved keenly as usual.

The lord made out in the summerhouse the figure of a noble lady in her ceremonial five-layer robe. She appeared to be playing the *koto*.[13] By her side sat a young man wearing a ceremonial *eboshi* hat and a hunting costume, listening to the sound of the *koto*. Delicate variations on the melody floated toward the lord's ears.

The lord continued to breathe hotly in his cold, enchanted world.

The sound of the *koto* stopped. The lady and the young man sat close to each other and began to talk happily. The color and shape of the lady's robe and the man's hunting costume were vague, half transparent, but the changing expressions on their faces were clearly visible.

Again the thick mist rose over the area and enveloped the summerhouse. Then the mist flowed swiftly away and the figures vanished. The lord found he had regained the use of his limbs. The color of the moon, the darkness behind the trees, and the sound of the river were the same as before.

The lord waited for dawn in a state of continuous and extraordinary excitement. When Mt. Kisen emerged, bright in the morning sun, Lord Motohiro commanded a night attendant to open all the lattice windows. The lord then sent for the old caretaker from the

13. A thirteen-string Japanese musical instrument. (NT)

servants' quarters and told him of what he had seen last night. The old man prostrated himself before the lord, and seemed to be trying hard to restrain the violent pounding of his heart. He too had seen it all.

"I have never known anything like what I saw last night," he said. "I was totally surprised. I have already told you about the princess and my silly grandson, but. . . ."

"Then you must still be hiding something else," said the lord in tones unusually stern.

"I did not mean to hide anything," said the old man, "but I'm sorry that I missed a chance to tell you more. I will keep nothing from you now." The caretaker's sunken eyes showed no deception.

"When the princess was still living," began the caretaker, "a young, high-ranking courtier used to come to visit her. He was from a good family. I understand that he also enjoyed the confidence of the retired Emperor. The princess and the young man were deeply in love. When he visited her, they always went to the summerhouse. He would walk ahead of her. He seemed to be concerned about my grandson."

A quick thought flashed through the lord's mind and he understood the general circumstances: "I see. Since the *kappa* is now away, having been sent to my son's residence in Kyoto, it was the young man who came last night," he said.

The old man apparently did not understand the lord's words, and continued:

"But, unfortunately, the troops of Kiso forced their way into Kyoto after having driven the Taira family out toward the Western region. They attacked the Hōjūji Temple, the retired Emperor's residence, setting it afire and shooting arrows. Many high-ranking courtiers lost their lives, and the young man was among them. It was most sorrowful. I do not wish to talk about the princess. Her pitiful, heart-breaking mourning for his death continued until her own. A little later, her father, the prince, also departed this world. I alone am left behind. . . ."

The old man stood motionless, head bowed. His tears trickled onto the wooden floor.

The lord took several deep breaths and for the first time felt peaceful. Since he had become the owner of the mountain villa, the depths and shadows of its hidden details, together with the various volumes in "The Ten Books of Uji," which he'd read with all his heart, had gradually deepened and widened. His soul and body had at times seemed to grow pale and thin with restlessness, at other times had seemed to gush up with delight. Now he'd ascertained where he stood.

The lord became aware of a strong desire to complete in the very best form this sad and beautiful beginning of a tale. Compared to the writing of poetry, to which he had initially aspired, the tale seemed an object throbbing with life. To the lord, who had lost his beloved wife several years before and had been lonely ever since, writing this tale seemed the most satisfying thing he might live for.

It was as if the leaves of Mt. Kisen—already showing signs of winter's blight—and the leaves still clinging on the trees along the river and near the villa, had suddenly put on green and were hurrying toward the lord.

While he cooled down his charged emotions, he did not forget the need to concern himself with more immediate problems.

"What shall I do with that carp-eating *kappa*? Shall I leave him with my son in Kyoto for a while? Or shall I call him back to be reunited with the old man in the servants' quarters? The old man would be glad."

He talked aloud to himself almost unconsciously, with a baffled smile. But he felt another strange presentiment rising in his heart.

"Would the young courtier stop coming if the *kappa* were here? That would never do! No, wait! By my heart's prayer, I'll try to make the *kappa* sit behind the princess and the young man."

TWO PRIESTS

Climbing eastward on the narrow path behind the Kimpu Shrine on the remote mountain of Yoshino, one comes to the top of the peak of Aone; descending from this point and going further east, one reaches the valley of the Otonashi River, a tributary of the Yoshino River. On a strip of level ground along the steep slope, there once stood a humble hermitage, known only to the inhabitants of the mountain and to religious ascetics.

The view from the hermitage was richly various. To the northeast lay the villages of East Yoshino and the low mountain ranges surrounding them, gray-blue, under the morning mist, like a wide expanse of ocean. To the south the view was strikingly different. Mt. Sanjō, home of the main temple of *Shugendō*,[1] rose among other prominent peaks, all thrusting their rocky walls high into the sky, the jagged sides of the mountains severely encircling deep ravines. The entire scene, sublime yet somber, guarding the sacred ground against the impure dust of the human world, was the will of the great earth itself.

Around the hermitage lay a deep silence. Only the sound of the great falls farther down the river rumbled, as if moving against the current, rising from the depths of the earth, intensifying the stillness.

Every year, during the long summer season of fasting and asceticism, one could see, small in the distance, the movement of white robes worn by the *shugenja*, followers of *Shugendō*. But when the season was over, only hunters and woodcutters came to this region. By the time everything was buried in deep snow, no one left his footprints but the most devoted of ascetics.

The hermitage had not been there very long. The hut had been built two years ago in the spring and had since then been occupied by a man in priest's garb, still many years from middle age. His

---

1. A religious sect blending Shintoism, Buddhism, Taoism, and Primitive Mountain-worship. Followers of this sect practice asceticism, self-mortification, incantation and prayer, and believe in the efficacy of magic. (NT)

broad shoulders and the steadiness of his hips revealed that he had once been a warrior.

This priest seldom left his hermitage. Every day without fail he recited the scripture three times, the intonation of his loud voice harsh and rough, as if he were confessing his soul's agony. Also, twice each day, he went down to the stream to bathe. On his way back he carried a pail filled with water.

Now it was March. The fact that he'd survived the pain of winter in this remote mountain hut meant that he had been victorious in his confrontation with loneliness, cold, and hunger. It was pleasant to drop off the burden of the past four months and abandon his heart to deep fatigue. But the muffled boom of the falls, suddenly much louder, fed by melting snow, rang like a gong commanding him to resume his discipline.

The beauty of sharp, geometrical lines, the white remains of snow in innumerable mountain creases, became more beautiful still under the awesome sunlight. The priest felt anew his deep sense of triumph.

Then, as the mild, quiet day was approaching dusk, the priest saw something astonishing: along the mountain slope facing the valley, at a level much higher than that of his hermitage, a streak of white smoke rose upward. He had never seen anything like it before. There had to be another hermitage where someone was living.

He had assumed until now that everything on the mountain—trees, rocks, earth, snow, and sky—was his alone. As he realized now that there was someone else who might know all that he knew, an unpleasant feeling began to rise up inside him; but it was immediately pushed aside by a rush of yearning for human companionship which came boiling up, exploding within him.

He quickly broke up some brushwood and, adding some dried grass, lit a fire. White smoke rose straight up, drifting only slightly.

Night came. The white smoke in the distance became a red star twinkling on the ground. The priest could not sleep; his chest danced with feelings at once happy and painful. As the night wore on he continued to burn brushwood.

The morning brought new warmth. A bird cried once shrilly, swept down near the collar of the priest, and flew away. The priest took a sip of millet gruel. He was muddled and blurry-eyed from lack of sleep, but the memory of the previous night was still fresh in his mind. Now his sense of victory over the severe winter cold was driven from his heart completely. As he read from the Lotus sutra, part of his regular morning confession, he felt as if somewhere someone was listening, and he finished reciting with a mysterious, deep emotion.

When he went down to the stream and bathed, he felt a sudden pain as if an arrow had struck the marrow of his spine. Gradually, as he regained his calm, he realized that a voice, deep and forceful, was reciting scripture, the sound reverberating, undisturbed by the roar of the falls.

He looked around and saw, on a large, protruding rock upstream, an older priest sitting in the proper, ancient way, with his legs crossed and his eyes closed. As the younger priest hastily put on his patched robe and approached, the older man opened his eyes. Surely, thought the younger priest, this was the man whose smoke he'd seen yesterday. The younger priest's lips grew tense and his breathing quickened.

The other priest—he was perhaps ten years older than the younger one—seemed a man of great calm and intellectual nobility. He was extremely thin, but there was a warm luster in his eyes. For an instant, the younger priest felt defeated. He seated himself down-stream, respectfully, but in his great agitation he could not speak with full decorum. Immediately he hurled himself at the older priest.

"Honored priest," he said, "I have been all by myself for a long time. I have suffered. Would you mind listening to my story? I feel that if I could talk about myself to someone like you, I would be able to continue my devotions in a better frame of mind."

"Tell me whatever you wish. I'll listen," said the older man. "I, too, have spent the whole winter here buried under the snow, suffer-ing. It gives me incomparable pleasure to be able to meet a friend on the same path."

He spoke these words in a serene tone, a faint smile revealing the composure of his mind. He had spent the winter in a temporary shelter on the flat rock near Mt. Sanjō, he said. Sensing the presence of someone living in the area, he had waited for the snow to melt on the mountain path and had come down. In short, he had expected this meeting.

The young man's eyes shone. "When I saw the smoke," he said, "I was convinced that I would be able to meet the most devoted of ascetics. I spent all last night without sleep."

"Is that so?" said the older priest. "From your appearance, I would guess you've been a military man. I dare say you must have had some profound reason for renouncing the world."

The young man was delighted that the older priest had so kindly invited him to talk.

"Let me take advantage of your offer," he began. "I was born in Bandō. Seveal years ago I went up to Kyoto as a retainer of Matano Gorō of Sagami. I served as a member of the Ōban² and was stationed at the mansion of Lord Yorimori.

"Two years ago this fall, when Lord Yoritomo, exiled in Izu, raised an army in hopes of restoring the Minamoto family, Lord Koremori of the Taira family set out for Bandō, leading the army as supreme commander, to fight Lord Yoritomo. As you perhaps know, before he could get off a single arrow, he was turned back at Fujigawa.

"The priests of the Tōdaiji Temple and Kōfukuji Temple in the city of Nara had for a long time been hostile to the Taira family, and at once they seized this opportunity to rise in arms. When the Grand Lord Kiyomori could tolerate the rebellion of the priests no longer, he had his son, Lord Shigehira, lay siege on the city of Nara with 30,000 troops. This was on the 28th of December. The fierce monk soldiers had been expecting the attack, and they'd blocked the main roads of Narazaka and Hannyaji with abatis. Violent fighting began."

The older priest responded lightly, "I am acquainted with the general story, yes."

"I had never seen such brutal fighting," said the younger priest. "I had two veteran soldiers as my attendants. But these two old men went into hiding, saying they were afraid of Buddha's punishment. It wasn't a battle at all, it was like beasts biting one another. In that narrow ravine, in the fierce northwest wind, everyone was struggling to take some other man's life."

The story was too much to be contained in the calm of the young man's recollection. His eyes turned up and his teeth chattered.

---

2. The title given to the group of soldiers who were sent on a rotating basis to the capital city of Kyoto and whose duty it was to guard the Imperial Palace as well as the city itself. (NT)

"The rumor of the brutality reached even this mountain," said the older priest, listening without moving an eye.

"Shortly before sunset, black smoke rose from the Hall of the Great Buddha. Horrendous pillars of flame shot up and became fiery whirls, and roof tiles blew about like flower petals. Angry voices, mad voices, wailing voices. . . . My nose and throat felt choked.

"By the time we'd pushed to the front of the Nandaimon Gate, the monk soldiers were nearly all dead. In their place, student priests rose up, not dressed in armor. They threw roof tiles and rocks at us. Flying arrows are not so frightening—you only hear them go past— but you can see roof tiles and rocks very clearly, so that you duck your head without thinking, and thus the marching order breaks.

"There was a young, tall student priest. He was wearing a priest's straight robe, his sleeves tucked up with a rope. He wouldn't stop throwing tiles at us, darting out from the cover of some piles of floor mats. A big ridge tile came flying down. It struck the left arm protector of the man standing next to me, a soldier in a dark-blue cuirass. He let his bow fall. Since my own bow had broken, I quickly picked up his, fitting an arrow to it, and twisted around to take aim.

"The student priest, lifting his right hand high, was about to throw a bell, an accessory of the Buddhist altar. It was a five-claw bell,[3] glittering like gold, reflecting the flames. It rang out sharply once. At that moment, my black-feathered arrow shot through the air. The student priest's body stretched out like a falling charred stick. His groan of frustration and rage is still deep in my ears.

"Then another one appeared. This one must have been a page,[4] he was very young and wore a young boy's hunting costume, a *suikan*. He was carrying a broken piece of a roof tile, but he picked up a halberd and brandished it.

"'My brother's revenge!' he cried out in a voice painfully sharp and clear, and again and again, recklessly, he tried to stab at me. Though he staggered under the heavy, unfamiliar weapon, he was an enemy not to be taken lightly. It was clear that he'd been devoted to the slain student priest. Before I knew it, my hand, gripping the long sword, swung sideways. The young boy fell."

3. A bell used in esoteric Buddhism, made of gilt bronze or plain bronze, so called because the bell has five claws at its closed end. (NT)

4. Many Buddhist temples, in which no female was allowed to live, employed young boys

The older priest covered his eyes with his hand. "What a pity! Such is a war!"

The younger man felt he had spoken too much, but he couldn't seem to check the torrent of words gushing out.

"Exactly," he said. "I drew close to the young boy and looked at his lightly powdered face. A thin stream of blood was coming from his mouth. His eyes were open. I still cannot forget his features, which had already slipped out of the world of hatred.

"I probed the front pocket of the boy's *suikan* and found a silk amulet case in which there were two sheets of paper. On one of them, someone had written, in a poor hand: 'May the enemies of Buddha be driven away quickly,' with the signature, 'Sakuramaru.' The other was a charm issued by the Kimpu Shrine. I supposed the student priest had been among the reserves from Yoshino who came as reinforcements to the priests of the Tōdaiji Temple. Sakuramaru, the young boy, must have volunteered to serve as the student priest's attendant."

"Splendid young men!" said the older priest. "Their performance did them credit. They were not inferior to warriors!" He continued to listen with his eyes lightly closed, chanting in a low voice.

"Though they'd won the battle, the soldiers went back to Kyoto with heavy hearts. On New Year's Day nobody would drink *sake* to celebrate the New Year. The wrath of Mt. Hiei and the Mii Temple was boundless. The whole world lamented the destruction of the Hall of the Great Buddha. I came to understand now the feelings of my attendants who had forsaken their long-time master in fear of Buddha's punishment. It became unbearable to me that I had killed two young disciples of Buddha with my own hands. My being a soldier became detestable. Finally I entered the priesthood to pray for the welfare in the next life of those I had slain.

"In the spring of the following year, I came to Yoshino, the place these young men had originally come from, to build myself a hermitage. Even though the Kimpu Shrine had lost many of its priests in that battle, there were still a great many people around, and I felt

---

between the ages of twelve and fifteen, whose duties included cleaning and waiting on visitors. They wore a young boy's hunting costume called *suikan*, put on light makeup, and used feminine language. (NT)

that such a place would be a hindrance to my discipline. And so, I chose this place, farther from human habitation.

"It has been two years now, and still I haven't attained peace of mind. The truth is I'm afflicted with nightmares day and night. I am filled with shame."

So the younger priest finished his long confession. He knew it had no eloquence of triumph in it; it was simply an outpouring of the lonesome yearning that had lain secret in the depths of his heart for three years and now happened to find words.

The older priest gave a light smile and said, "No, no. You have a rare, devoted heart. These things were not your fault but what all fighting brings about. The two young men will certainly enter the Pure Land. Tell me—I suppose you have a wife?"

For the first time, the younger priest smiled grimly.

"Alas! It is awkward to speak about this. I had a wife. We were getting along well, too. My wife's father was of the Hōjō family. But as soon as Lord Yoritomo's power reached Izu, my father-in-law took my wife away from me and married her to a man of influence in the service of Lord Yoritomo. At that time I was in Kyoto, and to my great mortification I could no nothing."

"I'm sorry to hear that," said the older priest. "But, if I may say so, you ought to consider that your father-in-law and your wife acted by the will of Buddha, so that you might be able to carry out your virtuous renunciation."

The younger priest nodded slightly.

"Let me ask you another question," said the older priest. "What did you do about food and fuel during the winter months?"

"During the season of ascetic disciplines on Mt. Ōmine, I went to the Zaōdō Temple or the Kimpu Shrine every day and worked for half a day as a carrier, woodcutter, or cleaner. They gave me rice and barley, which I saved. For fuel, I gathered and stored dried wood, fallen branches, and dried grass. I picked acorns and beechnuts for storage, and found some herbs, which I dried for future use. I also cultivated the soil around the hermitage where the sun shone, sowed some grain, and harvested it in the fall."

"Well, well!" remarked the older priest. "You made careful preparations—I would surely never have thought about such things. You will without a doubt attain enlightenment. Do not forget to keep adding to your well of ascetic virtues day by day and month by month."

"I have every intention of doing so," replied the younger priest, "but I feel helpless when I think of the future. It must be Buddha's kind design that I have now found my spiritual master. Please guide this imperfect disciple."

"No, no. Don't humble yourself! I was deeply moved by your story today. In the near future I will offer you my own confession. It might amuse you. I will let the smoke rise as a signal. My place is about five *chō*[5] southwest of here. You'll find it easily if you follow this narrow path."

The older priest quietly stood up. The younger one, though reluctant to part from him, also rose and returned to his hermitage. The encounter with a real human being, especially a superior priest, in this strange, unreal region gave him immense satisfaction. He felt ashamed yet relieved now, realizing his own insignificance.

The stars were clear in the evening sky. The young priest could not fall asleep; the sound of the falls was like the older priest's voice.

Now it was the morning of the fifth day after the meeting of the two priests. A rain, which had started during the night, slackened. As he watched the soft splashing, the younger priest felt his heart fill with emotion. Around noon, the rain stopped, and the valley became bright. As the vapor rose, the mountain peaks, the trees, and sky shimmered in the heat. Just then the young priest saw pale-blue smoke rising in the southwestern sky.

"So today is the day," he said to himself. "I'll go!"

He went up the steep rocky path in one rush. Stumbling a few times, he walked several *chō* until he came to a small, flat space on which stood a humble cottage. The inside was extremely small but tidy. The dirt floor was covered with dried grass. There was a small reading table on which lay several volumes of the Buddhist scripture. Next to the table stood a bronze water jar. A spare monk's robe was hanging casually on a cedar branch. There was nothing else.

The older priest smiled, elaborately thanking the younger priest for their meeting the other day. Then he began his life story.

From this hermitage one could look down at a span of the famous

5. One *chō* is about 119 yards. (NT)

thousand cherry trees that grew on the inner mountain. Their young buds were crimson, urging the pure white blossoms to open. It was a beautiful sight.

The older priest closed his eyes, quietly unfolding his recollections.

"I was born into the family of a fairly well-known Buddhist painter in Kyoto. (A painting of mine is on one of the doors in the main hall of a Buddhist temple built by the Taira family.) One summer morning six years ago, a dove flew into the Judas tree in our front garden and began to sing in a gentle voice. I scattered some parched beans about, then stood and watched as the dove flew down to peck at them.

"As I stirred to go and get my painting brush, the dove, perhaps frightened, flew up. Just then, an arrow crossed so close to my eye that it barely missed cutting me. The dove folded its wings and looked as if it were floating in the direction of the arrow, but the next moment it fell to the ground, flapping its wings wildly. Even now I cannot forget its round eyes looking up at me, appealing for help.

"As I stood there in dismay, a nobleman in a hunting costume, carrying a wicker bow, came bursting through the inner gate. Behind him came a young attendant wearing a cuirass over an under-robe with narrow sleeves. The nobleman was the oldest son of our next door neighbor, of the Taira family.

"'Look! My arrow pierced straight through the breast! My aim's as good as ever!' The nobleman in the hunting costume turned to his attendant, laughing loudly. The attendant snatched up the dying dove. Anger rose in me, I could no longer be patient. I said, '*I'll* bury the poor dove!'

"The nobleman, eyes narrowed with anger, hurled back a contemptuous laugh. 'Doves live to be eaten by man,' he said. 'It's the same with everything.'

"The two men disappeared, laughing. At that moment I felt a shock as if I had been hit on the head with a hammer. I sank to the wooden floor.

"'It's true!' I thought. 'Man lives on the destruction of life! Man eats birds, animals, fish, rice, barley. Man works the silkworm to death for silk and fells trees to build houses. All our life comes from death! How can such contradiction be permitted?'

"From then on, day after day, I wrestled with this question. My wife watched my pale face in trembling fear. My friends dismissed the matter with a laugh. They said, patting me on the shoulder, 'Your heart is too pure. We understand your logic, but it's a problem even Buddha with all his wisdom could not solve. Come, cheer up and let's drink *sake!*'

"At that point, such lukewarm friendship meant nothing to me. I reached the conclusion that there was no way to save myself but by escaping the human world. There were a number of barriers at home and with my family, but I closed my eyes and leaped over them all to land here.

"I chose Yoshino simply because of my deep admiration for En no gyōja.[6] Years ago I painted a portrait of him at the request of the Daigoji Temple. I felt now a deep need to feel with my own body the mountain's sacred atmosphere, created in the olden days by En no gyōja.

"And then there was this: I'd heard that in his youth Saigyō, the pure-hearted priest, twice came up to Mt. Ōmine to practice ascetic disciplines. I was determined to follow in his footsteps.

"Since I came here, I have not eaten any fish, birds, or grain. Neither do I take any cooked food. I keep myself alive with a small amount of water and weeds. Even this is not enough. Eventually I wish to be able to melt somewhere between heaven and earth, eating cloud and mist, and to attain Buddhahood while still in the flesh. No doubt it will be a lifelong task.—Well! What an endless story I've told! It must have been tedious listening!"

The priest's smile was lonely, otherworldly, even though he had an air of confidence. The younger priest was shaken to the core of the five organs, so that he could hardly think.

"I'm completely overwhelmed by your rigorous austerities," he said. "My heart has been cleaned, listening to you. Please forget all about the story of my renouncing the world. I am ashamed no end."

The older priest said in a subdued tone, "In truth it was the words of the nobleman next door that made me think of renouncing the world. If he hadn't killed the dove, I'd have ended an empty life licking brushes as an ordinary town painter.

"That nobleman, shortly after the incident, went on an expedition to the northern territory of Kiso with his attendant soldiers. There,

---

6. A famous religious figure of the late seventh century and the founder of the religious sect, *Shugendō*. See footnote 1. (NT)

together with his followers—so I've heard—he fell from a cliff on Mt. Tonami in the dark of night and died. Every morning I pray for the peace of the soul of that unusually enlightening man."

The evening haze rose stealthily before the two men knew it. The mountains were now tinted with pale gold.

The older priest stood for a long time, watching the young one climbing down the rocky path.

The younger priest could not sleep at all that evening. He had become doubtful of the result of his ascetic discipline, now that he clearly understood the difference between the greatness of the older priest and his own littleness. He said to himself, "You have not renounced all you should have renounced. The older priest has renounced everything. You will not obtain what matters most without total renunciation."

He regretted his meeting with the older priest, but also he remembered that just sitting near him, he'd felt his spine straightening and his blood running clearer.

After that day, the younger priest kept waiting for the smoke to rise in the southwestern sky, but he never saw it again. When he went down to the stream to draw water, he never saw the older man.

Then one day, the young man saw a bronze water jar flying from somewhere, drawing water, and flying back. It was the same water jar that he had seen in the older priest's cottage. The water jar appeared several times after that. When it flew up from the surface of the water, it nodded its head lightly two or three times, as if to greet the younger priest.

"Why doesn't my master come himself?" he wondered. "Has he confined himself to Mt. Sanjō? How I wish I could follow him! But *I* cannot live on the grass alone." No matter how hard he thought, he could not understand the priest's withdrawal.

The cherry blossoms had now turned to green leaves. As he watched the summer clouds flowing unhurriedly over Mt. Sanjō, his loneliness increased until even the color of the trees and grass seemed to fade. His longing for the older priest grew day by day.

It was an unusually peaceful morning. As he was reciting the Kannon sutra, his daily task, the young priest found himself mysteriously warming to the recitation. He had reached in the scripture

the section of Buddha's reply, "the *brahmana* who are to be saved
. . . the monk, the nun, the devout layman, the devout laywoman
. . . the wife of the rich man, the wife of the householder, the wife of
a prime minister, and the wife of a *brahmana* . . . a boy and a girl
. . . a dragon, a devil, a heavenly musician, a demon, a golden-
winged bird. . . ." He recited with increasing force.

Before the young priest's eyes, the foreign land of two thousand
years ago,[7] the strange world of Boddhisattvas, angels, boys and
girls and goblins, unfolded itself. He saw, as clear as actuality, a vision of the smiling older priest as Buddha, looking down at the earth
from above the clouds.

The young priest wrung his hands. "If I indulge in this kind of
sweet dream," he thought, "I will never be able to endure religious
austerities. How could I ever face the older priest again?"

The young priest thus severely reproached himself even as he
enjoyed his ecstasy. Nonetheless, he felt helpless and increasingly
doubtful about his future as an ascetic.

When summer was half over, the days became sultry in the valley.
The dark green of the huge trees gave an oppressive sense of weari-
ness; the shrill voices of cicadas were helplessly swallowed up in the
evening shadow of the mountains.

Shortly before the closing of the season for ascetic disciplines on
Mt. Ōmine, the number of lay devotees coming to the mountain from
the Kumano area increased. Those who belonged to the Shōgoin
Temple of Kyoto spent many days making a pilgrimage to the places
set aside for ascetic exercise in the mountains, with the Kimpu
Shrine of Yoshino as their final stopping place. Then they went
down to Rokuta, a village on the southern bank of the Yoshino River.
Crossing the river, they returned to their respective homes in Kyoto.
The young priest remembered the young people from his homeland
of Izu, who, clad in white and carrying octagonal white-wood canes,
had climbed Mt. Fuji, worshipped at the Asama Shrine, then returned to the village.

A group of ascetic devotees clad in white chanted a *dahrani*, or
magic formula, and shook their crosiers. Their doleful incantation
of exotic words lingered on, tremulous. The young priest involun-

---

7 Referring to ancient India, the birthplace of Buddhism. (NT)

tarily cried out to them, "Sirs, as you went from peak to peak, didn't you see a tall, thin priest practicing his austerities alone?"

Five or six men raised their faces from the tall grass, and one said, "Such a man was meditating alone on a flat rock on top of Mt. Sanjō. He looked like a true master of asceticism. He was sitting in the proper ancient way, with crossed legs, and his figure against the evening clouds was exactly like a stone image of Buddha. He was on top of a cliff that we couldn't reach by foot."

Then the five or six men resumed their incantation and continued down the path. The young priest felt a feverish chill flowing downward through his body.

"Oh my master! If only you would talk with me!"

But now it was clear that the older priest was living permanently in a world too high for the younger one to reach. This realization was in every respect a severe blow to the younger priest.

A few days later, something completely unexpected happened.

A great thunderstorm arose. In the afternoon of that day, as the sun was going down, the wind died away. Then, in an instant, many of the mountain peaks turned black. The wind began to blow again across the valley, making a thin, trembling sound. In the night, all at once, torrential rain struck. The roof of the young priest's cottage became like the meshes of a net from the force of the downpour. His round straw mat bobbed up and down on the floor in the accumulating rainwater.

Peals of thunder reverberated in the valley with tremendous intensity, drowning even the sound of the torrential rain. Dozens of fiery lightning bolts, bursting forth from rifts in the sky, zigzagged in all directions, their lower ends piercing the mountain peaks.

The younger priest was terrified but also he was deeply concerned about the safety of the older one sitting on his flat rock high on the mountaintop, exposed to the wind. The younger priest prayed over and over that his master would overcome the disaster through his long-practiced ascetic discipline.

The following morning the rain stopped and the sun came out. The mountain peaks, even clearer than usual, looked somehow lost in thought. The raging current of the stream rushing downward, crushing rocks and fallen trees in its way, was a reminder of last night's nightmare.

The younger priest was now exhausted, both mentally and physically. The grain he had stored was now all soaked. He had no appetite. He groaned.

"A man like me can no longer endure living here. The reality of Yoshino is as severe as expected. It was most naïve of me to consider myself a victor."

He carried utensils and food outside to dry on the millet field. It would have been better if the thunderstorm had come a month later. The roots of every plant had been washed away; the heads were broken. There was nothing he could do to save the crop.

As he vainly got up and sat down again, evening came on. The stars were beautiful. The moon came up. The weeds which bore blossoms had all been knocked down. Only the shadow of the remaining pampas grass was visible, feeble and helpless.

Late that night, something astonishing appeared—a multitude of squirrels. Perhaps because their acorns and chestnuts were washed away by the thunderstorm, countless families of the squirrels, large and small, drew around the young priest. Chittering like sparrows, jumping and rolling around and whisking their tails, the squirrels pushed heads of millet up to their mouths. A little squirrel put its mouth to a big one's and received its share from the big one, who dexterously worked his small teeth. Occasionally a little squirrel jumped over the big one's legs.

The young priest watched like a child. He became envious of the squirrels. The hardships of the past three years suddenly seemed meaningless. He recalled his former wife. He remembered his old mother. There was a squirrel which resembled his wife's father who had taken her away from him. Finally he shouted with all his strength—

"I'm going home!"

His words rumbled in the darkness, surprisingly decisive.

When the morning sun was bright over Mt. Ōdaigahara, the young priest took the mountain path eastward. He was carrying only a cane, a hat, and a small amount of food in an itinerant priest's bag. He abandoned his cottage, his field, and everything else. All his austerities and the convictions that he had maintained until the day before, he renounced in order to return to his former life.

Nevertheless, it was painful to look back at the grass and rocks, his familiar friends, receding higher and higher as he climbed down the mountain.

He thought of taking the Yoshino path toward the Zaōdō Temple and the Kimpu Shrine because he wanted to worship, but stopped. His feet would not move in that direction. He went down to the great falls, the place dear to him because it was there that the older priest had kindly listened to his story. Then without stopping at Miyadaki, he proceeded from Ryōmon to Murou, and passing through Nabarino, chose the Ise passage.

"I'm beaten," he thought. This sense of defeat would not leave him. But even so, as Mt. Yoshino and Mt. Ōmine grew smaller and dimmer in the distance, his spirit gradually lightened.

In less than twenty days, he arrived at his own village of Tahi in Izu. For over half of the way he had walked with the early autumn sea on his left and Mt. Fuji on his right.

"How wonderful!" he said, looking up again and again at the northern sky.

His old home was in bad repair but was not as dilapidated as he'd expected. His aged mother, at the sight of her son, when he returned unexpectedly in the form of a thin priest, began wiping her cheeks continually in silence. The farm hand who had been in service since the young priest was a boy uttered a loud cry and hid his face. On his left arm he had a shrivelled scar from an arrow wound.

There were no young men left in the village. They were fighting the Taira family in the far western sea. The young priest's house felt empty.

"What happened to Koyata?" he asked the aged farm hand. Koyata was the second husband of the young priest's wife.

The farm hand answered, faltering: "Master Koyata joined Lord Noriyori's forces and was said to have been killed in battle at the River Sunomata in Owari."

"Really?" said the young priest. "So, Koyata died. What about old Shigehisa?" Shigehisa was the father of the young priest's former wife. The young priest hated him.

"The old master followed Lord Kajiwara to the western region, as the supervisor of the provisions collected from the Enoura Bay area."[8]

8. The village of Tahi, the young priest's home, was on Enoura Bay. (NT)

The young priest wanted to hear about his former wife. He looked from his mother to the old farm hand. Her expression showing mixed feelings, his mother checked the old man.

That night, the young priest slept beside his mother. It was many years since he had done so. She drew near to him and whispered in his ear. After Koyata had been killed in battle, the wife would come stealthily to clean the young priest's house or to tidy the rooms. From time to time she would come while it was still dark to look after the field. The young priest understood why the rooms were neat.

Four or five days later, the young priest put out to sea in a small rowboat. The water was clear to the sandy bottom, where red and white shells winked their eyes. He enjoyed the boat ride as if he were a little boy again.

The sun was going down. From the beach he went up a narrow path among the rocks and passed under the pine trees, where he came upon his former wife, who was apparently returning from the field belonging to his family. Stiffening, the woman put the blade end of her hoe on the ground, set both hands on the top of the handle and bowed. He recalled that the nape of her neck had once been white.

Soon the two sat down side by side on a pine-tree stump. The evening came on quietly while they remained for a long time in the same position.

Two months later, one could see the woman working devotedly around her former husband. The wrinkles on his old mother's forehead decreased. But even though the young man became content with his present life, his yearning to talk with the older priest, whose position was beyond his reach, did not diminish. In fact the older priest was now among the group of Boddhisattvas the younger man worshipped every day.

The long period of civil war finally ended, and people's lives became stable again. The shogunate government was established in Kamakura,[9] and the relationships among the warriors altered dras-

9. Five years of civil war between the Minamoto family and the Taira family had ended with the defeat of the Taira family in the western sea. In 1192 Minamoto Yoritomo, the leader of the Minamoto family, assumed, for the first time in Japanese history, the title of *Shogun*, or generalissimo, as head of the shogunate government established in Kamakura. This government represented, in theory, only the military authority of the emperor, but in practice it con-

tically. The young man, as a matter of course, went to serve under the leadership of Lord Hōjō. This elevated position, which had been held by Koyata, his wife's former husband, came to him without any conscious effort on his part.

When the young man's grandfather inherited farm land from his mother's side of the family, he moved to this area from the village of Kazo in Musashi. The principal image on his family altar was a replica of Fudōmyōō,[10] enshrined in the Sōganji Temple of Fudōoka, a village next to Kazo. The young man had two additional images of Kimkara and Cetaka[11] made and placed them one on each side of the main image as attendants. These were for the repose of the souls of the student priest and the page whom the young man had killed with his own hands in the midst of the raging fire at the Tōdaiji Temple.

Every morning when the young priest opened the family altar to pray, the visage of the older priest seemed to appear in the awe-inspiring eyes and lips of Fudōmyōō.

It was not until ten years later, when the young man became the father of two children, that he came to understand the true intention of the older priest. At first, the older priest had tried to teach him asceticism, but he had soon realized that it would be impossible for a man born among farm people who worked the earth, engaged himself in working the earth, to become completely a man of religious austerity. And in any case, the older priest had seen that the war itself had redeemed the younger priest's killing of the two young men. Therefore, the older priest had chosen to leave the younger one to himself so that by his own wits he might decide to return again to the earth.

---

trolled all of Japan, while the Emperor (who remained in Kyoto) was the country's figurehead. (NT)

10. The god of fire, Acalanatha in Sanskrit. (NT)

11. Two of the eight attendant pages to Acalanatha. (NT)

CHIKUBU ISLAND[1]

A tall pine tree rises prominently on the east side of the spacious garden in front of the main temple. Under the tree three pages[2] stand talking. One of them points to the surface of Lake Biwa which lies beneath his eyes. Another glances around the lake, shaking his head. A third counts white sails and fishing boats. They all look very serious. Finally the pointing fingers of all three pages are focused on a pale blue point blurred by the watery haze on the surface of the lake in the distant north.

On the northeast side of the main temple stood several buildings where priests lived. One of the priests, Jishō, had been watching the three pages from where he sat on his round mat in the wooden corridor outside the easternmost building. He was resting after his scripture reading. The place was the Daijōin Temple, a famous temple in the Mudōji valley of Mt. Hiei.[3] At the time of this story, Bishop Jien was the chief priest. His grave is still there.

Bishop Jien was the younger brother of the *Kampaku*[4] Kujō Kanezane. Jishō was from one of the lesser branches of the clan and had entered the priesthood at a relatively late age. He had many sisters. His youngest brother, on whose future had rested much hope, died of an epidemic at the age of seven, and it was his death that had prompted Jishō to become a Buddhist priest. At age twenty, he went to the Daijōin Temple, relying on Bishop Jien, who tonsured the young man and gave him the religious name of Jishō. Having endured the seven years' *kaihōgyō*, the most rigorous of all the as-

1. A small island in the northern part of Lake Biwa, the largest lake in Japan. (NT)
2. Many Buddhist temples, in which no female was allowed to live, employed young boys between the ages of twelve and fifteen, whose duties included cleaning and waiting on visitors. They wore a young boy's hunting costume called *suikan*, put on light makeup, and used feminine language. (NT)
3. Mt. Hiei is the location of the headquarters of the Tendai group, a powerful Buddhist sect. (NT)
4. The most powerful post of regent for an adult Emperor. (NT)

cetic disciplines practiced by the devotees of this temple, Jishō was granted the rank of priest.[5] But Jishō had not chosen the Daijōin Temple because Jien was the *Kampaku*'s younger brother, or because Jien was a bishop. It was, in truth, because Jien was an excellent poet.

He was among the best poets of the period, and left the largest number of poems. In the *Shinkokinshū* anthology[6] alone, sixty-two poems by Jien were entered. These poems were not inferior to those by Teika, Karyū, Yoshitsune, or Saigyō.[7]

It was only natural for Jishō, a lover of literature, to wish that he could be like this master poet of his clan and that at least one of his own poems might be chosen for inclusion in an imperial anthology. Even after Bishop Jien died a few years later, Jishō never forgot to read the *Shūgyokushū*, a collection of Bishop Jien's poems, for this purpose curtailing his sleep after the evening's ascetic disciplines.

Jishō put on a pair of high clogs and went up to the pine tree. The eyes of the three pages all came to greet him. The morning breeze was gentle and comforting on the mountain in early summer. At the foot of the mountain, the city of Kyoto had already celebrated the Aoi Festival of Kamo.[8] Jishō could not help feeling a faint, tremulous yearning for the human companionship he had left behind in a corner of the capital.

"Hello, there! Have you found something interesting?" asked Jishō.

"Ah, sir, how I wish I could fly over to that island like a waterbird," replied the mischievous one of the pages, the one who most resembled the priest's dead brother.

"I wish I could see all kinds of fish," said the quiet one.

"Sir, I wish I could watch the crowd of young monks of that island

5. Much as in the Anglican and Roman Catholic churches, a priest (*sōzu* in Japanese) in Buddhist churches ranks next below a bishop (sōjō). (NT)

6. The ninth imperial anthology, containing a little over 1900 poems, c. 1234. (NT)

7. All are well-known poets. Teika (1162–1241); Karyū, also called Ietaka, (1158–1237); Yoshitsune (1169–1206), a son of the *Kampaku* Kujō Kanezane; Saigyō, usually called Saigyō the priest, (1118–90); Bishop Jien (1155–1225?). The priest named Jishō is a fictitious character. (NT)

8. The most important and most elaborate festival of medieval Kyoto, held in the Fourth Month of the lunar calendar (now on May 15) in commemoration of the two Shinto shrines— Kami Kamo and Shimo Kamo. The festival was attended by everyone—from the Emperor down to the humblest citizens. The people of medieval Kyoto were said to live for this annual festivity. (NT)

swim. I hear they're all wonderful swimmers," cried the most active one.

Jishō felt his boyhood again, running wild through the minds of these three pages.

"I see. In other words, you all want to go to Chikubu Island, eh?"

"That's right! That's exactly right!" The replies from the three bounced back all together.

The Daijōin Temple was about ten *chō*[9] to the south, below the central hall, Kompon Chūdō, the largest structure on Mt. Hiei. The view from the Daijōin Temple was said to be the best on all the mountain. Sky and clouds blended with the elusive outline of the lake. On its absolutely flat surface, many boats were afloat, like small insects. The tracks of the insect-like boats spread quietly in transparent radii, then changed to formless waves. Bamboos, reeds, and rushes, some standing, some bent over along the lakeshore, showed no interest in joining the change in the season but remained asleep, carefree, curving themselves to the shape of the lake.

To be truthful, Jishō had been thinking of a visit to Chikubu Island for reasons of his own. Because of his devotion to poetry, he wanted to enclose himself at the island's shrine of Sarasvati, god of poetry and music. For years, it had been popular for devotees of poetry to pay a visit to Chikubu Island for this purpose. They would cruise on the lake, go sightseeing on the island, and then, in their desire to win the increasingly competitive poetry contests, race to the island shrine to pray for success.

Jishō had been reciting chapter fifteen of the scripture called *Konkōmyō Saishōōkyō*, the chapter dealing with the power of the god Sarasvati. As his belief in the scripture deepened, Jishō found it impossible to suppress his wish to prostrate himself to his heart's content before the sacred image of Sarasvati, the scripture's embodiment.

If he could go, he would like to take the pages, so that their dreams, too, should be realized. After all, there was nothing in the mountain to warm the hearts of children. Jishō decided to request permission from the chief priest of the Daijōin Temple.

He asked the three pages, "How would you like it if you could all go to the island soon?"

---

9. One *chō* is approximately 119 yards. (NT)

"Could we go? We would be really happy if Buddha would allow us to go!"

The three saw the priest off, almost worshipping his retreating figure. Instead of returning to his quarters, Jishō directed his steps toward a large building near the main temple.

The bishop or chief priest of the temple readily consented to Jishō's request, for he knew Jishō's daily devotion to ascetic disciplines. Jishō was allowed to take not only the three pages but also two older boys called *daidōji*. The pages, whose duty was to serve inside the temple buildings, came from relatively well-to-do families of Kyoto, but the *daidōji*, who did outdoor labor, were sons of poor peasants of neighboring villages. Neither the pages nor the *daidōji* knew the sea or the lake.

Jishō was also allowed to take two young student priests who were under his guidance. It was almost the time of the Bon Festival,[10] when a great memorial service was held and a large number of people came to the temple. Jishō began to prepare for the two-day journey by boat, which he planned to begin on the day after the Bon Festival.

At dawn on the sixteenth of July, the group of three priests and five boys climbed through the mist down eighteen *chō* of the steep slope from the Mudōji valley to Sakamoto. Another path on the eastern slope from Tōdō, or the East Tower of Mt. Hiei, would have been much easier to follow, but Jishō purposely avoided going that way, since it was the regular route for the wild monk soldiers[11] of Sakamoto. On their way down, the priests and *daidōji* frequently had to carry the young pages on their backs.

They reached the foot of the slope and hurried through the busy streets of Sakamoto. Since an arrangement had been made in advance with the boatmen at the port, a new passenger boat was already waiting at the landing place. Many other passenger boats and freighters were moored there, but not a soul was visible, probably because it was still early.

In the light of the still invisible sun, the outline of Mt. Shimei

10. The Buddhist All Souls' Day, the fifteenth of July. (NT)
11. Large temples and monasteries maintained armed monk soldiers as security forces. Often the monk soldiers were ex-convicts or fugitives from the law. (NT)

emerged, as if carved in relief. The boat began to move, and the young boys shouted with joy. Three oarsmen rowed rhythmically. A moderate south wind came up, and the sail was raised. The boat's speed suddenly increased. The water of the lake was very clear. Large and small fish darted about quickly and easily.

"I wonder what that long, black wriggly thing is?" said one of the pages, gazing down.

"That's an eel. Eels are in the stream in the rice field, too," answered one of the *daidōji*. Suddenly, there was a strange noise overhead, as if a stone were falling. The next moment, a big bird flew up from under the water, flapping its wings and carrying the black wriggly thing twisted around its beak.

Jishō, showing his wide knowledge, said, "That is a bird called the little grebe. They live in lakes and make floating nests. They are often celebrated in poetry."

"We call them helldivers," one of the boatmen corrected him. "They're thieves who steal fish from the traps the fishermen make in the shallow waters."

Perhaps because they had left early that morning, the pages soon became hungry. At Jishō's signal, the student priests opened a box made of thin wooden boards. The box was neatly packed with rice cakes. The pages clapped their hands.

"How delicious!"

"We haven't had these since the memorial service for the Holy Priest Dengyō last month. We had only a few even then."

Jishō watched the boys with a smile. When their boat crossed the straits of Katada, the wind became stronger and the expanse of water suddenly became limitless. The fishing boats, scattered about at short intervals, looked as if they were dancing. Along the east bank, several rivers flowed silently into the lake, cutting through the endless green of rushes swaying in the wind. There were only a few houses and inhabitants in sight.

Jishō talked with the boatmen for a while and then turned toward the pages.

"Listen, my children. We have made much more rapid progress than we expected. It's seventeen *ri*[12] from Sakamoto to Chikubu Is-

12. One *ri* equals about two and a half miles. (NT)

land. From here to the island it's about twelve *ri* more. I'm told that
if we continue at the present speed, we'll arrive there before dark.

"Since we're going to have a retreat tonight in the shrine of Sarasvati, we don't have to hurry, so let's pay a visit to the Chōmeiji Temple on our way. It's a temple associated with our own temple in Mt.
Hiei. They're very closely connected. And before we leave, we'll buy
some of the famous *magari*[13] cookies."

The pages responded with another shout of joy.

At the mouth of the Yasu River, the boat's prow turned eastward,
running into the wind. The boatmen shifted the sail so that the boat
heeled slightly and its speed did not diminish.

Before very long, they saw a tall mountain which appeared to be
floating on the lake. At the foot of the mountain lay a harbor with a
pier. Jishō's party landed there and climbed the long distance up
808 stone steps. The Chōmeiji Temple stood opposite Mt. Hiei across
the lake. The architecture of the temple was magnificent and the
view from there was as fine as that from the Daijōin Temple on Mt.
Hiei.

"I didn't know that the Hira mountains were so big and so high,"
said one page.

"Mt. Hiei is so low and drooping," remarked another.

Jishō turned to his young disciples and exchanged winks. Climbing down the stone steps, they stopped at the teashop to rest and
bought *magari* cookies and melons.

Then they walked to the pier, where their boat was moored. To
their surprise, a nun was there. One of the boatmen, sitting in the
middle of the boat, called out brusquely, "Welcome back, sir. This
nun here asked if this boat's going to Chikubu Island, and I said yes.
She says she'd like a ride there. What should we do?"

The nun bowed politely to Jishō and clasped her hands. She
seemed a nice person, apparently somewhat over thirty. Her face
was pale and lusterless, and her cheeks were sunken. Her words
sounded as if she uttered them by tearing up the depths of her heart.
She was, and seemed to have been for many years, someone whose
heart and flesh could hardly sustain her sorrow, suffering, and de-
spair; her body was like living death.

---

13. Sweet, fried dough cookies made from wheat flour. (NT)

"If you please, sir, would you mind taking me with you? I have been waiting here for the ferry from Asazuma to go to Ōtsu. From there I was going to take a pilgrimage boat to Chikubu Island. But I was told that it would be a long time before the ferry from Asazuma would be here," said the nun.

"Oh, it's fine with us," replied Jishō in a cheerful, even cordial tone. "We are, just like you, going to the island. The boat can easily take one more passenger." The nun bowed repeatedly to the priest. The boat again moved on smoothly under full sail.

At the sight of the nun's weird face, the pages had become quiet. But she kept looking at them with a gentle smile, and before long they began to feel more at ease. Then one of the younger priests put his mouth to Jishō's ear.

"Sir, please look at the nape of that nun's neck. She has something around it—it looks like a white bag. I think inside the bag there's something alive."

Surprised, Jishō looked carefully; he saw the bag heaving slightly.

"You're right. There is something inside. Look!—a snake! Just now it stuck up its head and flicked out its tongue!"

The nun, while looking cautiously about, lifted her right hand and stroked the bag lightly. The heaving motion stopped immediately. Jishō, still gazing steadily at the nun, could no longer remain unconcerned.

He thought to himself, "Why is she carrying a snake around her neck? It must be the result of some profound karma. I'll ask her directly and see how she answers."

Apparently the pages, too, had seen what the nun had on her neck. They turned their dark eyes in different directions. They were sitting in the middle of the boat, the nun near the bow, and the boatmen near the stern. Jishō got up casually and sat next to the nun.

"My dear sister," he said, "it shows your deep devotion to choose the time of the Bon Festival to make a retreat at the shrine of Sarasvati. You must have some long-fostered wish that you hope will be fulfilled by making this journey."

The nun stared into the priest's eyes. Her shining tears wet the side of the boat.

"I am afraid you have already seen through the bag around my neck. How much suffering and how much pleasure have I had because of the thing inside this bag! My heart is broken in two, and I feel helpless. Day and night I pray to Buddha for help, but to no avail. Please, may I pray that you will help me!"

Jishō bowed profoundly. The nun's desperate words apparently did not reach the stern of the boat, drowned out by wind; but she no longer seemed concerned about such a thing.

The boat passed by Okinoshima Island. It was nearly all covered by a granite mountain, but along the shore, one could see more than a dozen homes of fishermen and the narrow space they used for drying their nets. Nearby, a group of sturdy men who were cutting stones stretched their backs and laughed at the strange-looking passenger boat gliding by.

The sun was now slightly west of its noon position. The cool breeze warmed a little. The surface of the lake reflected the sun with a blinding glare. Tired from their morning activities, the pages dozed off.

"My father was the *jitō*[14] in the village of Gamō," said the nun, beginning her long confession.

"I had a younger brother. We grew up, loved by our parents. My brother had such a gentle disposition and such a beautiful face our neighbors used to call him a living image of the god Sarasvati. In the summer of my sixteenth year, my mother told me to pick some flowers to dedicate to Buddha. I was about to go into the meadow behind our house, but somehow I was reluctant to go, and I asked my brother to go instead.

"He was bitten by a viper which appeared as if from nowhere. Apparently the bite was in a fatal place; he died a few days later. My parents' sorrow and disappointment were terrible beyond words, but the feeling in my heart was nothing like sorrow. Whenever I saw a viper, I chased after it or struck it to death. That was the only way I could vent my rage.

"My brother's body was buried in the graveyard of a temple. If you take the road east of the village toward the mountain, you will come to a bridge over a river of perfectly clear water. It's behind that

14. A steward sent by a feudal lord to his fief or estate to supervise the working of the land, to collect taxes, and to maintain peace and order. A *jitō* was often dreaded by the people of his jurisdiction. (NT)

bridge that the temple stands, with its gate and its large main hall—
an impressive building. I used to make it my daily task to go and
place some flowers there, and to apologize to my brother who had
become a new grave mound."

Jishō discovered that the nun's story had already linked his heart
firmly to hers. "So you have lost your beloved brother, and under
such circumstances!," he exclaimed. "How heavy you've made my
heart. Yes, in my heart, I too have tears for the sudden loss of a
brother I loved."

The nun's face became gentle, and she continued, "One day I
heard the rustling of garments behind me. A voice said, 'Why are
you so grieved day after day? You must have experienced something
very sad indeed.' I looked back and was surprised. I thought I saw
my brother, reborn as the god Sarasvati. It was a page of this temple.
He wore his hair in the pages' style and had on a snow-white hunting costume, a *suikan*. He looked amazingly like my brother, though
perhaps a little older.

"He listened to my story, putting his hand repeatedly over his
eyes. Then he said, 'I came to this temple three years ago. My gentle
mother had died and I was thoroughly tired of the world. I wanted
to become a priest, but the chief priest of the temple forced me to
become a page and refused to tonsure me. I am completely helpless!'

"According to the page, the chief priest was an extremely odd
man. He had told the page, 'Since you are an incarnation of the god
Sarasvati, you should try to be like a woman both in your heart and
in your body and should wear a woman's lined ceremonial robe in
beautiful colors.'

"By the chief priest's order, the page had to put on heavy makeup
and change the color of the *kosode* garment he wore under his *suikan* to pink, orange, or purple. The chief priest drank a large amount
of *sake* every evening and made the page pour for him.

"The page was sick of the temple now and wanted to escape, but
he could not because, again by the chief priest's order, a strong sexton guarded him constantly. I sympathized with the page with all
my heart and hated the chief priest. We promised to meet again, and
the page went back to the temple."

The nun's thin, pale cheeks turned crimson as she told this extraordinary story, making Jishō listen with absolute attention.

"This is astonishing," he said. "Can such things happen in this world? What happened next?"

In the nun's sunken, narrow eyes, a piercing, intense glow appeared.

"From that night on, a sweet, hot flame burned continually in my breast, consuming me, heart and body. Day and night, my brother's face—or the god Sarasvati's face—or the page's face—stared at me, never disappearing. I went to pray at the grave every day after that, but to my great disappointment the page was never there.

"Then early one evening, as I was leaving, giving up hope, I heard the page's voice. 'My dear sister, it's been so long! How I've wished, how I've wished to see you!'

"I also cried with joy. According to the page, the chief priest's behavior had become more and more eccentric. He ordered the page to stop wearing his *suikan* and to put on a young girl's narrow dress instead. When the chief priest drank *sake*, he would strip the page of his dress and underwear until he was naked to his waist. The priest would then order the page to put on a long, crimson, silk cloth called *hire* around his neck and over his shoulders, and to serve *sake* in a small *sake* bottle.

"'There is nothing like *sake* served by the naked god, Sarasvati!' the chief priest would say, smiling, and he would drink down cup after cup. The page begged me to hide him, as he intended to seize the first opportunity to run away. His clear eyes, filled with terror, never blinked.

"'Come any time,' I said. 'I will ask my parents to help you without fail.'

"After that I thought about nothing but saving him. I went to my brother's grave to pray regularly, as before, but the page did not come again, probably because he was being watched. Day after day I felt anxious.

"Autumn was half over. The rice in the field promised an unusually good harvest; the leaves on the mountain trees began to be tinged with gorgeous red. Then one day it began to rain, and the rain continued day in and day out. The peasants began to worry.

"Behind the temple stood a high mountain. On a plateau halfway up the mountain there was a reservoir that provided the rice fields with irrigation water and the temple garden with its waterfall. When I heard the villagers say that the waterfall was making a thunderous noise, I felt uneasy. I thought, 'If a landslide should occur, the page might be killed. If only the chief priest alone might die!'

"Too worried to sit still, I left home, wearing a bamboo hat and a straw raincoat. Of course I did not say anything to my parents. Fortunately it was raining less hard just now. When I reached the river bank, I saw the bridge gradually crumbling in a dark whirlpool of water, and its loose pieces washing away.

"I was startled, looking straight ahead. There was the page, running from the main hall. I stood motionless, my fingers and toes taut with fear. A little behind him the chief priest and the sexton were in pursuit. The page turned toward the temple gate.

"Just at that moment, I thought hundreds of thunderbolts fell, crashing, before my eyes; then I felt my whole body swaying. The water of the reservoir burst forth all at once, breaking the dam, pushing and rolling the mud, rocks, and large trees, and crushing the temple below. When I came to myself, I was standing stupefied, my hand pressed tightly against my closed eyes.

"The page was killed. So were the chief priest and the sexton. I could do nothing but cry. Even the sound of my parents' voices made me angry. I prayed to Buddha for my death. Then a few days later, at dawn, I had a strange dream. A handsome god of Sarasvati, with a red *hire* cloth around his neck, fluttering in the wind, appeared and tied a chaplet of prayer-beads around my neck.

"'Oh, my dear page,' I cried out, 'I'm so happy!'

"I was awakened by my loud voice. I stroked my neck and was surprised. A chaplet did seem to be wound around my neck. But in reality it was neither a chaplet nor a rope; it felt like a strange, cold, living cord. I got up immediately and opened a paneled door, holding a mirror in my hand. Then I almost fainted. I could hardly utter a word.

"'A snake!'

"It was a pale-green snake with black spots on its back. Its belly was transparently white with a tinge of red. It was wound round my neck three times. For several days I was ill in bed, unable to eat. My parents' shock and grief were beyond description. They covered my neck with a white silk cloth. Everything was kept absolutely secret from our neighbors.

"The snake neither strangled me nor struck my cheek with its tail, but moved its head gently from side to side, flicked its tongue in and out, and seemed to peep into my face. I was convinced now that the page's soul had come to me as a white snake, which is traditionally the messenger of the god Sarasvati. I was incomparably happy.

"For a long time after that I spent happy days with the snake. I could not go out during the day. Everything was done at night. At midnight I would sit down among autumn flowers, stroke the snake's head, or feel my heart throb with happiness as I walked with the snake along the moonlit river bank in a drift of falling cherry blossoms."

Jishō, as he listened, heaved a long, deep sigh. Before his mind's eye came a scene of the beasts' region from the large Buddhist painting of the six regions of delusion, where human souls were said to wander after death. This picture, displayed on the wall of the main temple only during the time of the Bon Festival at the Daijōin Temple, unfolded itself powerfully before Jishō's eyes.

"The more I hear of your story, the more deeply I feel the inevitable consequences of your karma. Please do continue," he urged.

In contrast to Jishō, who was growing more agitated, the nun became more calm as she spoke.

"My parents were full of anxiety. Any prospect of my marriage was blown away. My parents went to a great many temples and shrines to pray, but all to no avail. As for me, since I did not want to part with the snake, I prayed to Buddha that he not be concerned about me. One day my mother looked hard into my face and said, 'Lately you have been looking very tired. Your face has become emaciated. They say when a human being is possessed by a snake or fox, his soul is sucked out and then he dies. Surely that's what's happening to you.'

"In fact, I had begun to feel weak all over, and had no idea what to do about it. My mother said I could not be saved except perhaps if I became a nun and expelled the evil spirit of the snake by the power of prayer. I finally decided to shave my head. I felt very lonesome and sad, for it seemed that by becoming a nun, I had parted with the page.

"The snake, perhaps sensing it might be expelled, began to coil about my neck so tightly that it became difficult for me to breathe. I remained seated in front of the family altar and kept praying.

"One evening, a very old, dignified-looking itinerant monk came to stay overnight. He heard my story from my mother, and said, 'An ordinary prayer would not take effect on this case. There is no other way but for your daughter to go to Chikubu Island and to confine herself at the shrine of the god Sarasvati to pray for help. The snake is under the control of Sarasvati.'

"Following these words, I left home. My aging parents saw me off with tears and hopes. I was just waiting at the pier of Chōmeiji, when, through the divine guidance of Buddha, I was able to meet you, sir. Please have mercy on me and grant my prayer for your help."

The sun was going down, and the breeze felt cooler now. The pages woke from their nap and became lively again. They ate the *magari* cookies and melons which had been bought before.

A freight boat either from Kaizu or Shiozu passed by Jishō's boat, heading south. Ripples quivered over the surface of the lake, but the reflection of the sun on the water was no longer very strong.

The boat continued to sail due north toward Chikubu Island. The shape of the mountain on the island grew taller and larger every minute. It formed a sheer precipice on every side except the east. On the sunny side of the island, the green contour of the mountain shone with a dark luster, while on the opposite side, its shadow of solid black sank directly into the lake.

The mountains standing shoulder to shoulder on the borderline between the two provinces of Ōmi and Echizen embraced the lake-shore and protected the island from the rough wind coming from the north sea. Thus the mountainous island stood—quiet, gentle, majestic.

Jishō had no hesitation when he finished listening to the nun's story. He saw at once that it was Buddha's will.

"Your story is an extraordinary one," he said. "You may rely on me. I will do everything I can. To attempt an adventure into the world where no light reaches may also mean my own salvation."

By the time the northern peaks in the province of Yamashiro had emerged against the evening clouds, the boat, as if sucked there by some invisible force, arrived at the harbor on the east side of the is-land. Feeling tired and tense, Jishō and his party landed on the pier, pushing themselves up with difficulty as if carrying someone else's burden.

Trim buildings were pleasantly scattered among the rocks and trees along the narrow slope. There were fifty in all, though there did not seem to be that many. After worshipping at the Tsukubu-suma Shrine, built on a forbidding rock, and then climbing up the stone steps to pay their respects to the kannon, Bodhisattva of mercy, of the Hōganji Temple, the pages had nothing more in particular to look at.

To keep his promise to the pages, Jishō asked the priests of the temple about the monks who were said to be good swimmers. One of the older priests answered, scratching his head, "Ah, too bad! This morning, just before these lovely guests from Mt. Hiei came to visit, our young men took leave for Nagahama and Torahime, since the Bon Festival was over. We are truly sorry."

Since their hopes had been high, the pages were terribly disappointed. The buildings on the island, much smaller than those of Mt. Hiei and devoid of ornaments, now began to settle into the quietly approaching evening mist.

Immediately after the meal, the pages and the *daidōji* retired to a room in the priests' residence to sleep. After the recitation of the sutra in front of the kannon, the principal image of the temple, the student priests joined the pages.

Jishō and the nun went back to the shrine of Sarasvati to carry out the purpose of their retreat.

The Holy Priest Dengyō had chosen Chikubu Island as the location of the inner sanctuary of Mt. Hiei, and it was here that the god Sarasvati was enshrined. The statue was life-sized, an excellent piece of work, said to have been brought from China. It was a nearly nude body with a slightly bent knee, painted in brilliant colors. The long, pale-green *hire* cloth hanging from elbows to knees and around the fingers seemed to flutter in the breeze from the lake.

All around the firm and austere face, with its shining eyes, long, dark brows, and deep, compressed small mouth, some enchantment seemed to float. Above the highly raised hair, a white snake instead of a flower-crown coiled around several times, lifting its head and looking in no real direction—a fearsome sight.

Jishō and the nun sat side by side below the raised platform where the image of Sarasvati was placed. Jishō took out two volumes of the scripture from his front pocket.

"These contain chapter fifteen of the Book of the Great Sarasvati in the sutra called *Konkōmyō Saishōō*," said Jishō. "Here it is written: 'the sufferings from diseases, fights and quarrels, wars and battles, nightmares, demons and ghosts, the venom of poisonous insects, evil spirits, curses, half-dead corpses—all these evil-engendering things shall be completely destroyed.' In other words, through the efficacy of this scripture, the harm of the evil snake will be removed without fail. I am going to recite the scripture. You please repeat the incantation, '*om sarasvati sovaka*,' with all your heart and soul, and rub your prayerbeads at the same time."

Jishō's low voice reciting the scripture and the nun's thin, trembling incantation rose up. In the darkness of the shrine's interior, only the flames of two candles flickered.

Although it was not clear how many hours had passed by, it became a little lighter. It seemed as if the eyes of the image of Sarasvati blinked two or three times. Then the white snake on the image lifted its head in a large motion, thrusting out its tongue, and began to stretch itself, gradually moving away from the hair of the god Sarasvati. Jishō pulled the nun's sleeve. The white snake waved gently in front of the kneeling couple and looked up at the nun.

The silk bag around the nun's neck lifted slightly, and the pale-green snake crawled down from the nun's neck to her shoulder and then to the wooden floor, following the white snake. The two snakes, with the white one leading the way, slid outside across the threshold where the door had been left open. Jishō and the nun got up immediately and went after the snakes.

On the east side of the shrine was a gigantic precipice. The lake was directly below. Trembling with fear and amazement, the nun leaned over and looked down beyond her feet. Her astonishment became even greater. From all over the slope, snakes came flowing like water and leaped into the lake. Jishō turned back to the nun, and said, "This is an astounding sight. Let's call everybody right away!"

Leaving the nun behind, Jishō went to the priests' residence. In a little while, all the people came down the stone steps. The nun greeted them. Jishō was leading the party.

"The best viewing place will be over there!" said Jishō.

Everybody went to the edge of the pier where the boat which had brought Jishō's party was moored. The boatmen were already standing on the pier.

"Hello, sir, and everybody! You came to the island at a lucky time! Ever since we were small we have been told that the snakes of the island mountain are allowed to bathe in the lake only at the Bon Festival, by permission of the god Sarasvati. But tonight is the first time that we have seen them with our own eyes. Please, do look at them!"

The priest and the others stared at the surface of the lake. No one said a word. Could there be another sight in this world as fascinating and as beautiful as this? The waxing moon was low in the sky, but the entire surface of the lake was clear, shining with a bluish-silver color, and so smooth that one could have walked across barefoot.

Below the surface of the water, unexpectedly bright because of the penetrating moonlight, countless snakes, large and small, were visible. Black, blue, pink, yellow, or brown snakes, some with red stripes, or some with black spots—all were swimming joyfully, showing their shining bellies.

Two snakes were tangled with each other; two or three raced each other, side by side; one, standing on its head, sank to the bottom of the lake; some swam a short distance beneath the surface, making the part of the lake where they passed gleam briefly in small ripples, creating and breaking spreading circles of waves. Broken ripples overlapped other broken ripples and faded into the evening air.

The shrine and the temple spire on the shore, the trees surrounding them, and the black contour of the island mountain which rose, towering behind all these, seemed to have absolutely nothing to do with the countless snakes playing under the glittering water surface, but actually created a solemn and immense background for the dreamlike, rhythmical movements of the snakes.

All consciousness of time fell away. No one would stir.

Everybody finished a simple breakfast in the dining room of the Hōganji Temple. Despite the excitement and lack of sleep, they all felt cheerful. The nun's face looked exceptionally bright. The white silk cloth around her neck was gone. Jishō and the others climbed down the stone steps toward the shrine. The pages gathered around the nun. Could it be that she was enjoying a brief moment of playing mother?—or was she pursuing the image of her dead brother, or, rather, the figure of her lost page?

They all stood in a line in front of the shrine of Sarasvati and prayed reverently. The white snake had already resumed its former posture, wound around the hair of the image of the god.

It was another fine day. The pages returned to their childhood pleasures, climbing up or sliding down the rocks, or throwing the leftover *magari* cookies to the fish. The *daidōji* and student priests also joined the party, laughing and shaking their shoulders.

"Wasn't that an amazing sight last night?"

"We aren't sorry we came, even if we didn't see the monks swimming."

"I will be very proud when I return to the village."

In front of the shrine of Sarasvati, Jishō and the nun finished the thanksgiving recitation of the scripture and the incantation. The nun listened seriously to Jishō's words.

"With all my heart I sympathize with you for your many years of suffering. However, you made a very grave mistake. The spirit of the dead page possessed a docile snake which clung to your neck, unwilling to leave. You did have an enjoyable time together, but it did not last till the end.

"The spirit of the ferocious viper which you killed after your brother's death forced the page's spirit out of your snake and in turn possessed it. You did not realize the viper's vengeance but kept loving it, even as it sucked at your life. It was horrifying.

"Fortunately, last night you were saved by the divine protection of Sarasvati. Today, the snake which had wound round your neck began to live under the control of Sarasvati, along with many other new friends in the island mountain. Unfortunately, however, the page's spirit and the spirit of the viper you killed must still be wandering, unable to attain their salvation. You should pray to Buddha with complete devotion. When you have done that, not only you, but the page and the viper will be saved. No rigorous ascetic disciplines are needed to achieve this goal. The Daijōin Temple of Mt. Hiei, where I live, also has a shrine of Sarasvati. According to the legend, Sarasvati changed himself into a snake, made an appearance in Mt. Hiei, and then went back to Chikubu Island. When I return to Mt. Hiei, I will recite the scripture at the shrine of Sarasvati there every day as a prayer for you."

The nun bowed her head low and thanked the priest most reverently.

The boat carrying Jishō's party left the pier. The nun alone stayed behind to continue her seven-day thanksgiving retreat. It seemed that the pages found it difficult to part with the nun, who had become like a sister or mother to them.

Jishō's feelings were complex. On this boat trip, something completely unexpected had happened. Nothing could have been better than saving the soul of a woman. By this act Jishō was able to strengthen his experience in religious faith. The pages, too, were perfectly satisfied with the trip.

But what had become of his purpose in making the excursion in the first place? It could not be said that his heart's desire to see his poetry selected for an imperial anthology had been realized. On the other hand, it seemed to Jishō that by sitting at the same seat where those famous poetic masters had sat, and worshipping the god Sarasvati, he was now taking the same path they'd taken ahead of him, and thus closer to his poetic seniors than before. He was happy. He was full of deep emotion as he reflected on the time when he would be able to come again to this beautiful island.

Since the boat was tacking against the head wind, the boatmen rowed very hard, even though the breeze was quite mild.

The eyes of every member of Jishō's party continued to be fixed on the pier. The figure of the nun was motionless there, like a dark prayerbead on a chaplet.

THE ROBE

"Onoe, the mistress wants you."

The voice was gentle, but the tone revealed hidden feeling; the speaker seemed to laugh at the end of her words. Onoe was sitting at the entrance to her room, where the afternoon sun was shining. Two young handmaids assigned to Onoe were pulling white hairs from her head. As usual, she met the situation with a bold front.

"No matter what they may say, I am the most indispensable person in this mansion," said Onoe to herself.

Soon, after changing to a robe of subdued purple with a purple lining, Onoe disappeared into the lady's sitting room in the north building. After quite a long time, the sliding door of the room reopened. Onoe, very upright, walked, as if flowing, along the covered passageway on the way to her room. In the middle garden, the leaves of two maple trees had turned to their beautiful fall color.

Several waiting-women came out into the corridor and clustered there, talking.

"Something must have happened to Onoe the deer."

"The lady must have flattered Onoe, since her back is now so straight!"

"Some big question seems hidden behind her eyes."

There was a reason why the lady, wife of Lord Tameaki, Councillor,[1] had called the old waiting-woman, Onoe, into her private room. The Lord's wife, related by blood to the Minamoto family of Rokujō, was a devotee of poetry. With great enthusiasm, she was planning to hold a poetry contest on the shores of Ōsawa Pond, where she would take the waiting-women of the mansion when, in a few days, the season of red leaves had reached its height.

The lady planned to give the title for poetry composition to the rest of the waiting-women at the time of the contest, but she had decided to tell Onoe the title ahead of time. She did this partly as a reward

---

1. In the original, *chūnagon*, the second-highest-ranking official below the ministers. (NT)

for Onoe, who had been in service for many years, and partly as a means of insuring Onoe's full attention to the cooking and other necessary arrangements on the day of the contest.

"Onoe" was in fact a nickname. At the time of this story, women in service at the court or at the noblemen's mansions were customarily called by the official titles which their fathers or grandfathers held. Onoe's case was a little different. "Onoe" was derived from the old poetic phrase, "the deer of Onoe."[2] Just as the stag attacks its enemy with its antlers, so this old waiting-woman would knock down her opponent with her tongue.

Sometimes she was given another, faintly related nickname, "the six-eyed deer." Women of that day ordinarily shaved their eyebrows and painted on false ones. Onoe, however, never shaved hers. Perhaps she left them because they were very thin; but high on her forehead she painted on artificial eyebrows in addition to her own. Thus, from a distance, she looked as if she had six narrow eyes. In this sense, the name had affectionate humor in it. Onoe did not seem aware of these origins.

When Councillor Tameaki's father was the minister of *Nakatsukasa*,[3] Onoe's father had served for many years as a low-ranking official in the ministry, and he had also enjoyed the trust of Tameaki himself as chief officer in charge of household affairs. Onoe had begun her service at the mansion in her father's time, when she was young. Somehow she'd had very little chance with men. Without an opportunity to come into flower, she had developed only prosaic roots.

Now Onoe was the head cook of the kitchen in the mansion, where, presiding over more than a dozen other maidservants, she gave directions in a loud voice, sometimes hitting a cooking pot with her fist or waving a knife. Though she was a servant of low rank, she was always within the shadow of the lady of the mansion.

2. The word *onoe*, which literally means the trailing foot of a mountain, was often used as a kind of epithet for the deer in poetry. (NT)

3. One of the eight Ministries of the imperial government of medieval Japan. This office handled matters very close to the Emperor, including, among other things, preparation of imperial edicts, compilation of the official national history, and recording of the census registration. Because of the enormous importance of this office, the Minister was usually selected from among the immediate members of the imperial family. The fact that Councillor Tameaki's father was once the Minister of *Nakatsukasa* indicates that Tameaki was of imperial blood. (NT)

There was another reason the younger waiting-women felt contempt for Onoe. She was a heavy eater.

People of this period ate two meals a day. Women ate only a small amount of rice—unpolished and hard even after cooking. But Onoe ate two large metal bowl-fulls of rice at a meal. She was large-boned but small in stature, and her huge appetite seemed incongruous. It might have been attributed, this carefree eating, to her duty of carrying rice and other food to the kitchen, but in actuality it seemed to be because as a child she had been very poor.

The day of the feast of the red leaves arrived. For several days, the women had been making much ado about arranging their lined robes, until now, at last, the time had come. It was a fine day. In a caravan of ox-drawn carriages decorated with woven silk, some blue and some purple, all the women set out, led by the lady of the mansion.

From their residence at the corner of Nijō and Karasuma, the party took the main street which led to the Sujaku Gate, heading west. The swaying shadows of pedestrians, horses, and vehicles were reflected on the bright streets. The mountain range which included Takao, Atago, and Arashi, was unusually clear and bright.

Ōsawa Pond was very quiet, as if it had been forgotten. The breeze blowing over it stirred waves whose half-circles expanded endlessly until they disappeared. Trees surrounded it. The pond had once been an imperial garden and among the ruins stood cherry trees, maple trees, and lacquer trees, all blending harmoniously with a huge evergreen that deepened the crimson of their leaves.

Rolling out thin matting, the waiting-women took their seats. Young handmaids assigned to Onoe opened partitioned lunch boxes and distributed food. It was Onoe's proudest moment.

The lady of the mansion was quite accustomed to such occasions. She placed an inkstone on a small writing table, and, paying no attention to the appetite of her young waiting-women, she said, "Very well, then! The title for the poetry contest is 'Scarlet Leaves Along the Pond.' Can you see the setting of rocks behind the trees, there to the north? There used to be a waterfall there, where the famous poet, Shijō Dainagon Lord Kintō, once composed a poem:

The sound of the waterfall has long ceased;
Yet its fame still flows; its name is still heard.

You all know this poem, don't you? The great master of poetry is watching over you. Do the best you can! Let's see now, what should the prize be?"

The lady then looked casually to one side. The cook Onoe held a thin writing brush in her hand just as the other waiting-women did, but she picked up another, and using these two brushes as a pair of chopsticks, Onoe began to eat the food placed in front of the seated women. The women looked at her with their eyes wide, but since they were in the presence of their mistress, they desperately bit their lips. The lady lightly touched her mouth with the sleeve of her inner garment, trying to suppress the laughter which would have marred her careful makeup. Then, with superb tact, she spoke.

"Oh, Onoe, how well prepared you are! An excellent poem will surely come from you. I am most anxious to see it."

But Onoe's brushes never served their original purpose; the lady's expectation was in vain. After this incident, the women of the household stood in awe of Onoe.

During this outing, the lady's oldest daughter, who was married, sat at a little distance from her mother and looked at her attentively with sharp eyes and an ironic smile. Then she quietly drew near her mother and said, "I've been looking at your robe. I've never seen anything so magnificent. There is absolutely nothing lacking—the color, the beautiful woven pattern, the grace. . . . Really, my eyes have been held by it!"

The mother smiled calmly. Onoe looked back and forth from one to the other.

"Is that so?" said the mother. "Yes, a fine thing does show well, doesn't it? I've worn this once or twice before, although you may not have noticed. I understand that it was my father who bought this robe. It had been brought to the province of Tsukushi by a Chinese merchant ship. They call the woven pattern 'the Chinese rose'; it's supposed to be the most valued kind in China."

The daughter continued to smile coolly.

"Mother, wouldn't you like to give this robe to me? Would you mind? I think it would be simply beautiful on me. Hasn't it become a little too bright for you?"

The mother's countenance was rather stern for a moment. Then, again smiling calmly, she waved her hand several times. As Onoe watched these exchanges between mother and daughter, the color gradually fled from her face. Her two writing brushes fell to her lap.

All this happened on an autumn day. There is more to be told about this beautiful robe.

Since that day, a year ago now, Onoe became conscious of a change. She realized for the first time that her yearning for beauty exceeded her appetite for food. The thought that her youth was completely dark because she had nothing beautiful around caused her deep chagrin.

She closed her eyes and recalled the scene at the pond. The woven pattern of the robe, appearing in sharp relief in the bright, high-noon sun, had been like living pale-purple roses.

Onoe resented the thought that some day the robe would become a possession of the oldest daughter, who had never been beautiful at all, from childhood on. Starting with resentment, Onoe's feelings grew gradually more complex.

Then something unexpected took place. At the autumn ceremony for appointing high officials, the master of the mansion, Lord Tame-aki, received an imperial decree promoting him from *chūnagon* to *gondainagon*.[4] The *gondainagon*'s salary was more than double the *chūnagon*'s.

According to the custom of the period, when someone was appointed to the position of a minister or other high-ranking official, it was expected that he invite all the other ministers and courtiers to his home for a grand feast. Such an event required the rearrangement of the garden, remodeling of the interior of the house, purchasing of utensils, and careful selection of food and drink. All these preparations meant an enormous expense for the newly appointed.

Needless to say, on the day of the great banquet, the new *gondainagon*'s distinguished guests were dazzled by the magnificent screens displayed in the banquet hall and by the delicacies heaped up on the tables. Onoe worked as hard as she could and was delighted with the gratitude and praise of the lady.

4. The *dainagon* is the highest-ranking official immediately below the ministers. When an additional *dainagon* is appointed besides the existing ones, he is called *gondainagon*. His rank and official functions are identical with those of a regular *dainagon*, and he is treated as the equal of the *dainagon*. Each official position was also assigned a rank. The highest position, *dajō daijin*, was either the upper-first rank or the lower-first rank; the larger the number, the lower the position. The position of *dainagon* was in the upper-third rank. (NT)

Apparently pleased by her daughter's having teased for it the year before, the lady again wore the robe with the Chinese rose pattern. She had also given minute care to the color combination of the inner garments she wore under the robe. Onoe saw clearly the envious eyes of the wives of lords who were among the guests, all looking at the lady's robe.

Until that time Onoe had imagined that the lady's daughter was her only enemy, but on that day the number of her enemies suddenly increased, and her chagrin intensified sharply. And there was this, too: these middle-aged wives of the high officials were all sensitive to a thing of beauty, whereas Onoe, although she was always near her great mistress, had never even noticed the robe until the daughter had spoken of it.

"Ah, what a fool I've been!—But it's too late to cry!" she thought.

The feeling of inferiority which Onoe now recognized was to be the root of her increasingly complex feeling.

Several days later, Onoe was summoned to the lady's room. The lady spoke in a way at once compassionate and slightly probing.

"You don't look too well. I hope you'll soon be as energetic as you were at the excursion at Ōsawa Pond!"

Onoe bowed in silence and withdrew.

Before long, sleet began to fall from time to time, and as the cast of the mountains surrounding the city of Kyoto grew darker, the people grew increasingly depressed. But the city's activities were more bustling every day, until the old year came to an end.

Many days after the welcoming of the new year, the *gondainagon* made a novel proposal to his wife.

"At the poetry contest of last year's feast of red leaves we gave the women the principal role. Why don't we plan something different for this year?"

The two talked over the matter and made the following plan. For this year's excursion there would be no advance mention of poetry, and every member of the household would be invited. Instead of the feast of red leaves, the event would be a trip to the lord's villa in Uji in the summer, to fish for *ayu* or sweetfish, and to feast on them.

When the plan was announced by the lord's wife, the waiting-women and young handmaids were all filled with joy. Onoe was called in immediately.

"I am counting on your cooking the most delicious dishes for our Uji River excursion," said the lady. "What should be your reward, I wonder?"

Onoe was pleased.

"May I have that robe with the Chinese rose pattern. . . ?" But Onoe suppressed with her tongue these words which were about to spill out of her mouth. The lady had denied even her daughter's request.

After this, Onoe's appetite suddenly diminished. Her movements became slower and slower. The lady noticed these changes.

The day of the Uji excursion finally arrived. Onoe asked to remain at the mansion. The lady regretted this very much but in the end reluctantly granted the request. Besides Onoe, only the young hand-maids assigned to her, an old retainer, and a few servants stayed at home.

The lady and all the waiting-women changed to their new summer dresses, which had been made for this occasion, and started on their journey early in the morning in ox-drawn carriages, going away along Takakura Street toward Kujō Ōji. Most of the men of the mansion were on horseback. The breeze coming through the green leaves blew over the party's laughter and the bumping of the wheels in the ruts.

The whole house became suddenly quiet. Onoe was alone. Every section of the huge mansion seemed to lie in suspended animation, uncanny and hushed. After locking up the lattice windows and the sliding doors, the old retainer and other servants retired to the servants' quarters. The rooms of the waiting-women around the north building became so dark as to need candlelight.

Onoe decided to send her young handmaids, accompanied by the old retainer, on a shopping errand to the market along the road near the Shijō Bridge. She wrote down several kinds of food and vegetables on a piece of paper and gave it to the girls. These groceries were for the dinner to be served when the party of the *gondainagon* returned from Uji.

"When you finish your shopping, you may watch the *dengaku* dancers' performance at the foot of the bridge," said Onoe to her maids.

The three young maids, large baskets on their arms, ran out of the mansion in joyful excitement. The old retainer also got up, looking happy.

Onoe's nerves had been tingling, reaching out in all directions. Her face was white; her eyes began to shine dangerously. She had finally made up her mind. She imagined the figure of herself stealing the robe with the Chinese rose pattern from the lady's room.

The thought that this precious treasure from China should be forever someone else's possession had day by day become increasingly painful to Onoe. The will to find some rational solution gave way to the command that she act, and now she was determined to risk her life. Acting on her wish, she concluded uneasily, would be the only way to dissolve the sense of inadequacy she felt.

Since the lady and the waiting-women had all gone out in their summer costumes, she reasoned that no garment storage boxes except those for summer clothing would have been left open. Onoe carefully watched the movements in the servants' quarters, then entered the lady's room in the north building. The room was in terrible disarray, the storage closet left unlocked. Onoe had long studied the lock and had planned to use one of her ornamental hairpins to unlock it, but there was no need for that. As she put her hand on the heavy closet door, her body trembled, and she slipped inside, almost collapsing.

At first she could see nothing, but gradually it became lighter. The wooden-floored closet was not very large. Its three sides were solidly plastered; there was a small high window on the fourth side. In the semidarkness, as stifling as the bottom of the sea, several large, oblong garment boxes and some Chinese-style chests with stands rose up before her as sternly as a rock formation.

As Onoe had guessed, out-of-season clothes were stored in the oblong boxes which were piled in twos in the farthest recesses of the closet. She first opened one box on her right, which revealed, to her surprise, what looked like the robe she was searching for. She took it toward the small window to make sure. There was no mistake.

She felt almost disappointed that the search should have ended so quickly.

But as she looked at the robe, she began to feel a little drunk with the eerie charm of the pale-purple roses, which looked glazed in gold. Yet a part of her mind resisted the intoxication.

"Wait! Soon the young maids will come home."

Quickly, Onoe straightened up the room and closed the door. She looked around and saw no one. She went back to her own room in a hurry.

There was a part of the wooden floor of her room which was not fastened by nails, so that it was possible to clean underneath the floor occasionally. Too rushed for a leisurely view of the robe, Onoe hurriedly placed it in a garment box under a simple dress with narrow sleeves, a *kosode*. Then she nimbly crawled underneath the floor and planted the box in the north corner, which was the dead angle where no one could see it. She brushed dust off the *kosode* which she wore, tidied herself, and lay down to rest. Severe fatigue and stupefaction at once seized her mind and body. She felt a sickening pain under her chest.

"Well, I'm glad it's over! I'm glad!" she thought.

Then Onoe began to wonder why her young maids were not around.

"Why, of course, I sent them on a shopping errand to Shijō Street!"

In Onoe's mind, the events since the previous fall emerged and rolled backward at dizzying speed. She arranged her recollections in proper order. Before long, the young handmaids came back in great excitement, carrying baskets full of vegetables on their heads. The old man, too, looked happy, though out of breath.

Onoe roused up the courage of her trade and said, "Now I shall begin. I want you all to help me. You can count on a great feast."

At sunset, the *gondainagon*'s party returned. The lord was pleased with the big catch of fish. The lady was highly satisfied with the unexpectedly large number of good poems presented. Under Onoe's leadership, the kitchen maids worked together well, and in a short time, more than a dozen rows of small tables were splendidly arrayed with food. The men praised Onoe profusely; the women ignored her, silent with jealousy.

"Onoe the deer works with both hands and antlers," they murmured.

But the lady, feeling kindly toward Onoe, said tactfully, "I'm sorry you had to stay home today. But your accomplishment is by no means inferior to good poetry. What should your reward be?"

That night, Onoe could not sleep till very late. She felt knots in her stomach, and sour spittle filled her mouth. Her head was wide awake and her eyelids stiff. Finally she developed a curious theory with which she tried to convince and comfort herself.

"True, I did steal. But my stealing is a very small matter. There is no question that the Lord *gondainagon* is a great man, but they say his reputation at the court is not very good. Besides, look at these huge piles of rice and barley in the grain storage bins and in the servants' quarters. They were collected from the peasants of the lord's fief, who are suffering as a result. The lady has a graceful enough manner, but isn't she the partner of the great robber?"

Near dawn, feeling more at ease, Onoe dozed off for awhile.

Onoe was frightened again the following morning. The lady and the waiting-women set about carefully putting away the clothes they had worn on the previous day. The lady went in and out of the storage closet several times. Onoe nervously cast a sidelong glance at the lady, but nothing happened.

In the night, Onoe again became anxious about the robe. After listening carefully to the breathing of her young maids as they slept, Onoe opened up the wooden floor just a little.

"It's there. It's safe."

The same scene was repeated several nights in a row.

One day Onoe happened to hear the waiting-women speak cheerfully in the covered passageway. "Kagemune went to the mountain villa in Uji the day before yesterday. He's expected to return today with a huge catch of fireflies as souvenirs. Isn't that wonderful?"

The Uji River was famous for its fireflies. Kagemune, the young and bright chief household officer, and the lord's favorite, had gone to supervise the carpenters who had been working for some time on the remodeling of the villa. The politically powerful lord, it seems, was planning in the future to invite ministers, lords, and other high courtiers to the villa.

Onoe was attracted to Kagemune, though he was thirty years younger. When she saw him, she would relive the yearnings of her youth. She had now begun to feel that the robe had belonged to her for a long time.

Kagemune knew that the waiting-women were hostile to the high-handed old woman. He would therefore pass by the kitchen on purpose to annoy the waiting-women. He would speak a few words to Onoe and go away.

"Hello, Onoe! What a hard worker you are! I was wonderfully impressed with the *ayu* fish that you cooked the other day."

The evening came for which all the women had been waiting. No moon or star was visible. There was no wind, and the air was sultry. The huge, black shadow of a cluster of trees in the garden was reflected flat upon the surface of the lead-colored pond.

Kagemune, accompanied by two or three young servants, advanced toward the lady. The flow of the fireflies in the baskets these men carried showed in relief the oval face of Kagemune in his pale-blue hunting costume. The women's eyes at once focused on his movements.

Since morning, the lady had been reading the "Book of Fireflies" in *The Tale of Genji* and had transformed herself to the Book's heroine, the beautiful Tamakazura. Her excitement was therefore intense.

The baskets were opened. Several groups of lights, flickering like little stars, flew in circles one after another. The fireflies continued their dancing in the air for a while. Then the number diminished. Suddenly the young maids clung to each other and cried out, "How terrifying! They look like ship-ghosts."

Onoe was startled.

"What are ship-ghosts?" asked a young waiting-woman of good family, looking toward the young maids.

One of the maids, daughter of a provincial official of Aki, explained. "They say there are many pirates in Bitchū and Bingo. You know what a pirate is—a sea thief. When the pirates spot a ship sailing for the capital, they surround the ship with many small boats, throw a ship's crew and passengers into the sea, and steal the cargo of yard goods and rice. The ghosts of the people who die in this way wander in the air, sending out a pale light. They're called the ship-ghosts."

"Splash!"

Onoe's thigh had twitched suddenly and she had fallen halfway into the pond. She quickly grabbed the shoulder of a waiting-woman nearby.

"Ha, ha, ha. . . ."

Two waiting-women who had been the most hostile to Onoe laughed hysterically. The other women were scandalized. After that, a chill fell on the party. First the lady got up from her seat, then the waiting-women gradually withdrew. The phosphorescent light of the fireflies alone flickered aimlessly, as though tired, among the blades of grass beside the pond.

Five or six days later, the waiting-women's whispering was heard again.

"Onoe the deer is very low in spirits."

"Is she possessed by a ship-ghost?"

"She fell into the pond because she forgot herself in watching Kagemune. She ought to be ashamed—at her age!"

"She became so conceited about her *ayu* fish, she probably went crazy."

They were about right. Half consciously, half unconsciously, she'd brought herself to this. Called in by the lady, Onoe sat quietly, her face strangely dark and soft.

"Lately you seem to be out of sorts," said the lady. "Why don't you go home and rest for a while? I hate to see you continue in this condition."

These words flowed into Onoe's heart like steam. She repeated them to herself. Her gratitude changed to a choking sensation. But at any rate, things had turned out as she had planned.

Onoe went back to her home. On the night before her departure, she lifted the rose-patterned robe from its place under the floor, and tucking it underneath an old five-layer costume, she wrapped both with a sheet of oiled paper and placed them in a garment box. Her home was near the corner of Kujō and Mate no kōji. Her father had once lived there. The house then came down to her deceased elder brother. Now his daughter, Onoe's niece, lived in there with her husband.

The building was quite modest, but nothing was changed, so that the house, full of memories of her childhood, was dear to Onoe. There were a few mansions in the area, but mostly open fields. No one stirred around the commoners' houses. It was a quiet place, with many willow trees, whose thin, shaggy leaves rustled languidly all day long in the hot sun.

After she had left the lord's estate, Onoe felt much more at ease. Returning home had not been in her original plans; only when she'd begun to fear detection had she wanted to go home.

Yet here at home she was not completely carefree either. First, there was still the fear of being found out. Second, Onoe wanted to know what the waiting-women at the mansion were saying about her. Third, she began to have an unexpected worry—

"Is Kagemune becoming friendly with some other waiting-woman while I'm away?"

This last apprehension was very grave. The thought of Kagemune, affably smiling, irritated Onoe. As days went by, still another fear began to prick her heart:

"Isn't my niece secretly examining my belongings? Her husband is a petty official. Is he watching me at the request of my lord's household?"

Near her home was a vegetable field, where every morning deep-purple eggplants and yellowish-green melons had their fresh skins washed by the dew. Nothing gave Onoe greater peace than to walk along the narrow path through the field. Near it, three stone images of Buddha stood side by side. Onoe felt envious of their peaceful faces, as serene as those of sleeping babies.

One morning she saw something unexpected. Each of the three stone images had on a brand new white linen robe and a crimson silk cope. An old man wearing a small, wrinkled *eboshi* hat came walking toward her with a sickle in his hand. Onoe walked toward him.

"Why are the Buddhas wearing the copes this morning?" she asked.

The peasant turned to her seriously and said,

"These are efficacious copes. Any thief is supposed to be absolved of his sins as soon as he touches the cope and chants '*Namu amida-butsu.*'"[5]

Onoe felt as if she had been hit on the head with a hammer. That instant, the light of wisdom shone into her heart.

"How wonderful! Then why don't they wear the copes all the time?"

The old peasant spoke with deliberate dignity.

"If they wore them every day, their value would diminish. At the Jōrakuji Temple over there, they hold a monthly religious service.

5. An invocation of the *Amida* (*Amitabha* in Sanskrit) Buddha, meaning "Save us, merciful Buddha." (NT)

The Robe

The bishop recites the scripture. During this service only, if you touch the robe or cope of the principal image of the temple, all your sins will be absolved and you will be able to be reborn in Paradise. But for those who cannot come to the religious service that evening, the robes are put on the stone Buddhas for the following morning only. It is a wonderful thing."

Next day, Onoe carefully drew her eyebrows, put on a thin, pale-blue robe with a pale-purple liner and left home. Passing by the cattle barn and the irrigation ditch, she continued to walk until she reached the Jōrakuji Temple, surrounded by white oaks with green leaves. It was a middle-sized temple, consisting of the main hall, priests' quarters, a library of Buddhist sutras, and a three-story pagoda. The humble old bishop, chief priest of the temple, accepted with deep emotion the offer from a waiting-woman of the nobleman's mansion.

Leaving the temple gate, Onoe hurried home, kicking the bottom of her robe in her haste as she walked. She asked her niece to go shopping at the market. In a little while the niece got ready and left.

In her room, Onoe took out the robe from the bottom of the garment box and looked at it intently. The brilliant woven pattern of the robe did not look as attractive as before, perhaps because of the poor surroundings. Onoe felt strangely disappointed.

An intense sense of regret began to rise within her and prompted a quick decision.

"I am going to cut the threads of this robe and make it into a priest's robe. I will use the lining for a cope. How splendid the principal image of the temple will look when the special robe and cope are put on it!"

Exactly as when she'd first stolen the robe, thought and action came together in a way that seemed almost electrifying. Moving the scissors dexterously, she pulled the threads from the robe, and, before long it was reduced to a few pieces of cloth. The renowned masterpiece all too soon lost its glory. She felt disheartened. By the time her niece returned, Onoe had indifferently laid the pieces of cloth at the bottom of the garment box.

After that, the same scene was repeated until the cloth pieces began to grow into a new form, and their beauty was gradually restored. At last, Onoe's efforts were rewarded. Three days before another monthly religious service, she completed a robe and a cope, a *gojōgesa*, for the life-size image of Buddha.

Onoe was about to shed tears of deep emotion, alone in her room, when a servant from the lord's mansion arrived unexpectedly. Onoe was startled. The lady had had a large sack of rice and other delicacies sent to Onoe. At the end of the letter inquiring about her health, the lady had attached a poem. Onoe's deep emotion became gratitude and relief.

It had taken a month to transform the rose-patterned robe from the lady's closet to a priest's robe and cope in Onoe's humble cottage. For her, it was a month of daily strain.

The following morning, with a brisk breeze blowing, Onoe went to the Jōrakuji Temple, handed the robe and the cope still in a garment box to the bishop, who bowed many times. Then Onoe left the temple. For the first time, she felt light-hearted. It gave her pleasure to recall the pain of the past days. Now her dreams rested on Kagemune.

"How splendid Kagemune would look if he could put on the robe and cope I made!"

She decided not to think about anything else, but to wait for the religious service in hopeful expectation.

On the evening of the monthly religious service at the Jōrakuji Temple, people of all kinds and occupations gathered at the main hall. In the one-night paradise created by the whirlpool of incense smoke and candle light, all the people gathered there—peasants, soldiers, peddlers, carpenters, old women and wives—became gradually intoxicated, breathing in time with the whisper of the prayer-beads they rubbed. The bishop who led the service recited the *Amida* scripture loudly, while other priests and parishioners joined in unison. When the recitation of the words of confession in the scripture began, the worshippers seemed to vie with one another for the most pitiful tone.

Then when the formal part of the service was over, the bishop began his eloquent sermon, a eulogy with Onoe as its subject.

"My dear people, have you paid your respects to our principal image with devotion tonight? The Buddha is wearing a splendid robe and a cope. Their donor is a certain personage of the nobility. This person will go to Paradise without fail as a reward for this act. All of you should keep this well in mind."

Low groans were heard, and the foot of the principal image was covered by hands. Onoe, too, like a stranger, firmly grasped the bottom of the Buddha's robe and looked up at the Buddha's smiling face, then wiped away tears.

As the crowd in the main hall gradually shrank, Onoe went outside. Her thickly powdered cheeks smarted. The evening breeze of early autumn was gentle and refreshing. Several villagers walked past, loudly reciting Buddha's name.

When Onoe arrived at home, her niece, who had returned earlier, greeted her cordially.

"Dear aunt, wasn't that a huge crowd! You really have done a wonderful thing."

Since she asked no further questions, Onoe was slightly afraid lest her niece should have discovered her secret sewing. The niece knew nothing about it but she teased her aunt, saying, "Dear aunt, you have a halo tonight!"

That night Onoe had a dream. She was worshipping the large painting that hung on the wall of the temple's main hall, *Amida* with his two attendant gods and twenty-five Boddhisattvas greeting the soul.

"Look! The Boddhisattva playing the flute in the picture looks a little like me!" Onoe was about to say these words aloud, when she woke up.

On the following morning, for the first time since arriving at her home Onoe ate breakfast with her niece and her husband in perfect calm. During breakfast, another letter from the lady came as though following on the heels of the first one. A large amount of food accompanied this second letter as it had the first. Onoe looked carefully at the skillful penmanship on the paper, with a decorative design made of mica. She read:

"According to the messenger, whom I saw just after he returned the other day, you're blooming with health again. I would like you to come back as soon as possible. Without you beside me, I feel the cold in my heart, as if I were blown by the autumn wind while still wearing summer clothes."

Onoe continued to read, suppressing the warm tears that came welling up. Soon large teardrops trickled down her distorted cheeks, and her lips trembled.

"Kagemune, in the service of the lord, has died. He was overexhausted with the continuous tasks of preparing for the grand feast, clearing up after the feast, and repairing the mountain villa in Uji. Ironically, his being the lord's favorite turned out to be his misfortune. In that regard, you were spared."

Onoe remembered Kagemune's pale face as it was revealed by the light of the fireflies. When Onoe had stolen the lady's robe, she had convinced herself that the lord was a thief. But now she saw that Kagemune was his real victim. She felt a strong resentment against the lord and pitied poor Kagemune. It pained her to realize that filling in the great void left by Kagemune's death would be no easy matter.

A few days later, after some two months' absence, Onoe returned to the lord's mansion. The lady showed relief and pleasure. The waiting-women also spoke to Onoe with smiles. Many kitchen maids gathered around her, while her young maids clung to her sleeves.

"Onoe the deer seems to have lost her horns," whispered one of the most hostile of the waiting-women, but no one responded.

Onoe went to the edge of the pond in the front garden and stood at the spot where Kagemune had released the fireflies. Never before had she watched the autumn flowers with such affection and sadness.

She went back to the north building. The lady stood up and went inside her closet. Onoe could not help averting her eyes. Soon the lady emerged, holding a garment box in front of her. She put the box before Onoe. In the box was a folded, five-layer costume, on top of which was a pale-purple robe with the woven rose pattern. Onoe felt dizzy, but the lady began to speak quietly.

"From now on the wind from Mt. Kita will grow more fierce every day. So do take care not to expose yourself to the cold. Please take this robe and wear it. I chose the one I like the most for you. Though this is not of the best, it is a very good quality."

Faltering, Onoe barely managed to thank the lady.

"I am most truly grateful to you. The pattern and the dye are both of the finest. I believe you wore this robe at the festival of the red leaves at Ōsawa Pond."

The lady smiled lightly as if she had anticipated these words.

"Yes. I wore this kind of robe at the poetry contest at Ōsawa Pond. My oldest daughter wanted it and I promised her that I would give it to her in the future. I have put that robe away at the bottom of a

Chinese garment box at the far end of the closet. That one is genuinely the very best from China. Something like that would be completely ruined if it were soiled or damaged. So, some time ago, I had a master weaver in the weaving mill copy the original."

Again Onoe felt dizzy, but the next moment a strange vision sprung up in her mind.

Among many Boddhisattvas surrounding the *Amida* Buddha, who wore a pale-purple robe of the woven rose pattern, Onoe in the form of a heavenly maiden and Kagemune in the form of a priest stood on a cloud floating in the sky. Onoe could almost hear the sound of the flutes and harps played by the Boddhisattvas. She cried involuntarily, in a suppressed voice, "I am saved!"

MUSHI OKURI[1]

"This long rain is a real problem for both of us. You and I ought to try our best to prevent flooding. My lord minister in the capital[2] has expressed the same sentiment. Ha, ha, ha. . . ."

Morizane's face was bloated from drinking *sake* and buried in deep wrinkles; he was about twelve years older than his companion. He took off his ceremonial *eboshi* hat, casually placed it by his side, and cast a long glance at the heavy rain falling on an area covered all in green.

The mountains of Hitachi province, crossing the boundary of Shimotsuke province, became lower and lower as they extended northward, until at last they reached level ground. The River Kogai meandered along the edges of the mountain, dividing the land into east and west. Morizane was a lord who owned fertile rice fields in Abeoka village, on the mountain side of the river, but he never forgot his great obligations to the lord minister of the capital, lord of the fief.

"That's right," replied Morizane's companion Naritaka. "My people have been severely troubled by the flooding of the River Kogai in the past, and we sincerely hope that you will not cut the embankment this year. It is extremely annoying that our crop should fail because of the flood from the neighboring village, while our own water never causes any damage."

Young Naritaka felt extremely tense. He grasped the haft of his sword with his left hand and gazed piercingly at the breast string hung loosely on the ceremonial robe of the other man.

Naritaka was a landed warrior of Ōshima village, about two and a half miles west of Abeoka village. Since his grandfather was the

1. The title refers to a torchlight procession for driving away noxious insects from the farm; an agricultural ritual to pray for a good harvest. (NT)

2. A nobleman of high status, residing in the capital, who was designated as "the nominal owner or lord" of the fief or manor. The manor was actually owned and overseen by his "deputy," who lived in the locality. (NT)

Shimotsuke no jō,[3] Naritaka had lived in the province all his life. His family still retained its influence. Morizane, busily moving his *sake* cup, stared hard at the western sky. The cultivated and uncultivated pieces of land blended together and dominated the flat, low-lying scenery. Scattered trees and the thatched roofs of the poor stood like insignificant blots in the comfortless, swaying, drizzling rain; huge wooden roofs, backed against the Isoyama hill, showed distinctly the location of Naritaka's residence.

Morizane, like a sensible man, accepted Naritaka's candid plea with a smile. In future, he promised, the flood of the Kogai River would not be diverted toward the Gogyō River by any cutting of the banks, and if an emergency arose, no decision would be made without a mutual consultation.

Then the banquet began. Morizane's new wife brought several small, low tables on which there were large *sake* bottles and small dishes of hors d'oeuvres. The woman had long hair and a becoming orange-blue robe lined with crimson. At the sight of Naritaka, her eyes became suddenly fixed, but soon the smile returned to her face. Bowing her head quietly, she poured *sake* several times. Naritaka's look, however, was solemn.

"Your wife excells the report. You're a lucky man!"

Morizane nodded his head readily, spilling *sake* from his cup onto his lap. "Thank you for your compliment. She is considerate in everything."

Barely controlling himself enough to change the subject, Naritaka hurriedly left Morizane's residence. Morizane and his wife came out of the room to the edge of the open porch to see the visitor off, but Naritaka did not look back. Accompanied by two attendants, who were drenched to the skin, Naritaka crossed the rough wooden bridge. Naritaka looked at the ominous, foaming black water around the bridge posts and turned to his two men. "It looks very dangerous. We'll be in trouble if it doesn't recede soon."

On the embankment stood a man, his face anxious.

The River Kogai, on the east side, and the River Gogyō, on the west, flowed in parallel channels, a short distance apart, from north to south through this great plain. Both had their origin along the edges of the Nasu mountains, but because their sources and the geo-

3. The third-highest-ranking official in the province of Shimotsuke. (NT)

graphical features of their basins were not exactly alike, the two rivers soon became quite different from one another.

When the two rivers entered Hitachi province, further south, they became one, the Gogyō River being absorbed into the Kogai. Still further on, near the border of Shimousa province, the Kogai River was swallowed by the Tone River. The great Tone, in turn, flowed into the ocean. Such was the curious and capricious peregrination of the Kogai River over the distance of seventy-five miles.

In a few days the water finally went down, and sunshine brightened the plain. After a long absence, the purple-blue twin peaks of Mt. Tsukuba reappeared above Mt. Fukoku.

But in Ōshima village, the water in the rice nursery had risen and spoiled a great number of young riceplants, so that many villagers had to sow new rice seeds. The cause of this trouble was an overflow of water from the irrigation ponds along the river. Naritaka was chagrined. The shadow of Morizane's words a few days earlier, with their hint of hidden meaning (as it seemed to him now), flickered in Naritaka's mind.

"That man must have cut open some obscure part of the embankment and let the river-water flow onto our side. I thought the amount of the overflow was too great to be natural."

In Morizane's village of Abeoka, the transplanting of young rice plants from the nursery to the main rice field began shortly. The women's rice-planting song flowed gently and happily every day from one field and then another.

On Naritaka's side, the transplanting of rice was delayed by a month. The autumn harvest would be reduced by half. The peasants' faces grew darker. Two or three villagers disappeared; one of them became Morizane's servant.

The rainy season began. Every day was hard on Naritaka. Near the end of June, the rice was growing very well in the fields east of the Kogai River. Each plant was large and firmly rooted. Already young heads had come in sight. Besides, Abeoka village had, in addition to its level ground, many tablelands along the mountain slopes, where dry-land rice was grown and where the impact of the flood was hardly noticeable.

One day, when thin stems had finally begun to grow in the rice fields along the Gogyō River, Naritaka received a letter. It was from Morizane. The carrier of the letter was the man who had run away from Naritaka earlier. Naritaka read the letter, trying hard to contain his shame and anger. The letter read roughly as follows:

"Tomorrow night we will hold the torchlight procession for the villagers of Abeoka. Although this year's rice harvest is expected to be good, and although it is a little early in the season, we are going to hold the ritual in grand style, in order to ensure the finest crop possible. If your villagers wish to be favored by similar good luck, they may join the procession. My wife joins me in this invitation."

Without a word, Naritaka sent the messenger back. He, too, had been planning the ritual of the torchlight procession, but he had been postponing it until he could judge the growth of the rice a little better. Morizane's surprise attack was successful. He had schemed to make Naritaka lose face before his villagers.

Naritaka tore the letter into pieces. A scorching sense of mortification and rebellion welled up in him, and a single-minded desire to take action began to stir.

"It seems that Morizane knows of my relationship with his wife," he thought, "and is trying to make me angry. In order to protect her, he is planning to lure me to my death. In fact, I have long wanted to kill him and to snatch the woman. I wonder if he has read my mind."

Morizane's letter took effect all too quickly. Though an astute man, Morizane had not reflected sufficiently on the fact that success and failure are always just a hair's breadth apart. Could it be perhaps that both men were too eager to triumph?

Naritaka, on his part, turned the matter over in his mind all day long. A secret of this kind should not be revealed to anyone. However, he called his confidant, Gempachi, to his side. Gempachi was quick in action and showed flashes of wisdom. He was a little younger than Naritaka and lived in the latter's house.

"I have thought, my lord, that you might some day make a night attack. That man Morizane is truly a villain. He must have been seeking your life for a long time. However, I would doubt the wisdom of carrying out a raid under the pretext of the flood."

"Is that what you think? Are you afraid of following me?" asked Naritaka.

"No, not at all! I will follow you even to the grave. I will never part from you, my lord."

Gempachi left, straightening his shoulders. Next, Tomozō was summoned. He was some twenty-four years older than Gempachi, and had served the family since the time of Naritaka's father. He was a man of great physical strength and integrity. He lived near Naritaka's house.

"I understand your feelings, my lord. I, too, tried to fight a duel when I was young. If you are determined to kill the man, you should wait a little longer until he has proved himself to be a villain in everyone's eyes. If you should fail, there would be too many people who would blame you."

"Could it be that you have grown old and lost courage?"

"Oh no, no! My strength knows no age. But, my lord, have you spoken to anyone about this matter?"

"Yes. I have just told Gempachi about it."

"Oh, is that so? In that case, we can't keep it secret any more. You should do it as soon as possible."

Gempachi was summoned back again. The three men talked the matter over and decided to carry out the raid that following night. They would take the enemy by surprise and seize the initiative.

Later, when Naritaka was alone, he said to himself: "Neither Gempachi nor Tomozō knows my true intention. When I have killed Morizane and secured the woman, they will probably follow me, even if reluctantly. Just now I can trust no one but myself."

Besides the two men, there were many soldiers and servants, but none of them could be trusted. Naritaka knew all too well that his vehement will to succeed was dampened by his strangely oppressive sense of loneliness. But he could not turn back now.

When the dawn came, after a night of fitful sleep, midsummer seemed suddenly to have arrived. The wind blew hard across the broad, cultivated field, and the leaves of the roadside trees were hot. The small white flowers withered on their stalks. Naritaka looked around outside his mansion as if casually. All about him lay rice fields and hemp farms surrounding a hill Isoyama.

Naritaka's estate stood on a level slightly higher than the rice field and drew water for its moat from the wellspring of Isoyama. A small boat was floating in a ditch connected to the moat. At night he would hide weapons and armor in the bottom of the boat and row into the Kogai River. He would then moor the boat under cover, put on his armor, and commence his attack. Such were his plans.

The sun set and the wind died. Three or four bonfires were lit on the grounds of the Inari shrine[4] which stood near the embankment of Abeoka village. The flames flickered incessantly with the movements of the people. Quite a few from Ōshima village joined this crowd.

The moon emerged from the clouds. Suddenly there rose the long, hysterical screech of a trumpet shell, and torchlights began to flow in a vertical line along the embankment. The hollow, humorous sound of flutes, the quick beating of drums, the plucking of bamboo instruments, and the incantations chanted in hoarse voices all mingled randomly with an accompaniment of distant frogs.

Naritaka and his men had already left his house in Ōshima. Naritaka, accompanied by Tomozō, was now in the dry moat of Morizane's estate. Gempachi, squatting under the movable wooden bridge[5] across the dry moat, kept counting the number of people passing through the tower gate.[6]

Naritaka was clad in a braided cuirass of crimson over a dark-blue under-robe of loosely woven silk, and wore arm-protectors on both arms. He also carried a sword of which he was proud. Each of the other two men wore a black leather breastplate over a dark-blue linen under-robe and carried a small sword.

Gempachi crawled over to his master and said, "My lord, now is the time. Only a small number of men seem to be inside. Morizane went in a little while ago."

Naritaka trembled in every limb and felt an intense desire to urinate. But fear was gone and, like a man possessed, he felt full of fighting spirit.

"All right! Let's go! Gempachi, go first to the stable, cut the reins and saddle girths, and throw away the saddles. Then go over to the night watchmen's room. Tomozō, you go to the kitchen and take care of the people there. If you hear me cry out in a loud voice, come back to me at once. If you don't hear my voice, run away, for I will be dead."

The three men rose. Morizane's estate was built on levelled ground

4. The shrine, found in every locality, is sacred to the god of five kinds of grains. (NT)

5. The bridge consisted of wooden boards which could be removed easily to prevent the crossing. (NT)

6. *Yagura mon* in Japanese; the outer gate with a watch tower over it, built at the end of the movable wooden bridge (see footnote 5) and reached only by this bridge. (NT)

along the slope at the foot of the mountain. It faced the rice field on the west side; on the other two sides, the dry moat was covered with a thick growth of bamboo and weeds.

The central structure of the estate was Morizane's residence, built in the *buke* or warrior style. In addition, his large estate contained a warehouse, a stable, a farming tool shed, a manure shed, a granary, and several houses for retainers. The two men moved to the wooden fence on the outer bank of the dry moat, and at the corner where the moat turned sharply, they dug under the base of the fence with their swords. When they pushed at it the fence collapsed easily. The three men disappeared.

When he entered the stable, Gempachi saw four or five horses, tethered but unsaddled, and covered with mud. Only their eyes shone in the darkness. Gempachi ran directly to the night watchmen's room.

Tomozō soon went into the kitchen but saw no one there. On the wooden floor had been left two *sake* bottles which had perhaps been taken down from the kitchen altar. He sniffed and knew it was the finest kind of *sake*.

"This is a kind I have never tasted. Good!"

He drank up one whole bottle, but strangely enough, he found the *sake* tasteless. Just then a harsh, jeering voice was heard from the central building where Morizane lived; the sound of swords echoed once and died. Tomozō ran toward the building.

In the night watchmen's room, Gempachi cut three bow-strings, then rushed out toward the building from which the voice had come. Together the two men pushed the sliding door down so that it fell inward, and entered the room.

In Morizane's living room, a candlelight flickered, and his wife's gorgeous *kosode*, hanging on a clotheshorse, at once caught their eyes. A wooden tray had been set aside in a corner of the room. On the tray were *sake* bottles, *sake* cups, and large and small dishes of dried fish, dried shellfish, and fruit.

His sword thrown aside, Morizane lay on his back, beyond the mats on the floor.[7] The right side of his pale-blue under-robe was

---

7. In this period, only a small portion of the floor of a room was covered by *tatami* mats, usually by only two mats (each approximately three feet by six feet), while the rest of the floor was bare wood. (NT)

torn, and blood flowed out along the wooden floor, spreading gradually. Naritaka, with his blood-stained sword in hand, stood motionless, his eyes staring and mouth wide open. At the sight of his two men he blinked.

Suddenly, at that moment, a bamboo clapper rang nearby. In response, many more clappers sounded in various parts of the house, joined at once by the barking of dogs.

Naritaka and his men, as if in reflex action, fled outside. They crossed over the fallen fence, and, sliding down the slope, dropped into the rice field. Howling arrows pursued them. Men's heads moved in the watch tower above the movable wooden bridge, and a few more arrows followed, plunging into the rice plants. Naritaka put his hand on Gempachi's shoulder and said, "The rice field is slippery. We'll climb the hill on the other side."

It was the opposite direction from Ōshima village. Could it have escaped Naritaka that they would be moving away from the boat they had hidden? But since the thicket on the hill above their hiding place was so tall as to conceal the stars, there was no danger of the three men being spotted. They felt relieved and drank water from a bamboo canteen.

Just then the two men's eyes caught sight of an arrow stuck above Naritaka's heel. His face was twisted with pain.

"I was hit while we were in the rice field. What a piece of luck!—it came within a hair's breadth of missing me! At first all I felt was intense heat, but now it's hurting badly. Please, pull out the arrow and wrap the wound. Ai, how it hurts!"

The two men untied their master's waist sash, which had been tied over his cuirass, and wrapped his ankle with it while he lay on the ground. He took another drink of water from the bamboo canteen and spoke jerkily, as if he were choking up food stuck in his throat.

"I shouldn't have attempted a raid. It wasn't really necessary to go to the trouble of getting myself hurt in order to take the woman. Besides, she wasn't there. I'm very sorry that you, too, were involved. That man Morizane lunged at me with one terrific stroke of his sword. I parried his thrust and ran my sword into his side with all my strength. He must be suffering from the pain now."

The two men, in utter consternation, cried in strange voices.

"What? My lord, did you carry out this raid on account of a woman? We had no idea!"

The bamboo clappers were still ringing. The bonfires for the torchlight procession had been broken down, the flutes and drums stopped, and the trumpet shells no longer sounded. Instead, men cried piteously to one another.

Many of Morizane's retainers had joined the procession. His wife had gone to her father's home for the holiday. Those who had shot arrows at Naritaka and his men and those who rushed out at the sound of bamboo clappers now surrounded Morizane. A man skilled in archery put his mouth to Morizane's ear and said,

"I'm certain that my arrow hit that man's thigh. I heard the sound clearly. He leaned on the shoulder of the man next to him and looked hurt."

A faint smile came over Morizane's agonized face. Then he vomited a clot of blood and took a deep breath.

"I was surprised by the sudden attack. It was my mistake to confront the attacker, forgetting that my wife was away at her father's home and that I was not wearing my armor. Under such circumstances, he who hides himself and dodges his enemy is the winner. I should have gone to the chapel to drink the *sake* that was offered at the altar. For a man like me I lacked both wisdom and courage. Naritaka's wound is in a dangerous place. It will grow worse."

There were now more men sitting in silence around Morizane. But the doctor who had been sent for was not yet in sight; neither did his wife arrive yet. His old mother who had gone to the shrine was yet to return.

Naritaka hastened his flight. His two men took turns carrying him on their backs through the thicket, which adjoined a large mulberry farm. Naritaka frequently complained, "The pain's unbearable. Please, go and find some high-quality *sake*, and wash my wound with it and change the wrapping."

The two men laid their master on a straw bed in the grounds of the mulberry farm. Gempachi searched behind a farmer's house and was elated with his success. He now understood why all this time Tomozō had given out the smell of *sake*.

"Here it is! Of the highest quality! It's a long time since I tasted anything like this." He had found the excellent *sake*, surprisingly, at the corner of a manure shed that belonged to an old, run-down house. Removing a pile of rotten wall plaster, Gempachi had found an old jar. He emptied the bamboo canteen at his waist, filled it with *sake*, and ran. Unable to stop himself, however, he drank half the canteen of *sake* on the way. But, finding its taste strangely bitter, he stopped drinking and filled the canteen with water from the rice field.

The two men washed their master's wound. Naritaka was pleased. The area surrounding the wound was now swollen and hot.

"My lord, let's remove your sword."

Naritaka nodded gravely. The two men discarded their master's cuirass, arm protectors, visor and dagger. His sword, however, they placed beside Naritaka. They carefully wrapped his leg up to his thigh, even using a piece of cloth torn from his under-robe as an additional bandage. From time to time, they swatted at the striped mosquitoes attacking their master's face.

Their hiding place was not completely safe, they knew, since it was near people's homes. And the narrow path leading to the river might be covered by the enemy. Tomozō whispered, "Well, we have no choice but to go over there." He pointed to the temple graveyard. The big roofs of the temple's main hall and the upper half of the bell tower threw a dark overpowering shadow. The men carried the feverish Naritaka in among the five-stone monuments[8] and grave mounds and laid him on his back. It was a fairly large piece of land with oak, beech, and chestnut trees as well as various shrubs. The tall bamboo grass hid the river from view.

The two men lay down with Naritaka between them. They were not very tired, but their joints felt stiff. Naritaka's hard breathing prevented them from falling asleep, but gradually an aching fatigue grew on them and became so unbearable that they dozed off in spite of their uneasiness.

As for Naritaka, he couldn't possibly fall asleep. Neither the excruciating pain of his wound nor the sensation of burning heat diminished at all. Both his mind and body were under great strain,

---

8. A monument made of five stones of different sizes and shapes. (NT)

but in the back of his mind, as if he were close to delirium, rose an urge to talk. Naritaka stretched out both his hands and shook the two men.

"Thanks to you, I've recovered my calm somewhat. It's most mortifying that an arrow that had touched the mud should have struck me in such a vulnerable spot. I'm afraid my wound is a dangerous one. Some poison from the rice field must have got into it. Listen, a few minutes ago I told you that I made the raid on Morizane because of the woman. It was the truth.

"Morizane's wife is a beautiful woman, but sly. She knew very well that I had long wanted to marry her. During that long rain last year, I secretly cut a small part of the embankment in the middle of the night and saved her father's rice field. I'm sorry that, as a result, you people had to suffer, and I apologize for having kept it secret until now.

"She wept with gratitude and promised that this year she'd marry me. I was most impressed with her filial piety, but then near the end of autumn last year I learned that suddenly she'd married Morizane. I felt then as if I'd fallen on a muddy road on a dark, dark night.

"When I thought, I realized that it was my mistake to have been so foolish as to tell her everything. She'd learned the trick by which I'd saved her father's rice field. From now on, whenever her father's field yielded a good crop, I would be a loser. Thus she decided to have nothing more to do with me.

"But I think there's no way to know whether or not she would always have remained Morizane's wife. She's attracted to the capital—Kyoto. Do you remember the minister's chief officer for household affairs, a young man who's visited this area now and then? She wanted to marry such a man. I didn't learn of this until much later, of course.

"Even so, I made my last bet on that woman. Morizane will die deceived by her, whereas I, I made a bet though I knew her true nature! I am the winner, then. Now that I've told you everything, I feel more light-hearted. But I feel sorry for you two. I'm grateful that you've accompanied me this far. I have a favor to beg of you. It's about my younger brother, Narihisa, of Kugeta village. He has been friendly with Morizane for many years. Please tell him for me not to get into trouble with the villagers of Abeoka in the future.

"By the way, the water of the Kogai River and the water of the Gogyō River are incompatible, just as Morizane and I are. It's most regrettable, but it can't be helped."

Listening to this long and curious confession, Gempachi and Tomozō understood everything for the first time. As the night wore on, Naritaka, perhaps feeling more at peace with himself, fell into a deep sleep, sank away as if descending into the depths of the earth.

But the two men had mixed feelings. They shut their mouths tight, looking into one another's faces. In their minds, each of them compared what they had been until today and what they would be tomorrow. Before long, however, such thoughts turned into the semiconsciousness of shallow sleep.

Morning came at last. Under the dry, blue sky, the heat from the leaves of grass filled all the area. It was quiet. The two men felt hungry for the first time. Naritaka lifted his head slightly. His voice sounded hoarse, as if it strained through a sieve.

"My throat is swollen. I want some water. My body is hot but I feel strangely cold. My eyes are stinging. My head feels like someone else's."

The two men crawled among the grave mounds and found some cooked, unpolished rice in front of a new grave. They both ate the rice. In a wooden bowl dedicated to the grave there was some water, but they saw a worm in it; therefore, Tomozō cautiously poured some water from the pail at the well into the bamboo canteen hanging at his waist.

There were some movements of people inside the dimly-lit main hall of the temple. They seemed to be preparing for a funeral. Tomozō returned and gave his master some water. Tomozō and Gempachi talked in a low voice.

"We had better leave the lord alone for a while. When night comes, they may relax their watch. Then we can go to find our boat and take off."

"All right. But let's not be too hasty."

Though they were both impatient, they had to make a painful show of face before each other.

An oak tree thick with leaves stood on the north side of the graveyard. They moved Naritaka under the shade of the tree. Soon, five or six men emerged from the back entrance of the temple and walked toward Naritaka. They were Morizane's retainers and an old sexton with a spade. In the center of the graveyard, the sexton dug a hole, his back bent. After a short time, they all went back to the temple, talking loudly.

The sun rose higher. The gong began to sound in the main hall. The beating of a wooden drum continued languidly yet incessantly, and the unusually sad recitation of the scripture became audible. The unison invocation of Buddha's name, joining the recitation, mingling with the singing of cicadas, made the heat seem more intense.

Naritaka opened his eyes a little and faintly smiled. Putting his trembling hand on the haft of his sword which lay by his side, he said,

"Morizane is finally dead. I've won."

The two men noticed Naritaka's throat heaving strangely and looked at his face. Large drops of sweat shone on his swollen, purple cheeks, brown spots visible underneath. His eyes were sunken and there were pale black shadows over his eyelids. He breathed hard and fast.

The gong sounded unnaturally loud, and a crowd of people flowed from the main hall. The square coffin on an open bier moved along with them, guarded by men wearing breastplates. Two young men carrying white banners led the procession; women followed the bier, holding up bamboo vases with red and yellow wild flowers. Behind them came a number of old peasant men and women, their faces emotionless.

The young woman immediately next to the bier showed no sign of tears. Her hair was neatly combed down, and she wore only a pale-black robe over her unlined under-robe. Yet she was beautiful. The woman next to her had to be Morizane's aged mother, sobbing, her face wet with tears.

At the sight of the younger woman, Gempachi carelessly raised his face a little, and someone uttered a loud cry,

"The fugitives! Under the oak trees!"

The two men, acting by reflex, held their swords in readiness and twisted their left shoulders forward. Naritaka uttered a cry with all his strength. These were the only words of his farewell.

"Don't resist! You can't win. Forget about me. Run! Just run!"

The two men looked back briefly at their master. The next instant they kicked at the tree roots, slid down the slope of the graveyard and ran toward the river. Several men who were around the newly dug grave jumped out, struggling through the human walls. Arrows began to fly. Separated from their master, the two men became completely different and faint-hearted.

"Run! Run!"

"Let's run! Run for your life!"

The figures of the two men disappeared for a moment in the thick growth of weeds on the embankment, but soon reappeared at the edge of the water. They jumped into a manure boat which was moored to the log-landing jutting into the water. There was no oar. They untied the rope and used their swords as their oars. The boat became caught in the current. The two men plunged into the luke-warm river water with their breastplates still on them.

Meanwhile, gigantic white columns of cloud appeared in the sky and, floating unhurriedly, enveloped the mid-slopes of Mt. Tsukuba and Mt. Kaba. The sun cast the same force and heat on ripe fields and unripe. The bamboo forest along the river banks swayed gently, watching, emotionless, the fate of the two struggling lives.

Five or six men carrying bows and arrows lined up on the log-landing. The river channel was normally narrow and its volume of water not great; but its iron-black current, swollen with the recent rainfall, was much faster now than it had seemed. Gempachi took the lead. "Tomozō, can you swim? I'm all right. What a foolish thing our lord has done!"

Tomozō spouted water from his mouth two or three times, vigorously kicking and splashing with his legs. In no time several arrows converged around him.

"Indeed, our lord has done a stupid thing! I'm not a good swimmer. Please help me if I'm in danger."

Gempachi did not reply. Another arrow sank between the two men, leaving a hiss behind.

For some time both Gempachi and Tomozō had realized that the flitting image of Narihisa, of Kugeta village, was in their minds.

DISCONTENT

"I wonder if it's going to be chilly again tonight? As I expected, the weather here is quite different from that in Izu. I wonder if it's still too early for the bonito season at sea?"

Rokurō's sturdy cheeks and his two eyes, which still retained their simple dreams, shone in relief against the strong flame of the torchlight.

"Probably it is," his friend Kanezō answered. "But it seems the smell of the sea has mostly disappeared from your body, and the smell of the earth in the capital has started to seep into you. Of course, I didn't mean to include that section of the city over there." Kanezō turned to the right and pointed toward the darkness across the river. That area was called Rokuhara. Rokurō had just recently arrived in the city.

"You're right," said Rokurō. "Even though we wear armor, we were originally fishermen and farmers."

If it had been daytime, elegant ox-drawn carriages[1] would have been coming in and out past those dozens of magnificent structures which stood in a row, and swift horses driven by young warriors would have been galloping by, neighing and pushing aside the servants with huge loads on their backs, who came and went with hurried steps. That section was the very heart of the capital city. With what kind of noise would it be beating that night?

Rokurō and his fellow officer Kanezō, both from Taga, had left the gate of the guard station of *ōban yaku*[2] and were walking on the Gojō bridge, which was part of their foot patrol. Both men had been together, fishing in the sea or plowing on their small mountain farms, until they were chosen to serve as *ōban shū* in the capital.

1. Reserved exclusively for noblemen and high-ranking officials. (NT)
2. The headquarters of the guards or soldiers called *ōban shū*. Recruited from various parts of the country on a rotating basis, these men were sent to the capital city of Kyoto, and it was their duty to guard the Imperial Palace as well as the city itself. The *ōban shū* soldiers were supervised by their unit chief, called *ōban gashira*. (NT)

It was the last day of April. There was no moon. Recently the weather had been unseasonable; the cherry blossoms came out late with poor colors. That night the two young men could almost see their exhaled breath as they walked. In the morning, normally, this big old city, now fast asleep, would awaken and bustle with activity. But there was a reason why that would not be exactly the case.

One evening at just about this time in the previous year, a fire had started near the corner of Higuchi and Tomi no kōji, and one-third of the capital city had been destroyed. Concealed by the quiet darkness, the area to the northwest of the Kamo River was a wasteland of broken tiles and rocks and charred sticks. Poverty-stricken people who had turned robbers after losing their homes, and unruly monks who rebelled against the religious persecution of the Taira family, would nightly haunt the burnt-out area, robbing people on the road or setting fire to the temporary huts, so that the low-ranking *hōben*,[3] their supervising officers of *Kebiishi Chō*, and the young *ōban shū* guards had to repeat their investigations and prosecutions day after day.

Rokurō and Kanezō crossed the bridge and walked northward along the river. A short distance away stood a lumberyard, where they could make out a group of human figures. As Rokurō and Kanezō approached, two men stood up and started running toward the west. Behind them was left what looked like a fully packed jute bag. Kanezō ran quickly after the men, shouting to Rokurō, "Guard the bag!"

Rokurō was about to open the bag when he heard a man's desperate cry coming from underneath the bridge. He jumped down to the river beach, leaving the bag behind. At once the flat back of a man swimming downstream in the river and the wriggling figure of another tied to a bridge pole came into Rokurō's view. As he approached, splashing in the water of the shoals, he found an old man, limp and exhausted, with a draw rope bound several times around his neck.

Rokurō cut the knot with his sword, dragged the man to the sandy river beach and rubbed his limbs vigorously, but the old man never revived. Holding up the torchlight which he'd earlier thrown aside,

---

3. Ex-convicts who were hired by the police department—the *Kebiishi Chō*—after their release from prison and were especially assigned to arresting criminals. (NT)

Rokurō saw that the dead man was a peasant, about sixty, small in stature. He wore a coarse, dark-blue unlined top and a pair of short linen *hakama*.[4] He had a half-sandal[5] on one of his feet. Kanezō's loud voice sounded above the embankment.

"Hulloa! Come up, Rokurō. I've caught one."

It was one of the gang, a thin boy of fifteen or sixteen. The thud of Kanezō's fist resounded, and in a frightened voice the boy quickly confessed, drying his tears with his dirty *eboshi* hat.

The small three-man gang—probably people whose homes had been destroyed by the fire—had chosen this dark night and were preying on passers-by near the bridge. The old man, saying that he was from Fukakusa, had approached the gang and inquired about his destination. He had intended to deliver some rice to his sick younger brother, living in the burnt-out area. The old peasant had sighed and said, "I gathered only this much. It was as if I had squeezed blood from my own body." According to the boy, the gang struck the old man down before he finished speaking, carried him to the river, tied him up, and started to run away.

Rokurō and Kanezō began walking, Kanezō carrying the jute bag on his shoulder and holding the boy by the arm. Rokurō looked back toward the body of the old man, which by then had sunk into the sandy river beach. There was no sound but the lapping of the river waves, breaking and gradually retreating.

When Rokurō and Kanezō returned to the guard station, Rokurō was severely reprimanded by Miyake Jūrō, the *ōban gashira*. Removing his right arm-protector, his face turning crimson, Jūrō hit Rokurō with a broken bow.

"When you find a corpse," he shouted, "you must not dispose of it by yourself. You should run back and report it to the *ōban gashira*. Then you should lead him to the scene. The *ōban shū*'s distinguished services become the *ōban gashira*'s. And the *ōban gashira*'s become the Taira family's. If you do such a presumptuous thing again, I'll take your sword away and send you back to Izu."

Kanezō, who had captured the young boy, was praised and given

4. A divided skirt worn mainly by men for formal occasions, but also worn by some women (e.g., Shinto priestesses) performing special ceremonies. Here the man is wearing a short kind. (NT)

5. A short sandal that lacks the heel portion. (NT)

as a reward the quiver which Jūrō had used. From the next day on, dark shadows appeared beneath Rokurō's eyes. With exaggerated good will, Kanezō patted Rokurō on the shoulder and stuck out his chest.

"Say, Rokurō, are you not feeling well?"

Rokurō smiled a grim, silent smile. Spitting from time to time, he muttered, "I see that to take enemies' heads on the battlefield is not the only thing a soldier does. All is well so long as he kills other people, no matter what. It's disgusting."

The green leaves of the willow trees along the river had suddenly grown thicker. Women had made their seasonal change of clothing. But there was something heavy in the atmosphere of the town. Rokurō recalled the sun's bright reflection on the deep blue sea of the south.

"Oh, how I envy Hatsushima Island," he thought. "It floats lightly on the waves."

The summer was long that year. The daytime patrol was hard. To Rokurō, who had grown up with the sea breeze, the heat and humidity of the capital city were unbearable. Sweat spilled down from between the layers of small leather pieces forming his breastplate. He felt as if a burning moxa had been applied to his head under his soldier's hat.

In July, Taira Shigemori, who had been sickly, died, perhaps overcome by his father's eccentric perversity and by the intense heat. Shigemori's unlucky year[6] was to inflict a calamity not only on himself but on the Taira family and the court. Shigemori's death made people feel as if a clear stream flowing through the capital had dried up.

One evening after the first day of autumn, Kanezō and Rokurō went on patrol together as usual. The river breeze had turned cool, as might be expected. When the autumnal equinox arrived—it was not far away—sardine clouds would hang over Izu and the fishing season would begin. Kanezō, who by now had forgotten the sea, patted the haft of his sword, his chest stuck out. He had been promoted on account of the case of the rice thief.

6. Shigemori was forty-two years old, which is considered one of the unlucky years in one's life. (NT)

"I hear that at the end of this month the annual wrestling match will be held in the Imperial Palace. I wonder if strong wrestlers will come. I expect I'll be allowed to watch the imperial match, since I'm a *bangashira*."[7]

Along the river, the row of hastily rebuilt stores came to an end at a vacant lot covered with pampas grass which had survived the fire, the heads of the grass still brown, swaying heavily. A steep slope began near the roots of the pampas grass. Below, small waves reflected the moonlight, brightening both the river and the shore.

The river seemed to be quite deep here. A small boat was moored, and a young woman crouched in the boat. At the sight of the two men, she beckoned to them. It appeared that she was asking them to pull her out onto the slope. Rokurō immediately began to stretch out his hand toward the woman, when he recalled the old man of the other day.

"Kanezō, isn't she asking us to help her? Her body is wet. She may have tried to drown herself. Shouldn't we pull her up?"

Kanezō deliberately uttered a loud cry. "Pay no attention! That's a prostitute. It's a trick they have, acting conspicuous on purpose. Let's go; let's go!"

Rokurō started to say something but obeyed his superior's words. When they returned to the same spot after the circuit of their patrol, the boat was there as before, but only a woman's sedge hat and a pair of women's slippers were to be seen in the center of the boat. The two men slithered down the slope, holding on to arrowroot vines, and supported themselves against one of the wooden posts that stood along the river.

The woman's body lay at the bottom of the water, parallel to the boat. The torchlights carried by the two men threw countless shadows on the pebbles at the bottom of the river. From the woman's mouth, a stream of tiny bubbles arose and disappeared instantly on the surface of the river. Rokurō's heart pounded. He knew that by his native seashore, a drowned fisherman was always restored to life if his body under the water had sent out bubbles at the time it was pulled out.

"Say, look! She's alive! Bubbles are coming out of her mouth!"

"What of it? Do you want to be hit by the *ōban gashira*'s broken

---

7. The rank of *bangashira* is above the *ōban shū* and below the *ōban gashira*. (NT)

bow again? Go back to the guard station immediately and report to him. I'll yield the credit to you."

Rokurō ran back. The *ōban gashira* smiled with satisfaction and stood up with a whip in his hand.

"Well done this evening, Rokurō! Kanezō is commendable, too. Before long, I shall promote you to a *bangashira*. Now lead the way."

Rokurō went back to the river with five or six men, and they picked up the dead body and laid it under a willow tree. The immobile woman under the moonlight looked exactly like the goddess Kannon. The pale-colored silk garment twining round the lower part of her body looked like the embossed pleats on a statue of the goddess. It was a pitiful thing to see the water still dripping from the side of her mouth.

An old woman in a worn-out, lined summer robe appeared, escorted by a young soldier. At the sight of the corpse, she burst into bitter tears. The body was that of her daughter. The old woman's husband had been an official on the fief of Lord Narichika, who had been executed by the Taira family as one of the leaders in the Shishigatani incident the previous year. After the fief was confiscated, the father had died in poverty.

The daughter had become a *shirabyōshi*[8] dancer in order to support her mother. However, unable to make progress in her dancing skill and unwilling to degrade herself completely, she had apparently grown distraught and had chosen death.

Every day was painful to Rokurō. He became increasingly weary of his job as an *ōban shū*. Indeed he became sick of life. He could not help feeling on his patrol as if he were treading on the sleeping goddess Kannon. Meanwhile, the *ōban gashira* suddenly began to make him a favorite. This tortured Rokurō even more.

Near the place where the young dancer had drowned herself stood a small temple which had survived the fire. When Rokurō was off duty, he went there alone and bowed his head in front of the main image of the temple.

"You would have been saved if I had pulled you up immediately. I

---

8. A medieval female entertainer who danced and sang in male attire (consisting of a white hunting costume called *suikan* and a ceremonial *eboshi* hat), complete with a sword. A *shirabyōshi* was often identified with and acted as a prostitute, although some of these women never engaged in prostitution. (NT)

was a coward. Please forgive me! I am praying to Buddha on your behalf."

Raising his head, Rokurō stared at the gentle features of the image of the eleven-faced goddess Kannon. Without knowing it, Rokurō had learned the pleasure of worshipping gods and goddesses.

In this part of the fire-ravaged area, temporary cottages had only recently begun to appear. There was a sort of a restaurant among them. Several waitresses were trying to attract customers. All of them were young, and their manners were polished. Rokurō stopped and looked around him.

"I wonder if these women worked in the homes of the *Sesshō* and *Kampaku*,[9] destroyed by the fire? They're pretty. What's this? That woman, standing there farthest to the left, with the black mole and the long eyes—she looks very much like the drowned one."

Noticing that Rokurō did not move, the women poked each other in the back.

"That soldier's face is rather handsome to look at, but his head must be filled with pebbles."

"But his figure is manly. Say, you there, don't be standing around like a fool! Come on in."

"No, he must still be innocent. Leave him alone. We'll be sorry afterward. Ho, ho, ho. . . ." laughed one of the women.

Rokurō felt curiously happy. He bowed lightly and started to walk away. But how embarrassing! The *ōban gashira*, wearing a ceremonial robe and riding a dappled grey horse, happened to come by. Kanezō and his fellow guards all turned stiffly to look back at Rokurō. The *ōban gashira* glared at Rokurō with bulging eyes but did not utter a word, assuming an air of indifference.

Standing between the women who kept laughing and the men who were marching away, Rokurō kept gazing at the tail, swishing right and left, of the horse that the *ōban gashira* Miyake Jūrō was riding. Rokurō could not control the heartbeats springing to his throat.

After this incident, Kanezō seemed to avoid Rokurō. Even on their patrol duty, Kanezō would not walk side by side with him.

9. Both are titles for the most powerful post of regent for an Emperor, *Sesshō* being the regent for an infant Emperor and *Kampaku* the regent for an adult Emperor. (NT)

"Perhaps," Rokurō thought, "Kanezō secretly reported my solitary walk to the *ōban gashira*. He's a clever devil, this Kanezō."

Rokurō came to dislike Kanezō intensely, and on his part decided to make a conscious effort to keep his distance, both mentally and physically.

Sooner than he could know, however, the time was approaching which would allow Rokurō to set foot on his native soil again. The long-standing conflict between the ex-Emperor's court and the Taira family came to an end with the victory of the Taira family, headed by Kiyomori. The government of the ex-Emperor[10] collapsed, and most of the noblemen holding high-ranking offices were dismissed and placed under house arrest. The Taira family took over the power and fiefs which had belonged to the ex-Emperor and his officials, and it looked as if the whole nation would flock under the red flag of the Tairas. Soon the new year came. Ominous forebodings filled the air.

But the whirlpool of reaction quickly surfaced and began to spread in a cloud of spray over the entire country. The Taira family had the difficult task of devising countermeasures. It was decided that the young *ōban yaku* guards' term of duty should be extended and that they would be sent to their native provinces to collect and bring back food and forage as taxes.

The *ōban gashira*, who had been aloof to Rokurō ever since he had glared at the youth in front of the Kannon temple the previous year, called for him and, smiling cordially, handed him several sheets of paper. These papers were the letters demanding rice from the *jitō*[11] representing the Taira family in eastern Izu. There was also a small piece of paper addressed to Rokurō.

"Rokurō," said the *ōban gashira*, "I'm counting on you. I am sending this order with full confidence in you. Collect the supply of food and return as quickly as possible. I have just promoted you to a *bangashira*."

Rokurō was totally surprised, but he was glad, too. He felt life was worth living again.

10. A form of government called *insei*, in which actual powers were vested in an ex-Emperor. (NT)

11. A steward sent by a feudal lord to his fief or estate to supervise the working of the land, to collect taxes, and to maintain peace and order. A *jitō* was often dreaded by the people of his jurisdiction. (NT)

"Yes," he thought, "I have become a little jaundiced lately. Now I've got hold of myself."

Rokurō left the capital city, accompanied by several attendants leading pack-horses. Two or three rolls of the silk cloth of the capital were bound around the cantle of the saddle on Rokurō's roan. The light-green cuirass which he wore in celebration of his departure shone like gold in the morning sun. Kanezō, riding side by side with Rokurō on the city's main street, which was lined with willow trees full of young leaves, gave him encouragement.

"Well, good luck to you! From today on, you're the same rank as I am."

Kanezō's words seemed to imply something unpleasant, but Rokurō accepted them submissively and smiled.

Upon his arrival in his native village of Taga, the first things that seemed to greet him, as if with delight, were the navy blue sea of late spring and the familiar contour of Hatsushima Island. Needless to say, his aged parents were pleased with his promotion. Every day he was busy. He went hurriedly around among the *jitō* to deliver the order from the Taira family. But the looks which they gave Rokurō were dark.

"As you probably know," said one of them, "the rice crop is discouraging, since we've had bad weather for three years running. Around here there are even some who peel off pinebark for food. We have been praying desperately to Inari, god of harvests, but to no avail."

Still Rokurō persevered. As his efforts began to bring about considerable results, he was somewhat relieved.

But suddenly Kanezō arrived, accompanied by several attendants. They all came on horseback. They must have galloped all along the coastal roadway without stopping, for their eyes were sunken and their foreheads and jaws were covered with thick dust. The tassets of Kanezō's crimson cuirass showed large marks of saddle gall. Kanezō spoke.

"Rokurō, terrible things have happened! A rumor turned out to be true and Prince Takakura's plot to rebel was exposed. There was a battle fought at the Uji bridge, and the leader of the rebellion, Lord Minamoto Yorimasa, was killed. The prince, too, was struck and killed by a stray arrow. Meanwhile, it seems that the prince's secret message has been sent all over the country. The soldiers on *ōban yaku* duty will soon be sent somewhere to attack the insurgents. There's not a moment to be lost in delivering the supply of food. Here is a letter addressed to you."

Kanezō produced a sealed letter, all wrinkled, from the depths of his breast pocket. Rokurō's face immediately turned deathly pale. The content of the letter was to this effect:

"Kanezō shall supervise the delivery of the food supply. Rokurō shall remain in the province to follow the *jitō*'s direction."

In other words, Rokurō's position of *bangashira* was automatically dissolved. On the following day, Kanezō departed with twenty horses loaded down with rice and barley.

Rokurō could not understand the world. Putting his hand to his face occasionally, he again and again found tears trickling down of their own accord. He became thin, emaciated.

"What should I do? I have been forced to do a job which is as hard as pulling nettles in the mud every day!"

He learned that what gave him the greatest comfort was self-derision. He would burst into laughter wherever he might be and fling himself at the trunk of a pine tree with all his strength.

"Good lord!" whispered the villagers. "Look at Rokurō! He must have been sent home because he went crazy."

"What a pity! He was always as gentle as a girl, ever since he was a child."

The old villagers still retained their affection for Rokurō. But the anticipation of battle soon spread throughout the village. Men scoured rust from their swords and daggers and groomed their horses. Women dried small fish and sea weeds to store. The *jitō* checked the village register to prepare for the gathering of his forces.

"Now what am I to do? I'm thoroughly tired of fighting!" Then Rokurō thought: "I've got it! I'll enter the priesthood! A pilgrimage would do me good."

Rokurō walked aimlessly along the beach. What his vacant eyes caught was not the blossoms of the dayflower in the bush, but a torn straw sandal nearby and a solitary seagull which flew away from the bush.

When he returned home, Rokurō brought out an old hand-mirror that his mother used, and held a dagger with the point upward. Moments later, as he gazed at his severed topknot, excitement and contempt combined became an invisible whip which urged his heart to action.

After several days' continuous rainfall, the rare sight of August's full moon was revealed among the wet stratus clouds. Then instantly the moonlight disappeared as if flowing away. Rokurō remembered the drowning of the dancing woman in the Kamo River about the same time the previous year. Her sculpture-like figure seemed to be stretched out under the moonlight, and her pale face came floating before his eyes.

When Rokurō got up the following morning, it was no longer raining, but the sky was dark. A neighbor woman came running, the hem of her unlined linen robe fluttering. This good-natured old woman had lost her son when he was very young, but he would have been the same age as Rokurō.

"My son, there is terrible news!" she cried. "My husband has just come back from the *jitō*'s office. He told me, 'There will be a battle very soon. Many soldiers from this area have been in and out of Lord Hōjō's mansion, where the renowned personage from the capital[12] has been staying.'" She asked desperately, "Where can we escape? I'm scared, Rokurō! I'm scared!"

Rokurō felt a thrill of delight stirring within, as if seeing a sudden whirlwind blow away masses of rain clouds which had lain stagnant in the sky for months. However, he soon folded his arms, inwardly crying out, "What should I do now? How I wish I weren't a man!"

The old woman went away, seeing that Rokurō remained motionless, his mouth tightly closed.

Several years earlier, by accident, Rokurō had met the exile from the capital. This exile, Lord Yoritomo, had come to worship at the shrine of Izu Gongen, accompanied by about ten attendants, or rather, guards who looked after him.

Rokurō was on his way home from an archery practice contest with his friends. As he walked along the narrow, steep mountain path, he met the group, and Lord Yoritomo, as if to show his good will, turned back toward Rokurō and his companions with a smile

12. Referring to Lord Yoritomo. Everybody in the village knew the identity of the "renowned personage." (NT)

of courtesy. Rokurō had a fond memory of the man's graceful manner.

"Can a man of such gentle disposition really fight?" He wondered. "I would be glad to die for a general like him. Yes, I will entrust my life to that man!"

Rokurō at once derided his sudden change of mind. Yet his inmost will seemed to drive him hard toward the decision to act as he had said he would. Before long, when the report reached the village that Yoritomo's surprise attack on the Yamaki estate was a success, the hearts of the men of the village were stirred. Twenty years' oppression was now ended; people's lips began to move more freely, and this freedom led directly to action on the part of the young men.

The eagle soaring in the sky may call up the thunder. Only after the falling of the thunderbolts will the future of the land become bright.

The deputy provincial governor of Sagami, Ōba Saburō Kagechika, had been home for half a month, having finished his term of *ōban yaku* duty in the capital. Taking advantage of the Taira influence, Kagechika gathered a large number of men and began his campaign to quell the few rebels. Rokurō was swallowed up only too quickly in the tidal waves of conflict between these desperate wills.

Rokurō had formerly been assigned as a foot soldier among the personal retainers of Kurō Sukekiyo, a son of Itō Nyūdō Sukechika, a close friend of Kagechika. Sukekiyo had in past years shown kindness toward the exiled Yoritomo, but he could not escape his destiny to serve the Taira family.

Yoritomo had been exalted as the god of war incarnate by the former retainers of the Minamoto family, who had come from Sagami, Izu, and other provinces. He marched along the main road from south to north and set up his encampment on the sandy shore of Hayakawa. It must have been his plan to reach Kamakura, the place closely connected with his ancestors, where he hoped to assemble his former retainers from the provinces of Miura, Awa, and Kazusa and fight the decisive battle.

But unexpectedly, Kagechika's attack was overwhelming. Thus, Yoritomo was forced to retreat in haste about two and a half miles to the south and to bivouac on Mt. Ishibashi. The mountain, standing alone beside the small stream on the southern edge of the village of

Ishibashi, was not very high, but from the top one commanded a full view of Sagami Bay, which was embraced by the Miura peninsula on the east and by the Manazuru cape on the south. On its east side, Mt. Ishibashi dominated the road along the beach; on the other three sides, several prominent mountains which eventually led to the Hakone range were joined together and formed complex valleys. It was, in short, an excellent citadel for protecting a small armed force. Morever, numerous gigantic cedar trees growing on the hillside provided the best possible shield against enemy arrows and served to hide the actual size of the forces.

During the morning on August 23rd, it started to rain. From time to time the sea breeze drove the rain sideways. The troops of Ōba Kagechika surrounded the foot of the hill and impatiently waited for a lull in the storm. It would be hard work, fighting with bows and arrows while trying to climb up the steep slope covered with rain-drenched leaves and bushes. Yoritomo, on his side, had no wish to force an immediate battle, since the troops from Miura had not yet arrived.

At dusk, the rain finally stopped, and the time was ripe. Angry voices and the neighing of horses arose, but these sounds were soon pierced by the whistling of arrows and the clashing of armor, which in turn reverberated among the trees. Moments before sunset, however, the outcome of the battle was clear. The reinforcements from Miura had never come. Yoritomo's troops were divided into two groups, one wandering in the mountain and the other fleeing along the narrow, steep path along the beach.

Before he knew it, Rokurō was leading the pursuers, running southward along the coast. His arrows gone, he threw away his bow. He wore the same light-green cuirass, but it was no longer shining. The sun had set beyond the mountain range of Amagi, but bloodthirst still ruled the battlefield. Ahead of Rokurō, an enemy soldier suddenly threw away his sword and turned to face him. The pattern of his armor was utterly indistinguishable, but the man was brimming over with strength. He was the rear guard of the retreating troop, filled with courage born of desperation.

"I am the famous Usami Heihachi. Come! Let us have a wrestling match for everyone to see."

His calm, husky voice rang out strongly, and Rokurō knew the

name. Rokurō was not a good wrestler, but it was too late to with-
draw. Leaving everything to luck and with a roar that broke involuntarily from his mouth, Rokurō hurled himself at this black,
shadow-like figure.

Soon Rokurō found it difficult to breathe and felt dizzy, ready to
faint. As his strength gave way, his enemy began to overpower him,
until at last Rokurō was pinned to the ground, his nose pressed into
the dust of the road. Both of his ankles were dangling out over the
sea cliff, so that, try as he might, he could not rise.

Heihachi pulled a dagger from his waist, and in preparation for
beheading Rokurō, he put his hand into Rokurō's helmet through
its crown and tried to pull up his enemy's head by grasping his
topknot.

Since Rokurō's topknot had already been cut off, Heihachi could
find no hold. The strength of his grip suddenly relaxed, and Heihachi's body sagged forward. Rokurō was able to get his right hand
free. Pulling out his dagger, he drove it several times through the
slits of Heihachi's tassets, then got to his feet. He saw an arrow
stuck in the chest of his fallen adversary. Alas for him, Heihachi had
been struck by an arrow sent flying by one of his retreating fellow
soldiers.

Rokurō felt a strange sense of separation from the accomplishment of his other self, so to speak. He stared at the body of the enormous man, who looked as if he might awaken at any moment.
Rokurō breathed hard, his mouth dry.

"Whew! I'm saved!" he said to himself. "What a strong man he
was!"

Several fellow soldiers ran toward Rokurō and patted him on the
arm.

"Well done! Well done! An incredible piece of work! We'll be your
witnesses."

Rokurō shook his head as he picked up his sword. "No, no. His
own friends did it, accidentally fighting among themselves. I don't
want to claim the head."

"Don't be silly! I'll cut the head off. Be sure to have this recorded
in the head-count book."

One of the soldiers leaned over the body, his sword flashing. Another pulled a bowstring from Rokurō's bowstring spool, wound it

around the top-knot of Usami's head, and tied it to the sash around the waist of Rokurō's armor. Then the soldiers started back on the same road. As the weight of Usami's head pressed into his spine, Rokurō could not suppress a weird feeling of familiarity, as if Usami were his blood relation.

The mountains of Izu and Hakone formed a low range, creating a simple, undulating shadow in the uniform blackness of heaven and earth. One could count hardly any stars. The night air felt as usual. But the singing of insects in the bushes and the sound of the waves languidly rolling up the shore were sad to Rokurō.

At Hayakawa, where Yoritomo had set up his temporary encampment, Ōba Kagechika had curtained enclosures[13] spread in seven different locations. He was holding, simultaneously, a ritual of reading the head-count book and a banquet to celebrate the victory. Since the battle had been a free-for-all fought in rain and mud, on a steep slope and in darkness, even the victors were weary to the bone. As the relentless search for the retreating enemy dragged on for two or three days after the battle, the men began to feel their legs shake and their spirits weakening.

The prostitutes who were summoned from Yumoto and Kokufu-juku put on their makeup and busily ran among the deathly tired soldiers, to serve them.

Since Rokurō was not a heavy drinker, he did not join this beastly circle, but merely moved his chopsticks.

Ōba Kagechika had taken off his deep-blue leather suit of armor, leaving on other smaller pieces. Surrounded by his devoted followers, he turned with one hand the pages of the head-count book while emptying his large *sake* cup with the other hand. Suddenly he stopped laughing, his eyes fierce.

"I see Usami was killed. He was an excellent soldier. Who killed him? The record is not clear."

Miyake Jūrō, who was an *ōban gashira* during the *ōban yaku* duty in the capital city the previous year, had been Kagechika's retainer since his childhood.

---

13. Unlike tents, these were roofless enclosures made of curtains spread between upright wooden posts driven into the ground. (NT)

"It was Rokurō from Taga. I gave him a rigorous training in the capital. He isn't anxious to claim credit."

"Is that so? You did a fine job. Rokurō sounds like an interesting man. Bring him here."

Rokurō bowed when he was brought inside the enclosure. Kagechika laughed lightly like a man of importance, but looked suspiciously down at Rokurō's head.

"Rokurō, well done! You deserve great credit. You shall be rewarded later without fail."

"No, sir. It was not I who killed Usami. Credit should go to this shortened hair of mine and to an enemy arrow. That's the truth."

Kagechika's face instantly betrayed a mixture of emotions, but he assumed an air of calm. Taking a writing brush from his clerk, who was next to him, Kagechika crossed out Usami's name. Miyake Jūrō, his eyes angry, uttered a cry loud enough to tear the curtained enclosure.

"You damn fool! What nonsense! How dare you bring disgrace on me! If your hair is short, so much the better. Go at once and become a monk."

Rokurō went outside the enclosure in silence. The wind under the starry sky was strong. The waves beating the shore roared as their long forms rolled in unhurriedly on the sandy beach. Far out at sea in the darkness, numerous fishermen's torchlights flickered like living creatures.

Many thoughts passed through Rokurō's mind.

"They say Lord Yoritomo rowed out to sea safely in a small boat. I wonder if it's true?

"I hate the Taira family. I hate Kagechika. I hate Kanezō. I hate even more the big eyes of Miyake Jūrō. I don't want to become a monk, now that Jūrō told me to.

"Lord Yoritomo, who was nice to us, will surely return, with torchlights blazing on hundreds of boats, just like these fishermen's torchlights tonight.

"When that time comes, the world will change. And I might begin to like people."

Rokurō folded his arms and went on gazing at the horizon. Two men came out and began to urinate on the beach.

"Say, Rokurō, what are you doing? You aren't thinking of committing suicide, are you, because you've been dismissed by Master Ōba?"

"Absurd!" he answered. "I'll be damned if I'll die! A new world is coming!"

The two men did not even look back toward Rokurō but went back inside the curtained enclosure, moving their hands and feet in a tipsy dance.

A young woman came out and raised the hem of her gaudy robe. Then she threw the fish bones heaped on a big plate out over the receding waves and dried her legs with the hem of her robe as she lowered it.

"Dear me! You! What are you doing? Can't you drink!"

Rokurō stretched out his right hand and pointed to the sea.

"Soon he'll come. He will. Then life will be easier."

The woman looked Rokurō intently in the face, smiled sweetly, and stepping back, disapeared. Rokurō felt happy.

"I wonder if only that woman understood my feeling."

Rokurō gradually regained his calm. What floated before his mind's eye were pictures of the old man who was robbed of his rice and murdered by young men under the Gojō bridge of Kyoto, and the Kannon goddess who could not support her mother and drowned herself.

For a long time he went on listening to the sound of the waves.

ESCAPE

The attack on Lord Taira Kiyomori's estate in Rokuhara took place about 10:00 a.m. on December 27th, 1159, the first year of the Heiji era. It ended in defeat for the troops of the Minamoto family.

Two hours earlier, about eight o'clock, the Minamoto forces had overpowered the Taira forces, aided by the psychological advantage of being inside the Imperial Palace. Then, in an ill-considered burst of overconfidence, the Minamoto forces had left the Imperial Palace, taken in by their enemy's clever tactics, and pursued the retreating Taira troops. Although the Minamoto forces broke open the magnificent main gate and entered the Rokuhara estate, they were outnumbered from the beginning and suffered great losses. Minamoto Yoshitomo, the leader of the attack, had no alternative but to gather his routed soldiers at Rokujō Gawara. Unable to withstand the counterattack of the Taira troops, now riding the wave of victory, Yoshitomo's entire force became restless and unruly. Already, the most devoted retainers of the Minamoto family, and the landed warriors and their attendants in the famous Seven Parties of Musashi, who had participated in the attack, had divided into several small groups and were acting at their own discretion. One by one they fled from the battle scene, protecting their exhausted horses in the wind so cold that it froze the reins.

Most of these men had come to Kyoto only two weeks before, responding to Lord Yoshitomo's emergency call from that city. Intoxicated with a dream of great victory, they had ridden westward on horseback day and night. Their horses were equipped with new hames and cruppers, and with them came spare horses carrying food and forage, also provision-bearers carrying leather-covered boxes containing spare weapons. As soon as they arrived in the capital, they had to take their share of the unexpected misfortune.

While he was victorious, Lord Yoshitomo looked like a kind of god in his all-black military attire, giving orders in his shrill voice.[1] But now that he had been reduced to little more than a scrambling corpse, the number of his followers diminished steadily.

Lord Yoshitomo and his son, eight of their lifelong retainers, some twenty surviving warriors of the Seven Parties of Musashi, and their attendant foot soldiers, pressed upstream along the Kamo River and then moved northward through the narrow valley of the Takano River. Knee-deep snow on the mountain path and numerous icicles of every size, forming on the curves of the path or on the tree roots, again and again baffled the footing of the horses.

Yoshitomo's party avoided crossing the Kirara Pass, which led to the sacred region of Mt. Hiei and was crowded with monk soldiers. Instead, the retreating group chose a route further north over the Ryūge Pass. The strategy proved futile. Even there the party was attacked by the monk soldiers of Yokawa, who had been on the watch. Running for their lives, the party barely escaped the ambush, and those on foot learned the limit of their physical endurance. Though not one of the men on foot was injured, they were forced to discard the food and spare weapons they had carried on their backs. Still wearing their breastplates and short swords, their eyes bloodshot, they tried desperately not to lose sight of the men on horseback ahead.

When all these men, who could barely stay together, came near the Wani river, those on horseback became separated as a matter of course from their foot soldiers and provision-bearers. The distance between the former and the latter gradually increased until the horsemen began to cross the river, disappearing southward without even looking back.

The men left behind all dropped down into the dry grass as if at a signal. Without uttering a word, they looked straight ahead.

Under the dark-gray, snowy sky, spread out endlessly before them, the low mountains of the northern region dimmed, trembling. Immediately in front of them, Mt. Reisen's large, white slope—an extension of Mt. Hira—seemed to stretch down toward them, but it would not touch the exhausted group.

---

1. Literally a devil, referring in Buddhist belief to one of those said to live in the region of demons. (NT)

"Those warriors wearing the crimson or cherry-blossom patterned cuirasses are all coldhearted, as I suspected. Only at a time like this can we find it out." The name of the young man who spoke was Buichi. He was taciturn but sturdy in build, and always calm. He was a peasant, twenty-five years old, from the village of Yorii in Musashi province. Serving as a provision-bearer for Inomata Koheiroku, Buichi had gone through the famous battle of Hōgen three years before. That time, his side had won.

Buichi stretched out his right hand and pointed at a spot in the distance. It was the horsemen, who looked like a school of small fish sucked into the heart of Lake Biwa.

"Look at them! How sad it is to see their backs! In peacetime they hold up their swords proudly, and bullseye the target with their bamboo bows and rattan bows, but now, now that they're defeated, they behave like that! As for us, let us try to get our feet on our own native soil again, no matter what."

Of the seven men, five were young provision-bearers who were from villages lying close together. The other two were middle-aged foot soldiers for the warriors who had run away. After whispering to each other, these two men got up and tried to run after the horses. Buichi stopped them with his outstretched arms. Fire sparkled in his eyes.

"Don't! Don't go! Your horsemen will certainly be attacked by wandering soldiers, but they will probably be able to get away from the attackers. Then who do you think will take the brunt of the fight? From now on, we must concentrate on how to survive by ourselves. All seven of us have to live. Will you do as I say? What's your answer?"

The stillness of the place seemed to sink into the hearts of the six men. The four younger ones looked up at Buichi in silence. The two middle-aged men nodded repeatedly.

"Yes. You're right. You're quite right."

It seemed as if they were trying to convince themselves by uttering these words. But when Buichi told the men to discard every weapon and every piece of armor, he was met with violent opposition. He insisted strongly, as if prepared to knock the others down.

"Listen carefully. If you carry arms, you will be attacked. If you're attacked, you'll feel like fighting. From now on, we shall be beggars.

Nobody will notice beggars. We must become beggars in order to live."

Now the six men obeyed unquestioningly. The most convenient hiding place seemed to be a small shrine, a little to the south, surrounded by dry reeds and cedar trees.

"It will be dangerous to move in the daytime around here. Let's wait until nightfall."

With fatigue and relief surging up at once, explosively, the men fell into deep sleep as soon as they lay down on the rotting wooden porch of the shrine.

Buichi was far from being able to sleep. He gathered the cuirasses and short swords of the seven men, tied them together with a rope he had worn around his waist, and left the premises of the shrine, carrying the bundle on his back. The six men remained motionless, but as the evening wind blowing from the lake seemed to tear at their skin and as their frostbitten fingertips began to itch, they awoke involuntarily.

Buichi, who had returned unnoticed, stood there smiling, with a bag on his back. Behind him was an old man with a face like a monkey's. He, too, carried a bag on his back, to be filled with joy. The little monkey-faced old man gradually began to show signs of friendliness. "You are lucky to have escaped without injury. Thanks to the Taira family, I was reduced to what I am now," he said.

The old man had been one of the monks in the West Tower of Mt. Hiei. Five years before, in the autumn, when the resident monk soldiers were about to enter the city of Kyoto carrying the portable shrine of the Hiei Temple,[2] the old man had joined the procession as a bearer of incense and flowers. As the procession approached Shirakawa,[3] it was attacked by the Taira soldiers who had been lying in ambush there. The old man hid himself in the monks' quarters of Sakamoto, but, fearing for his life, he had returned here to be a peasant. Today, his sympathy greatly stirred by Buichi's story, the old man had persuaded his fellow peasants to accept the arms in exchange for food. His eyes shone brightly.

2. Also called the Hiyoshi Temple, located at one of the entrances to Mt. Hiei. (NT)
3. The northeastern part of the city of Kyoto. (NT)

"The two bridges of Seta are no doubt closely guarded by the Taira forces. Tonight I will give you a boat. It is best to cross the straits of Katada and go toward the Yasu River."

The seven men decided to follow this kind advice, and waited for nightfall in the sanctuary, eating the rice-balls offered by the old man. In the meantime, he went down to the lakeshore, rowed his boat over, and hid it behind a shed.

When night came, the vast sky hung darkly over the large lake. There was neither moon, nor star, nor wind. The boat carrying the eight men moved eastward, breaking the frozen surface of the lake. No one spoke.

At midnight, the boat entered the delta of the Yasu River. The lame old man knew a small wharf there. Their strange association now ended with a hurried farewell.

"Good luck to you! Let us hope the Taira family is defeated soon. They are terrible villains!"

The life blood had apparently started to flow again inside the small, shriveled body of the old man. Raising one hand, he pushed the bow of the boat out into the dried reeds. Gradually his figure disappeared.

The seven men searched for the east road, crunching underfoot the frozen snow on the narrow path which stretched through the endless rice fields and swamp. As it began to grow light, they came to the front of a temple surrounded by trees and mud walls. Over the small temple gate was a tablet with the name of the temple, Busshōji, written on it. Buichi took a chance and stepped inside. The chief priest, who was drawing water from the well, invited the whole group in. This area was the territory of the Ōmi branch of the Minamoto family. The men were not only invited to sleep at the fireside but were also treated to the gruel breakfast.

The men went out through the temple gate. The sky was clear, but there were no people moving on the road. The seven arrived in the post town of Kagami. The round top of Mt. Kagami, overhead, was covered with snow and looked like a round, mirror-shaped rice-cake. They came upon a group of three women, an old man, and a horse, resting at a peasant's hut near the edge of town.

First Buichi approached them and inquired about the horsemen from whom he had been separated. He was answered by the pret-

tiest of the three women, twenty-one or twenty-two years old, who wore a man's ceremonial *eboshi* hat, a man's white hunting robe, and a pair of crimson *hakama*.[4]

"Yesterday, shortly after noon, we were crossing the bridge of Seta, when about twenty mounted warriors galloped past us. In a little while, terrible screams came from the east end of the bridge. Without thinking, we clung to the railing. After it became quiet again, a group of warriors coming from the opposite direction passed by us. We heard they were of the Taira family, but they didn't carry a single enemy soldier's head. I assume the first group must have managed to escape. Three or four Taira soldiers seemed to be wounded."

She was a singer of *imayō* ballads[5] from the post town of Hashimoto in Tōtōmi. The other two were both about fourteen or fifteen years old. One carried a flute, the other a small copper cymbal; they were the singer's accompanists. The sturdy-looking old man was a groom.

They had come to Kyoto in the hope of making money during the New Year's festival, but without recommendations from the households of the ministers or of the Taira family, they could get no engagements at the noblemen's estates. Moreover, the situation in Kyoto looked very threatening. Large numbers of warriors were gathering from the various provinces. And so the woman and her attendants were now on their way home. It so happened that immediately after their departure from Kyoto, the city had become a battlefield.

"We are extremely uneasy about the journey ahead. Would you please take us with you? Please, have mercy on the helpless. We will do anything you ask to repay you."

Tears welled up in the heavily shaded eyes of the singer in male attire, who otherwise wore only light makeup. The two girls also

4. A divided skirt worn mainly by men for formal occasions, but also worn by some women (e.g., Shinto priestesses) performing special ceremonies. The description of the woman's clothing here indicates that she is a *shirabyōshi*, a medieval female entertainer who danced and sang, in the male attire as described here, complete with a sword and a hat. Her singing included the *imayō* ballad (see footnote 5). A *shirabyōshi* was often identified with and acted as a prostitute, although some of these women never engaged in prostitution. (NT)

5. The *imayō* ballad is a verse form which gained its popularity in the middle of the medieval period of Japan and consists of four lines, each divided into two parts of seven and five syllables. (NT)

trembled, their shoulders shaking. The six men shut their mouths to keep from smiling. Buichi breathed deeply, his eyes closed and his arms folded.

Presently Buichi opened his eyes, unfolded his arms, and spoke in a stern tone of voice.

"I understand. I wish we could escort you safely. But we have enemies. It would be most tragic if their cruel swords hurt you. At a time like this, it is best for everyone to think of his own safety. I wish you all good luck. I'm sorry, but we must part. I wish you a safe journey."

The singing woman tried to understand Buichi's words, and spoke, as if resigned, in a brave tone.

"Well, good-bye. I deeply appreciate your kindness. I wish you good health. Be good to your wife."

The seven men got up and started to walk along the main road. They felt suddenly awkward and did not feel like talking, but unconsciously they quickened their pace.

On the east side of the road was the forest of Oiso, where numerous gigantic cedar trees grew thickly, forming a hilly outcropping that nearly blocked the road. Here the men saw something unexpected. A bay horse with a gold-dusted, lacquered saddle was eating clumps of green grass along the roadside. Nearby lay a soldier with his face up, wearing a crimson suit of armor, his back and buttocks buried in the snow. Buichi ran toward him.

It was a young soldier whose name was Seki Hachirōta, a member of the Yokoyama Party and one of Yoshitomo's surviving warriors. He said he had received a sword wound in his left side during the fight at the Seta bridge on the previous day. He was a handsome man, and spoke in a broken voice, his lips twisted.

Buichi nodded and said, "Is that so, then? How well you've held out! Never mind, you'll be all right now that we're here."

Hachirōta continued his story as if talking about someone else.

"I was forsaken both by my friends and by my horse."

As he bent over the man to check his wound, Buichi looked up at the four provision-bearers, who each closed one eye as a signal.

"There is no need to pick up someone now who has abandoned us before. Let's go," murmured one of them.

Buichi stood up and spoke in a loud voice, probably so that Hachirōta could hear. "I shall take this man with us. We flee only because we hold our lives dear. It is the same with him. I save him because I hate him. The more I hate him, the more dear our lives become."

Buichi lifted Hachirōta in his arms, placed him on the saddle, and started to walk, holding the reins in his hand. Hachirōta clenched his teeth. The provision-bearers and foot soldiers followed, their faces expressing mixed feelings. In a little while, one of the foot soldiers pulled at Buichi's arm. "Look! I see five or six men moving in the shadows of the forest. Those wandering soldiers are after armor and horses."

Buichi nodded. The number of wandering soldiers rapidly increased. Hachirōta also became aware of them and stretched out his arms to hold onto the horse's neck.

"I don't want to die. You picked me up. Please save my life! We should quickly find a strategic spot to hide ourselves in ambush. When they come, we will chase them away. There's no alternative. I will command, but I will not give up my armor. It is the soldier's symbol."

Buichi and his party came to an open field of pampas grass. The snow was thin there, probably because of the direct force of the wind. Though a single path pierced the field, there was neither a house nor a large tree in sight. Hachirōta felt for his stirrups and dismounted from the horse as if he were another man.

"This is it. Nobody would believe we'd be hiding in such a place as this. We'll get behind the shrubs. When you see the wandering soldiers come, set fire to the dried grass."

One of the foot soldiers led the horse into a grove of shrubbery. Buichi, too, straightened himself up.

"The wind is excellent. Let's go!"

Presently fifty or sixty dirty-looking men approached shouting, carrying rusty weapons and farm tools in their hands. Buichi took out his bag containing flint and steels. No sooner was a thin column of smoke seen rising than it suddenly moved forward, spread sideways, and changed to a flame. The snow melted and turned into smoke. Under the smoke, red, hot tidal waves broke loose, and the ground seemed to rumble. In a short time, the surrounding area became a wide, black, sandy field and stillness returned. No one moved or talked. Buichi's sides alone shook with laughter.

"Ha, ha, ha. . . ."

The sense of uneasiness suddenly called for a tone of voice which was at once cheerful and scornful. But Hachirōta brought his face close to Buichi's and said, "Please help me take off my armor. I'll leave it as a souvenir for them. I've now come to understand the danger of wearing it."

Hachirōta placed his helmet over a still-smoldering shrub. He then untied the knots at his shoulders, removed his armor, and placed it underneath the helmet. He looked at his helmet and armor intently. It looked as if Seki Hachirōta, known for his crimson armor and bay horse, were finished there.

"From this day on I am your comrade," said Hachirōta, patting Buichi on the shoulder. "You are my senior."

Buichi also patted Hachirōta on the shoulder.

When the two older men whispered something in his ear, Buichi nodded. The two men removed their wide sashes from around their waists, tied them together, and wrapped Hachirōta's wound with them. At the lakeside on the previous day, when the weapons and armor had been surrendered for food, the old men had not given their sashes to Buichi but had kept them.

The seven men began to move out, and Hachirōta followed them on horseback. Because of Hachirōta's injury, the other men walked at a slower pace, but they all felt some mysterious strength rising within them.

Since the checking station of Fuwa[6] seemed a dangerous place to pass, they waited for nightfall, went through the barrier of Kozeki,[7] and entered the province of Mino about midnight. The snow was deep there, probably because of the fierce wind blowing from Mt. Ibuki. Now that they had taken their first steps into the eastern region, their tension diminished greatly.

With the checking station behind them in the west, they found that the morning of the New Year's Day holiday was like any other

6. One of the three most famous barriers or checking stations of ancient Japan. The Fuwa station was in the province of Mino. (NT)

7. A smaller barrier or checking station than the Fuwa station, located almost a mile west of Fuwa. (NT)

day. After that, they were confronted with hardly any danger. Every day their journey was like that of carefree priests.

They saw with their own eyes that the people in Konan and Mino were surprisingly poor. It was clear that in Musashi, by comparison—with its rich meadows and prosperous horse raising—there was much room left for farming and further development of the land, and that there was hope for the future of people's lives.

When they arrived at the post town of Hashimoto, several large houses of *chōja*[8] caught their eyes. Leaning against the railing of the Long Bridge of Hamana,[9] Buichi looked at the horizon in the setting sun. The broad, wintry sky was slightly tinged with brown from the rays of the sun which had just gone down, but the brown was gradually blending with the color of the sea. On the vast expanse of water, there was nothing to see but a few fishing boats, moving without haste, like small black cracks on the surface.

"That singer also held on to the railing of the bridge of Seta, didn't she?" Buichi said to himself.

The recollection of the ten days' flight now became for him a fond memory. Three women in dancing attire passed by. One of them approached Buichi, smiling. To his amazement, it was the singer.

"What a surprise! I am most grateful to you for your kind help the other day. Thanks to you, we were all able to return safely."

After passing the checking station, the woman said, her party, sensing the danger on the land route, had gone to Kuwana, hired a boat there, and returned to Hashimoto by the sea route.

Buichi's heart swelled with happiness. When he had refused to lead her party, she had accepted his blunt words submissively and had borne no grudge, recognizing risk involved for her party.

He repeatedly wiped the tears which came welling up. Through the singer's good offices, the eight men were invited to stay overnight at a *chōja*'s home. After they took a bath, *sake* was served. For the first time, they laughed as they told the stories of their hardship. One of the two old men of the party asked about the horsemen.

---

8. A *chōja* is in general a successful and wealthy businessman, engaged in agriculture and other businesses and using many employees. Here, the reference is specifically to those who operate inns for travelers. (NT)

9. *Nagabashi* in the original story, literally, long bridge. It was a wooden bridge about 650 feet long, located at the southern end of Lake Hamana. (NT)

A woman pouring *sake* spoke. "Several days ago, I've heard, a few dozen mounted soldiers went by. I didn't see them myself, as I was polishing candlestands in the back of the house."

While Buichi assumed an air of indifference, Hachirōta listened intently and did not lift his *sake* cup.

"Hachirōta, aren't you drinking?" Buichi asked him.

Hachirōta suddenly became serious.

"Brother, I'll give up *sake*. It is bad for my wound."

The next morning, the *chōja* presented the men with a large amount of food—probably another result of the woman's resourcefulness. The time came for the men's happy departure. To everybody's surprise, Hachirōta decided to stay.

"I want to see a doctor and recover quickly. I am anxious to be able to hold the bow again. Besides. . . ."

The singer cast a quick glance at Buichi from behind Hachirōta and then hid herself. In the eyes of this strong-willed woman could be discerned a desperate plea. Buichi nodded and smiled a forlorn smile. Dividing the food among themselves to carry on their backs, the seven men started their journey again on foot.

Hachirōta uttered a cheerful, loud cry from behind the men, patting the neck of his bay horse.

"Thank you all for your kind help, brother. I promise to take good care of her. I'm sorry."

Buichi was sad. Strength was the reverse side of weakness, he realized now for the first time. From the shores of Lake Biwa he had come all this distance, trying to give courage to his fellow travelers every day; it had been a happy journey, after all. He had never expected that such an outcome as this would await him here. It was a painful experience for him.

The men reached the post town of Mishima. The great shrine of Mishima was magnificent, complete with the middle temples and the small temples. The middle-ranking priests who went in and out of the chief priest's residence were in their proper traditional attire. The shops standing in a row near the shrine were well stocked with merchandise. But surprisingly enough, a crowd of about a hundred beggars awaited the travelers in front of the large temple gate.

Buichi stopped and looked at each of the beggars. He felt a fit of laughter welling up inside. The beggars stood like fat scarecrows, bundled up with every piece of rag they could find to protect them from the cold.

"Let's give our rice to the female beggars only. What do you say?" asked Buichi.

The six men agreed, clapping their hands.

"In three more days, we'll be in our own town," said one of the men.

At Buichi's signal, the beggar women came running and gathered around the seven men. Buichi gave each three handfuls of rice. When the male beggars tried to come near, the female beggars shoved them aside with all their strength. The seven men laughed again. Buichi shook the emptied rice bags. "Some fun, eh? We'll take these bags as souvenirs."

The sky was blue; there was no wind. Mt. Fuji looked enormous. The snow covering the entire mountain gently absorbed the sunlight and made the mountain seem even more beautiful and friendly.

Two or three young men poked Buichi in the back. An old foot soldier pulled at Buichi's hand. He turned his face, its lines beginning to relax. For some time he was motionless. His features had never been so bright as now.

"I guess a man feels happy when he's worshipped by women," he thought.

Lord Yoshitomo had been killed seven days before in the village of Utsumi in the province of Owari. He was thirty-eight years old.

THE MESSAGE

It had been a long day. The sun was about to set in the northern sea, leaving the sky dyed yellow, but the hot air rising from the earth was not yet gone.

The warriors who had scattered over the battlefield gathered naturally in several groups. The battle was over. The soldiers' sunken cheeks were covered with spotty whiskers, their eyelids incrusted with greasy sweat. The ornamental ear-covers of their helmets were half torn; their neckplates were pierced with arrows. No one there looked like a victor, and yet they had finally won the battle of Shinohara.

The defeated soldiers were no longer on the battlefield. In every part of the pine forest, on the sand dunes which lay from north to south between the sea and the long inlet, the low branches of the trees were broken and the grass trodden; headless corpses and dead horses with their legs stretched and stiffened lay motionless, as if part of the landscape. Torn pieces of straw sandals, broken swords and halberds, and tattered cloth badges were strewn all over like dirty refuse.

The hatred and fighting among men had resulted in pitiful ruins. When one looked at the countless arrows piercing the fallen pines and the tree stumps from north to south, one could easily grasp the tragedy of the battle.

Having suffered tremendous losses at the successive battles of Mt. Tonami and Mt. Shio in Etchū province on the night of May 11, in the second year of Juei era (1183), the troops of the Taira family had only repeated their defeats and retreats. They barely escaped the enemy's pursuit at the shore of Ataka and finally arrived at the post town of Shinohara in Kaga province. In the meantime, they were severely pressed by their enemy, the Kiso troops, who followed them relentlessly.

At noon on May 21, with their helmets burning and armor scorching, the Taira troops fell victim to the enemy's final annihilation operations. In a few hours, the battle cries, archers' shouts, noise of clashing weapons, and clatter of horses' hoofs had stopped, replaced by the sound of distant sea-waves.

In the center of a curtained enclosure in the temporary encampment, the commanding officer sat on a folding chair, while his most trusted men knelt around him. One after another, horsemen arrived, carrying enemy soldiers' heads tied to the saddles of their horses. Dismounting, each horseman placed his enemy's head on a small wooden stand, which was then offered to the commanding officer for inspection. Nearby, a clerk with his portable case of ink and brush recorded the individual achievement. Then the head was immediately turned over to the attendant outside the curtain.

By nightfall, more than thirty-seven hundred heads of the Taira soldiers were collected and displayed along the roadways.

In the gathering dusk, flickering bonfires began to appear. The victors were to camp here for the night. At that moment three horsemen returned, followed by their attendants. They brought with them three men of the Taira troops tied with ropes. The captors looked like woodsmen who until recently had caught wild boars and deer with their hands in the remote parts of Shinano province. They drove the three captives unceremoniously inside the curtain.

Two of the three prisoners were apparently peasants, wearing plain armor. No matter what question was asked, these peasants had no courage left to answer fully and merely repeated the same words, "Please let us go home right away. We are here simply because we were taken away from our mulberry field."

The middle-aged soldier who had been interrogating the prisoners held the clerk's right hand and looked up at his master, the commanding officer. The latter nodded. The interrogator understood and said, "Take them to the foot of the big pine tree to the west."

A group of men went outside the curtain. Shortly after, a shout of rebuke was heard two or three times, followed by the reverberating sound of the beheading sword. Then all was quiet. The face of the captive who had been left behind suddenly turned pale. He was exhausted by battle, a man of about thirty, clad in fine armor. Over his pale-yellow, twilled under-robe, he wore a suit of round armor, called *dōmaru*, in varied shades of purple. He had no helmet on, and his left shoulderplate was gone. It was noticeable that he wore a crystal chaplet of prayer beads around his neck and that his manners had ease and grace.

In consideration of the captive's status, the interrogation was taken over by the commanding officer in charge of the day's battle. This commanding officer's name was Yoda Saburō, a relative and follower of Nenoi Koyata Yukichika. As a man experienced on the battlefield, Saburō began in a tone deliberate yet stern.

"You, state your rank and family name."

The prisoner of war, who had been sitting on the ground with his legs crossed, looked up as if in disbelief, and said in a quiet but clear voice, "I have never in my life been addressed in this manner. I shall refuse to answer."

To his credit, Saburō understood and said, "That was rude of me. Please accept my apology."

The tension of the prisoner's eyes relaxed; he even smiled.

"My name is Itō Noritsune, deputy magistrate, a vassal of Lord Tomomori, a new *chūnagon*," he said. "Because my family has served the Taira family since my grandfather's time, I am treated like one of the Taira sons."

"As a man of such importance, how have you allowed yourself to become a prisoner?"

"I am not a prisoner by choice. The other two men were. The fact is, I just happened to be near them."

"If you are not a willing captive, were you caught because you failed to leave the battlefield in time?"

"No, no. That was not the case. I was about to hang myself with my own hands when I was captured."

Saburō's face turned pale. The men surrounding him also put their hands on the shafts of their swords.

"After today's battles," said Noritsune, "many of our fifty or so soldiers were either wounded or killed, and the survivors ran away. I decided that I must die in order to deliver the dead into Buddha's hands. I tied the horse's reins together and was in the midst of hanging them over a pine branch when I was caught."

Saburō somewhat regained his calm as he listened to Noritsune's quiet speech.

"That was an admirable intention so far as it goes," said Saburō. "You obviously are already prepared for death. According to the custom of the battlefield, you shall be beheaded. Please leave any message you wish to be conveyed."

Noritsune became extremely disconcerted.

"No!" he cried. "That won't do! That won't do! I have been a true believer in Amitabha Buddha since my early childhood. I have heard that if a man dies maimed in his body he may not attain his soul's salvation in the Buddhist paradise but will be condemned to Asura's hell. In order for me to send our soldiers who died of arrow and sword wounds to Amitabha Buddha's Pure Land, I must not maim my body. I entreat you. Please let me hang myself."

Saburō moaned low and long. His men got up all at once and surrounded Noritsune. One of them drew his dagger and held it with its point downward. They exclaimed indignantly:

"My lord, I can't stand the sight of such a man!"

"What an effeminate man! What a simperer!"

"If he doesn't know the law of warriors, kick him to death."

A shout was heard outside the curtain.

"My lord, please give me the man. We'll hang his head on a pole along the roadway together with the two other heads we've just cut off."

Without waiting for their master's words, five or six men set upon the prisoner. Noritsune was unexpectedly strong. He deftly moved his head and neck and jerked at the men's elbows, even snatched the dagger from the man's hand. But finally the men held Noritsune's head and decapitated him. The crystal prayerbeads were scattered about, mingled with the blood. At the same time, a large, oblique crescent moon was carved into Noritsune's right cheek.

Saburō sat on his folding chair without uttering a word. He remained there, his eyes closed and his arms folded, showing no signs of getting up, until a snowy heron cried in the starry sky.

At the edge of the village, far from the battlefield, stood a wooden hut in which materials for fences against wild boars and deer were stored. Inside there sat a man. He was dressing a swollen spot on his left arm with an ointment, and wrapped the wound with a piece of cloth torn from the sash tied around his cuirass.

He was one of the most trusted followers of this same Noritsune who had been decapitated earlier. His name was Tsuneshichi. He had seen how Noritsune, helping his surviving soldiers and servants flee the battlefield, had been unable to get away himself; and he had seen how just when he made up his mind to hang himself, the enemy soldiers ran toward him. Tsuneshichi had run for his life, until he'd banged violently into the trunk of a pine.

He felt a burning pain in his arm and cried like a child. As he cried, his mind was somewhat diverted from his pain. When he tried to dry his tears, he found that he was unable to move either hand. He shouted in astonishment, "How strange! Now the nape of my neck is stiff and ice-cold. I can't stretch my legs! What in the world has happened to me?"

His eyes were wide open. Through an opening in the hanging straw mats which were used in place of regular wooden shutters, a white mist floated in. It gradually formed a distorted round object, which became a man's face, until at last there appeared before Tsuneshichi the sorrowful features and part of the body of the lord, so familiar to him. The brand-new wound, a large, red opening on the right cheek, was horrid to look at. Tsuneshichi closed his eyes, chanted a prayer at the top of his voice, and then, almost sobbing, appealed to the apparition,

"My lord, please forgive me! I was a coward. When you fell from your horse, I couldn't help shouting, 'Ah, it's all over!' At that moment, for some reason, that woman's face suddenly floated before my eyes.

"I could neither draw my sword nor could I stand in front of you as your shield. Instead I ran westward, kicking the sand of the dunes, until I found myself alone. Please forgive me. I lost my senses because of the heat and that woman."

The sorrowful face with the wound on its cheek seemed desperately to make a request, but since his eyes were tightly closed, Tsuneshichi could not see. Gradually, as the outline of the face began to fade, Tsuneshichi regained his strength and was able to move his hands and legs again. Everything was the same as before inside the hut. Tormented by loneliness and remorse, Tsuneshichi could not remain there but rushed outside.

He turned his steps to the southeast. Here the shore of the inlet formed an intricate, saw-toothed indentation, and the tall rushes grew thick, casting dark shadows. Nearby stood five or six poor fishermen's cottages, their roofs almost touching one another. There was one, however, which stood apart from the rest.

Tsuneshichi burst into that isolated cottage. The moonlight, coming through the window which let out smoke from the sunken hearth below, revealed the figures of five women. To his surprise, the best-looking one, who was also the oldest, was beside herself and the other four were trying to pacify her. The woman shook her hair loose; convulsions seized her arms and legs; she did not even try to dry the greasy sweat flowing into her eyes. It was obvious that she was in a trance.

These women were all the daughters of peasants in the country outside Kyoto. Owing to the failure of crops for two successive years, between forty and fifty thousand people had died of starvation in the capital city. The daughters of poor peasants became prostitutes in order to save their parents from famine.

The five women were the daughters of peasants who lived near the manor of Tsuneshichi's master. Tsuneshichi had brought these women, entrusted by their parents, to the capital. He soon became friendly with the most beautiful one of the five and never failed to communicate with her every day.

There were over two hundred of these newly made prostitutes who had come from various places to Kyoto. When the Taira troops departed on their campaign against the Kiso forces, these women had also started their march in the rain—it was during the rainy season—carrying their own food on their backs and casting their hopes over the sky of the northern country. Among them were the five girls entrusted to Tsuneshichi.

At the night battle of Kurikara Valley, these women were all at the Taira troops' quarters. Many of them, caught among the fleeing warriors, fell into the pitch-dark ravine and died. Fortunately, these five had survived, and after that night, Tsuneshichi had taken special care of them.

On the day of the battle of Shinohara, as Tsuneshichi was leaving the older woman just before sunrise, they had exchanged these words:

"Whether we win or lose our battle," Tsuneshichi had said, "let us return to Kyoto eventually. Then I will marry you without fail."

"That's what I've understood from the beginning. After all, I followed you, and I have survived only to endure all sorts of misery. But can everything go that well?"

Now, the same woman was bawling and squalling, her vacant eyes wide open, her mouth foaming.

"Oh, how disgusting!" she raged, "What a fool I am! Why did I come to a place like this? What a terrible mistake! Can I trust Tsuneshichi? I doubt it! I'm full of uncertainties. I hear his master is an excellent man, but I'm afraid he may be deceived by Tsuneshichi. I must see the master in person and by all means ask for his help so that Tsuneshichi may become an honest man."

The spirit who had possessed her had seen into Tsuneshichi's mind and exposed it. Feeling both shame and horror, Tsuneshichi jumped up and disappeared.

The woman's eyes were still half open, but she soon closed them, joined her hands and bowed her head reverentially. Her movements became much calmer. She spoke.

"My goodness! Are you Tsuneshichi's master, sir? You were gracious enough to appear as soon as I spoke your name. I don't know how to thank you. Please see to it that your humble servants may make a living. I will follow your words without fail."

Nodding repeatedly, she now spoke in a much lower voice, as if engaged in a conversation with her shadowy companion. Suddenly an expression of disappointment appeared on her face, and the movement of her lips stopped.

She looked exhausted, but after a while she opened her eyes and looked around her. The other four women, too, had been straining their ears, half absentmindedly. Now they took a deep breath for the first time. They told her that Tsuneshichi had come earlier but had run away. She became angry and said, "Oh, is that so, then? How cruel of him to have burst out without a word to me!"

The four women told her what the invisible Noritsune had spoken through her. It was something like this: that he was captured and decapitated in the early evening of that day; that he would like to let his wife in Kyoto know of his death; that his cheek was injured at the time of decapitation; and that he would like his wife to pray so that the wounds in his neck and cheek might be removed.

The woman finally came to herself and said,

"I must have been talking like one in a delirium. Now that I've heard what you've just told me, I feel I understand. But there is something rather strange. When the figure of the master became faintly visible, he showed me a piece of white paper in his right hand and tried to tell me a number of things, but I could not hear him well. He sounded full of arguments. I still don't know what he would like me to do."

There was nothing she could do, since Noritsune, whom she had trusted, was dead. There was no alternative but to rely on Tsuneshichi again, who was still alive. Without listening to her four companions' remonstrances, the woman ran into the dark pine forest. She searched like one mad, in the bushes and among the sand dunes, but Tsuneshichi was nowhere to be found, and the strain of hunting in the darkness became too much for her.

Exhausted, she returned to the cottage. Her distrust of her lover exploded, and she wreaked her anger on her female companions.

After a while, the five women lay down. An unspeakable fear was growing in them. They huddled close together, held each other's hands, and closed their eyes.

The older woman could not sleep. Two great anxieties occupied her mind. The first was whom to rely on during the present retreat following the disaster. The second was whether or not, under the circumstances, she could return home safely.

A man named Kojirō, a year younger than she, now came to her mind. He was a young fellow who since boyhood had been brought up by an old, low-ranking officer of Noritsune's manor. Since she had from time to time brought products from the farm to the manor house, she had spoken to Kojirō. She liked his gentle nature. He seemed to find her beauty and her sisterly manner appealing. Before very long, their relationship developed to the point that they had secretly promised to marry in the near future.

The woman was pleased with Kojirō's gentle disposition, but at the same time, she often found him rather unexciting. Then the time came for Kojirō to follow his master to the battlefield, and the woman saw the young man off in tears.

At the battle of Shinohara, Kojirō had received an arrow wound in his left side and was unable to follow his master's horse when his master was captured and beheaded.

The other four women seemed to fall asleep. The figure of sturdy

Tsuneshichi disappeared from in front of the woman's eyes, and in its place appeared thin Kojirō. She went outside, impatient for dawn.

With the smoke from the cooking fire as a guide, she walked, wandering in the pine forest, until it became lighter. The survivors of the previous day's melee were crouching for shelter, each according to his inclination. Even young men looked suddenly aged. The dried, cooked rice which they'd carried in bags tied to their waists they now soaked in hot water, and they sipped the food like children.

Fortunately, Kojirō was alive. The woman wept aloud. When she learned that his wound was unexpectedly shallow and his strength undiminished, she was overjoyed.

The woman told Kojirō as fully as she could about the mysterious event of the previous night.

"Please let the master's wife know the circumstances of his death," entreated the woman, and, taking Kojirō's hand, she dropped tears onto his knees. "When we return to Kyoto, I will definitely do what we have promised before. Please forgive me."

Kojirō nodded vigorously and rubbed his eyes.

In a short while, the morning sun appeared like a fireball, and the retreat began. One after another, the soldiers discarded their suits of armor. The pain caused by the shoulder straps of the armor was unbearable to the exhausted soldiers, to say nothing of the intense heat beneath their under-robes. Even luxurious suits of armor with intricate woven patterns, even armor made of white leather or silk, were abandoned like old straw coats.

The men whose duty it was to carry provisions were especially miserable. When they went over a narrow mountain path, they were helpless against the soldiers who attacked and killed them. The horses, too, understood the defeat and limped on without neighing. The women regained their courage and walked barefoot when they learned that they would reach Kyoto in three days.

When the survivors of the defeated troops finally came again to the Ushinoya Pass, on the border between the provinces of Echizen and Kaga, they saw anew the geographical advantage of the place. In order to ensure their safe and orderly retreat, and to be ready to engage in a counterattack if a chance should arise, the Taira troops set up layers of wooden fences and laid abatis along the path. Then the exhausted soldiers felt perfectly at rest and fell into a deep sleep.

The enemy, however, had shrewdly kept track of the Taira troops' movements, and late on this moonless night, they launched a surprise attack. This time it was not torches on bulls' horns but burning arrows that assaulted the Taira troops.[1] The blazing flames revealed the locations of the soldiers and at the same time burned the wooden fences and abatis the Taira troops had built.

Here it was not at all like the battle of Mt. Tonami. This time the soldiers knew their way, since they had walked the same road by daylight. They ducked the shower of burning arrows and ran down the steep slope in a large body.

The enemy had planted many archers along the mountain path. Suddenly there rose the fierce sound of arrows singing through the air, and moans reverberated in the valley. Gradually all became quiet, and the sky lighter. Kojirō, who had wrapped his wound with a piece of cloth and joined the counterattack forces, was dead. He must have fought bravely, for there were five arrow wounds on his body.

The woman wept. She grieved over his misfortune and felt a deep sense of loneliness enfolding her. It had been only the previous day that she had made a definite promise to marry Kojirō, and she had revealed the secret to no one. If she had foreseen his fate, she would have boasted of him to all her companions and thus have felt less desolate. Her regret was great, but there was nothing she could do now.

The survivors of the defeated troops gave up their counterattack and retreated into the province of Echizen under the hot sun. From the Tochinoki Pass they took the Hokkoku roadway. Then they proceeded south along the shore of Lake Biwa and finally arrived in Kyoto in the first part of June.

The news of defeat had already reached the capital city, so that

1. In the night battle of Mt. Tonami, which had taken place earlier on May 11, the Taira troops were defeated because they were attacked by 600 bulls who carried burning torches on their horns. In the present battle described here, the enemy attached oil-soaked cotton to the points of arrows, ignited the cotton, and shot the burning arrows. (NT)

the townspeople stood silent, as if receiving a funeral procession. Two months before, one hundred thousand young warriors, full of courage, had left the city. Now they returned as ruined men, their minds and bodies hollow. Their number was short of twenty thousand.

Their return deepened the sorrow of the people of the capital. The deaths of husbands, sons, or brothers were confirmed, now that witnesses had gathered in large numbers. Everywhere one went in the city, one could hear sobbing voices or the sound of temple gongs struck for the repose of the dead. The imperial court ordered Mt. Hiei to offer a prayer to expel the Kiso forces. But the prayer did not seem efficacious.

Of the five women, four barely managed to return to their respective homes in Matsugasaki, outside Kyoto. They told their parents that the older, beautiful woman became intimate with a middle-aged provision-bearer and that one night they had run away by themselves.

The late Noritsune's residence was at Hachijō Horikawa in the capital. His wife spent uneasy days in the family chapel, reading parts of the three volumes of the Jōdo sutra that Noritsune had finished copying just before his departure for the recent northern campaign. Confirmation of the death of men who were decapitated by the enemy was often difficult; the difficulty was especially great if a soldier met his death alone.

On the evening following the return of the defeated soldiers, Noritsune's wife was reciting the Amitabha volume of the Jōdo sutra. The older of her two sons, who sat on the floor next to her, listening, suddenly stood up and went down to the garden. He picked one of the lotus flowers blooming in the pond and, returning quickly, tried to place it in a vase.

As his mother watched him, full of doubt, the petals of the cut flower flew about and gathered on her sleeves and on her long hair. The son, sitting down again, held the flower stem tightly, but the sleeves of his hunting costume began to sway violently back and forth. Next, his body, still seated, floated high in the air and then came down on the wooden floor. As he stopped swaying, his face turned pale, and he began to mutter rapidly in a low voice. His tone was that of a complete stranger. His voice was clear.

"I am Kojirō, a servant of the master of this place. Unfortunately I am no longer of this world. I report to the lady that the master died in the early evening of May 21 in Shinohara. He especially regretted that he could not die in the way he had hoped before his death. He also left a message for his wife, asking for her prayers so that he might attain salvation even though his body was maimed.

"There is one thing more. I understand that he held something like a piece of writing and spoke at length, but I don't know what he meant at all. I must hurry. Good-bye."

The rigidity of the son's body gradually diminished, and he returned to his normal self. Even though they had more or less anticipated the report of Noritsune's death, his wife and sons became so heartbroken that their tears stopped flowing. Gradually their despondency turned to resignation.

No one but the wife knew about the piece of writing. For generations, Noritsune's family had provided chief officers for the household affairs of the Konoe family. Consequently, according to the custom of the period, Noritsune's family had designated the Konoe family as nominal lords of the land and property which Noritsune's family actually owned. When, later, Noritsune's family became followers of the Taira family, they transferred, for the sake of convenience, the nominal lordship from the Konoe family to the closely related Taira family. Realizing that the Taira family was doomed, Noritsune had told his wife, before he left for the battlefield, to return the nominal lordship to the Konoe family, according to his ancestors' tradition.

Noritsune's wife shed fresh tears when she realized that her husband had taken minute care of family affairs, looking beyond his death. From that time on, she spent her days devoting herself solely to prayer.

The day of Noritsune's forty-ninth day ritual[2] happened to be during the week of the Bon Festival.[3] The family altar was purified, flowers and incense offered. It was a quiet evening, with a cool breeze blowing. The wife, who was small in stature, had been recit-

---

2. A ritual performed on the forty-ninth day after a person's death, the day death occurs being counted as the first. (NT)

3. The Buddhist All Souls Day, the thirteenth of July. (NT)

ing the Buddhist sutra for some time. She had had her hair cut and let down;[4] over her white robe with a blue lining, she wore a yellowish-brown cope called *gojōgesa*.

In the rising smoke of the incense, Noritsune appeared to his wife for the first time. It might have been exactly the hour of his death on the battlefield. Instead of his armor in varied shades of purple, he now wore a white robe like a priest's, with wide sleeves. Behind his head hung a pale-golden mist.

The look on his face was peaceful. The sword-wound on his right cheek was gone. Joining his hands, he spoke in a thin voice which sounded as if it emanated from the other world.

"I would have liked to see you immediately after my death in battle, but I did not wish to show the scar on my cheek. For that reason, it took a great deal of trouble to convey my message to you. Please forgive me for having taken, against my wish, such a long time. Thanks to your prayer, I hope I will eventually be able to enter the Pure Land. I believe that Buddha saw the circumstances of my death. I shall be watching over all of you."

The wife looked intently and saw, close behind her husband, several white, half-transparent men. They were probably her husband's retainers who had died with him at Shinohara and who had since been under his protection. One of them looked like Kojirō. Noritsune's figure gradually faded away until it mingled with the quivering smoke of the incense.

On July 25, in the second year of Juei era, the surviving members of the Taira family and their followers fled from the capital city toward the western sea. Shortly afterward, the fifty thousand Kiso troops invaded the capital and engaged in destruction and plunder. Fortunately, Noritsune's family escaped the calamity. Half a year later, the Kiso forces dissolved.

In the spring of the following year, the Taira family sank to the bottom of the sea and perished. Consequently, the relationship between Noritsune's family and the Taira family was automatically terminated. The past traditions of Noritsune's family were restored and passed on to his sons.

4. She had renounced the world, but according to the custom of the period, she did not shave her head. (NT)

The Message

In a corner of the ancient battlefield of Shinohara, there was once an exceptionally large pine tree. According to legend, it was on one of the branches of this tree that Noritsune had tried to hang himself. From the spot where it stood, one can see the low, dark surface of the Shibayama inlet. At the foot of the pine tree there used to be a small, moss-covered five-stone monument. The local people called it the nun's monument. It is said that it bore an inscription to the effect that it was erected by Noritsune's wife, who became a nun. Neither the pine nor the monument has left a trace.

THE CAMELLIA MANSION

The rain which had started in the morning was still falling. The lattice windows were all closed. Only one of the sliding doors on the east side was slightly open, but the weather was not cold. Near the door stood a large white plum tree, its blossoms a little past their prime, though just now one could not see them. There was only the fragrance of the blossoms in the darkness of the night.

Suenaga, a nobleman, a middle-ranking official in the Ministry of *Shikibu*[1] and also a *kurōdo*,[2] was leaning against his low desk in the east building. He was reading a long letter from his maternal uncle, Nakanori, the governor of the province of Awa—reading as if he were enjoying a book of fiction. It was Nakanori's second letter from his new post, much longer than his first, probably because he was now more familiar with the area. Suenaga again poked the wick of the candle.

The estate at the corner of Shijō and Mate no kōji streets did not belong to Suenaga. He was still dependent on his father, who was growing old but held on to his position of *shōnagon*,[3] keeping up with the other noblemen of the Imperial Palace who had higher family status.

Suenaga occasionally raised his head and tried to imagine his uncle's slender figure and the surrounding scenery of the southern region. The letter, written in Chinese, said something like this:

"It is already more than a month since I arrived here. I hope you are in excellent health. I too am in good health, and have become

1. The Ministry of *Shikibu* was in charge of rituals, ceremonies, and the civil service. Normally, the head of the Ministry was chosen from the Imperial family or the relatives of the Imperial family. In the original, Suenaga's rank is identified as *shōyū*, a middle-ranking position in the ministry. (NT)

2. A *kurōdo* was an official serving in the office called *kurōdo dokoro*, the office in charge of matters related to the Imperial household. (NT)

3. A middle-ranking official, approximately of the same rank as *shōyū* (see footnote 1), but in a different category. (NT)

familiar with the locality. I have gained a general understanding of the office of governor and the administration of the province. Here the sun is comfortably warm, the wind gentle. The rape-blossoms are in full bloom. I am reminded of the words that my late father, Koremori, the governor of Shinano province, often spoke, while he was still living.

"As you probably know, my father was unfortunately involved in the civil war during the winter of the first year of the Heiji era, and had to spend his days as an exile here. My mother remained in Kyoto and received several letters from him. I understand that in the letters there were no complaints of an exile's hardships, but only poems singing the views of the south sea.

"The fact deeply impressed my young heart. Even though Awa is not a large province, I decided to take my new appointment gladly, since it would fulfill my desire to visit a place dear to my deceased father's heart."

Suenaga could well understand that this middle-aged lover of literature had been excited in his quiet expectations. As he continued to read his uncle's letter, Suenaga felt as if he were receiving some mysterious revelation.

"About one and a quarter miles east of my official residence is a bay called Kagami ga ura. The waves are calm and the surface of the sea looks as if the blue-green sky is melting directly into the water. Imagine Lake Biwa[4] and you have the right idea. Off shore there are two small islands next to each other. They look like Chikubu Island and Oki Island.[5]

"It was a fine day yesterday. I hired a boatman and, as an experiment, went over to the western island. I was surprised when I landed. The entire island was covered with tall camellia trees, the camellias now in full bloom. I cannot find words to describe their beauty.

"I was surprised again when I reached the highest point of the island. I discovered a stone image of Buddha, its height about two-thirds that of an adult. It was the image of Sarasvati[6] with the eyes half closed, quietly holding a lute in his arms.

4. The largest lake in Japan. (NT)
5. These islands are both on Lake Biwa. (NT)
6. The god of poetry, music, and good fortune, called *Bensaiten* in Japanese. (NT)

"One could guess the age of this stone image from its hands and feet, draped with white moss. The sea and the sky were bright, the woods dark, and the flowers red. It seemed as if the strings of the lute might any moment begin vibrating with sound."

Suenaga held his breath, feeling an unusual excitement, and closed his eyes. Then he resumed his reading.

"In the boat on my way back, I learned from the boatman that this island's Sarasvati is a divided spirit of the Sarasvati of Chikubu Island.[7] It was enshrined by the Reverend Sokaku, the ancient priest of the Nago Temple, who was well known for his extraordinary virtue. The big roofs of the Nago Temple's main hall and its three-story pagoda rise up from the mid-slope of the mountain on the mainland, directly east of this island. The temple is very much like the Chōmeiji Temple on the eastern shore of Lake Biwa.

"Many years ago, in the autumn, the shrine was blown away by a strong west wind. Since then, so I've heard, the image of Sarasvati has been standing out in the wind and dampness.

"Now I am back in my official residence, but that Sarasvati has never been absent from my mind's eye. To me it looks like the most beautiful thing in the world. I feel that I will have perfectly enjoyable days from now on."

Suenaga was usually a calm man, but when he finished reading his uncle's letter, his heart was beating hotly. Yet he felt happy.

The sound of the rain is diminishing.

When Suenaga, lying down, noticed this thought in the back of his mind, he felt so tired that he almost lost consciousness. He had even forgotten that he had gone to bed.

Suenaga felt well in the bright sunshine the following morning. He felt that his uncle's letter was too precious to be kept in his mind alone.

"Toshisuke," he called, "I have something to show you." Toshisuke was younger than Suenaga and served Suenaga's family as chief officer for household affairs. Suenaga and Toshisuke had both been wet-nursed by Toshisuke's mother, since Suenaga's mother had died shortly after he was born.

---

7. The spirit of the Sarasvati of Chikubu Island has been separated into two parts, one of which now occupies the new image. (NT)

Toshisuke had been on duty the night before. He appeared, straightening out the high collar of his plain, light-blue ceremonial hunting costume. Without words, Suenaga handed the letter to Toshisuke.

"Ah, is it yesterday's letter from Awa?"

"Yes. Sit down and read it right here. It's interesting."

As Toshisuke, without reserve, sat at the low desk across from Suenaga and began to read, Suenaga followed the movements of Toshisuke's features eagerly. Toshisuke went through the letter at a stretch, put it back in the envelope and straightened up. Suenaga could hardly wait.

"Isn't it tremendous? What do you think?"

Toshisuke answered with complete unconcern, as if to dismiss the subject, "It could be that the image is beautiful, but there's a world of difference between a stone image and a human being."

Suenaga was slightly angered. "Do you mean to say that nothing but a human being would interest you?"

Toshisuke's light smile held a touch of criticism. "My young lord, haven't you heard of the Camellia Mansion?"

Suenaga nodded coldly.

"My lord is the stone image of Buddha—the stone image of Buddha without ears. The front garden of the Minister of the Middle[8] is a camellia forest. But more important is the princess, his daughter. The courtiers of the Imperial Palace call her Princess Camellia. I hear that she will receive no letters from anyone."

"Is that so? I did not know that. What a majestic lady! I suppose she wishes to become the wife of a minister."

"She may—or she may not." He glanced at his lord. "I hear that she wants for her husband a man whose tastes are exactly like hers in every way."

"Toshisuke, you are really a mysterious man!"

But there was nothing mysterious about it, though the servant's words were polite and devious. Each time Toshisuke accompanied

8. In Japanese, *Naidaijin*, sometimes translated as "the Minister of the Center." The position was immediately below the Minister of the Left (*Sadaijin*) and the Minister of the Right (*Udaijin*), who were the highest officials under the Emperor. Toshisuke is of course covertly suggesting the real reason for Suenaga's interest in the letter—his interest in the princess. (NT)

Suenaga's father to the Imperial Palace, he would meet one of the attendants of the Minister of the Middle. A glib talker, this man was always glad to gossip. His name was Sadamoto. He had an aunt who was known as Emon.[9] This elderly woman was a maid of the daughter of the Minister of the Middle. Most of what went on in the princess's mind was conveyed to Sadamoto through this connection.

Toshisuke gave the explanation, smiling proudly. Suenaga's expression became serious. In his mind, he contiued to paint a picture of the idol of Sarasvati on the camellia island in the bay of Kagami ga ura in the southern province, transformed into a human being.

From the next day on, a new world opened for Suenaga, a world that lay behind him and yet seemed to be tied directly to his heart. But he could not find its entrance. He felt impatient. The dream-filled words which came out of his mouth were constantly passed along to Toshisuke in their conversations. Toshisuke easily fathomed and caught at his young master's wishes, which were then relayed to Sadamoto with a few slight changes in content and tone. Suenaga's thoughts flowed on from Sadamoto to his elderly aunt Emon. At the same time, of course, everything about Suenaga's daily life was scrutinized and distilled, until a sharp outline of his personality was shaped in the minds of the two attendants.

Toshisuke and Sadamoto, leaning against a stand on which rested the shafts of an ox-drawn carriage, laughed loudly together, like good friends, drank the *sake* they had secretly brought with them, and patted each other on the shoulder.

"You and I are now important middle men. Let's set to work and play matchmakers to the young lord and the princess. Judging by our information, they would make the best possible couple. After that, let us ask the lord and the princess to find wives for us!"

At the present time, Suenaga was busy. His duties involved both service as *kurōdo*, a clerk of the Imperial court, and as a young bureaucrat in the Ministry of *Shikibu*. In the latter office, he was being worked to death with the preparations for the Aoi Festival[10] of Kamo, which would be celebrated in a month.

9. In this period, women were not identified by their given names but by the positions their fathers or grandfathers held. Here, the father or grandfather of Sadamoto's aunt was an *Emon*, an official of the City Guard Unit. (NT)

10. The most important and the most elaborate festival of medieval Kyoto, held in the

In truth, however, Suenaga did once visit the residence of the Minister of the Middle, taking time away from his heavy load of work. It appeared that the plans made by Toshisuke and Sadamoto over *sake* had come to fruition through Sadamoto's aunt Emon. In a detailed letter to his uncle in Awa, Suenaga immediately reported the result of his visit.

After the visit, Suenaga's face became more luminous than before. He also began to talk frankly to his stepmother, with the result that she would look intently after him as he left for his office in the Imperial Palace.

It had become hot and humid; it was the time for women to change their winter clothes to summer ones. On one of these days, Suenaga's day off, he was working hard on a poem. He had recently become enthusiastic about writing poetry. He was trying to compose a poem about the evening dusk gathering in his front garden, when an old man brought him a thick letter and left. The old man was the chief officer for household affairs of Suenaga's uncle Nakanori and looked after his master's residence in Kyoto in his absence. Suenaga immediately unfolded the envelope.

"I am glad that you are well and busy," the letter began. "Thank you for your letter. I was most pleased with it, for I had never before received such a long one from you.

"I love the unreal camellia god, and you love the real Camellia Princess. How wonderful! There is a tremendous difference between myself, a widower, and yourself, a man of great future.

"According to your letter, the lady loves you, and you would like to receive her as your wife. So far, so good.

"However, when both parties are great personages, the outcome can be unfortunate if they do not agree in every respect. You must not hurry. You ought to know how to exercise your passion and reason properly. You are learned and she is wise. In this regard alone, nothing is missing.

"Now, around the provincial government office, there are some imperial estates and other pieces of land which have belonged to the Ise Shrine for generations. In the rest of the area, however, there is

---

Fourth Month of the lunar calendar (now on the fifteenth of May), in commemoration of the two Shinto shrines—Kami Kamo and Shimo Kamo. The festival was attended by everyone— from the Emperor down to the humblest citizens. The people of medieval Kyoto were said to live for this annual festivity. (NT)

far more wasteland than I had imagined. Following the directive sent from Kamakura several years ago, the land reclamation work has progressed greatly, carried out by laborers who were formerly warriors, men who lost their properties and lords at the battle of the western sea. This work, of course, has nothing to do with the provincial government office. The natives here tend to neglect agriculture and prefer fishing, which generally gives them a better return in proportion to their labor.[11]

"To the northeast of the Bay of Kagami ga ura there is still much swampland. My servants, who accompanied me from Kyoto, are diligently working on its reclamation. I wish to choose for my burial place this land with its beautiful scenery. I feel sorry for you, there in the city. It seems that the stagnant air of the ancient capital does not agree with me. Recently I have been feeling better than ever before, probably because the climate is right for me.

"I have come to the conclusion that I wish to be another Yoshishige Yasutane[12] in the remaining year of my life. His book, *The Record of the Arbor in the Pond*, gives me immense pleasure.

"On the island I have made a new shrine for the idol of Sarasvati to live in. It is a small place, but it will protect the god's skin from the sea spray.

"I do think much about your Camellia Princess. I'll be waiting for another letter from you. May I pray that you take good care of yourself."

It was a surprise to Suenaga that his good and respected uncle was planning to retreat forever into that far-away world. It made him feel lonely.

"From now on, I will walk alone," said Suenaga to himself, defiance and confidence arising together within him.

At last the day of the Aoi Festival came. It was the time when the year-long dreams of the people living in Kyoto would for just one day turn into reality. The sky was clear and the wind light. Added to the heat of mid-day, the warmth of the huge crowd made the air stuffy.

---

11. The reclamation work lies outside the jurisdiction of Governor Nakanori and the provincial government office. Nakanori's official concern is with the people of the province, to whom, as he explains, the reclamation work is not very important. (NT)

12. A medieval man of letters (A.D. 934?–97) who later renounced the world. *The Record of the Arbor in the Pond* (*Chitei no ki* in Japanese) is one of his well-known works. (NT)

The ox-drawn carriage of the Minister of the Middle, with its red and white silk ornament, stopped at the corner of Ichijō and Taka-kura streets. The Minister's wife and the elderly maid Emon took another look at the princess in her brand-new lined summer robe.

The procession was led first by the officials of the police department, the *Kebiishi Chō*, and those of the provincial government of Yamashiro.[13] Then came the imperial envoy in his splendid ceremonial court dress of starched silk, and the imperial messenger to the Kamo shrines, followed by a group of attendants clad in white, carrying large, plain, wooden Chinese-style chests with stands in which lay offerings to the shrines. Next were the officials of *kuraryō*.[14] For a moment the commotion stopped, as there came in sight the procession of the courtiers on horseback, who would play as accompanists for the performance of court music, the *gagaku*. The eyes of the women who, in their summer dresses, had gathered closely along the road, were all concentrated on this group of young courtiers.

The wife of the Minister of the Middle and her companion focused their eyes on only one man in the procession. Emon turned happily and proudly, and the two women nodded emphatically at one another.

"No matter where you look, there is no one like Master Suenaga!" said Emon.

At the end came the well-known flower-hat procession of the low-ranking *hōben* of the *Kebiishi Chō*. On this day only, these ex-convicts turned policemen were allowed to put lipstick and powder on their faces and to wear large bamboo hats decorated with artificial flowers of the four seasons—roses, peonies, rhododendrons, irises, and hibiscus. When the men wearing these large hats passed by, the crowd greeted them with shouts of joy. At that moment these townspeople's dreams were coming into bloom. But the three women did not move their heads.

On the same night, a poem from the princess was delivered to the exhausted Suenaga. The foreword read: "Thinking of your figure as seen among the bright green leaves." Toshisuke looked over his master's shoulder and said, "Just like her! She knows where to strike, eh? Lord Buddha, what a lady!"

13. Kyoto was in the province of Yamashiro. (NT)
14. The office in charge of the storage of the imperial treasures. (NT)

Though Toshisuke urged him to send his poem of reply, Suenaga did not, partly because he felt bashful, but also because he was reluctant to sell his heart cheaply.

Alas, his act could be interpreted as a disregard for the other party's sincerity, though in his inexperience he did not realize this fact. But at any rate, the princess's offensive was to continue.

A few days later, the deputy chief officer for household affairs of the Minister of the Middle brought a letter from the princess. Suenaga's stepmother sent the messenger away with a generous gift. Suenaga's eyes were drawn to the dignified yet elegant flow of writing in India ink on the thick Michinoku writing paper.[15]

"The west building in which I live has grown too small, and the work of enlarging it has recently begun. I would like to borrow a young man from your household to help rearrange my rooms."

There was no poem attached to the letter, but a slightly dried, two-leaf hollyhock was enclosed. It probably came from the hollyhock plant she had tied to the bamboo screen that hung in her room on the day of the Aoi[16] Festival.

Suenaga idly repeated the word *auhi* or "hollyhock" in his mouth until his tongue moved to say, "a-u-hi" or "the day of meeting."[17]

He immediately wrote a letter of consent.

On the following day, Toshisuke went to the residence of the Minister of the Middle and returned late at night. He held many gifts in his arms and seemed unable to stop laughing.

"My young lord, it was quite a structure! One could almost call it building a new house."

"Is that so? In that case, most would-be bridegrooms could not compete."

"Well," replied Toshisuke, "I seemed to smell a desire to receive you as the chosen one floating in the air. The Minister of the Middle is a descendant of the imperial family and won his present power on

15. Semitransparent paper with smooth surface, used mainly by men. Often this kind of paper was used for copying the Buddhist scriptures. The princess's use of this particular kind of paper shows her to be a woman of forceful personality. (NT)

16. *Aoi* means hollyhock. (NT)

17. A play on words. The word *aoi*, meaning the hollyhock, was pronounced "auhi" in the medieval period depicted in this story. The same word *a-u-hi* (each syllable more distinctly pronounced than *auhi*) also means the day of meeting. (NT)

his own merits. It seems fairly likely that he's looking for a young lord with similar qualities."

Suenaga hurriedly waved his hand back and forth.

"All right, I understand," said Toshisuke. "By the way, I saw a tremendous collection of books!"

Suenaga always felt challenged when he heard about someone else's book collection. He himself had a considerable number of books.

Two or three days later, at midnight, Suenaga groaned, thrusting aside his sleeved coverlet.

"Now I see. To call Toshisuke for help was part of the princess's campaign."

Suenaga opened the lattice window halfway to cool his head. It was the first day of the month and there was no moon. The trees in the front garden stood motionless, as if standing guard. Suenaga was still trying to put on a bold front.

But Toshisuke had been unable to stop laughing for a different reason. During their talk, Emon and Toshisuke had come to an agreement. If the nuptials of Suenaga and the princess should be held, Emon's niece, a white-complexioned girl, would be given in marriage to Toshisuke. Suenaga was of course ignorant of this fact.

In the morning, while Suenaga was getting ready to leave for the court, the poems from the princess arrived. Under the title, "According to the 'Song of Unending Sorrow,'"[18] there were two poems written on the thick writing paper called *hōsho shi*, deep-blue in color with an arabesque design of silver. Since that day, as it happened, Suenaga had urgent business to attend to, he got into his carriage without sending his poem in reply.

Suenaga left his office in the Imperial Palace early and went to Kangakuin,[19] where he borrowed a biography of Yōkihi[20] entitled *Yōtaishin Gaiden*, published in China. He read it through with un-

18. *Ch'ang hen ko* in Chinese or *Chōgon ka* in Japanese, composed by the Chinese poet Po Chu-yi (Hakkyoi or Hakurakuten in Japanese) (772–846). The poem is about the tragic love of the aged Emperor Hsuan Tsung (Gensō in Japanese) (685–762) for his beautiful young consort Yang Kuei-fei (Yōkihi in Japanese) (719–56). The translation follows the original in using the Japanese pronunciation for each name. (NT)

19. A private academy established in 821 by Fujiwara Fuyutsugu, the then Minister of the Left, originally for the offspring of the Fujiwara family. (NT)

20. See footnote 18 for the "Song of Unending Sorrow." (NT)

usual excitement. Picturing in his mind the Camellia Princess of the Minister of the Middle in Chinese costume, with a Chinese outer-robe and a long silk *hire* cloth fluttering in the breeze, Suenaga felt a strong desire to see her.

On the day when he was off duty, Suenaga performed his toilet with care. His high silk ceremonial *tate eboshi* hat, his pale, bluish-purple *nōshi* robe,[21] and his wide *hakama*[22] with the woven pattern of wisteria[23]—all fitted him perfectly. Toshisuke, who was helping Suenaga dress, uttered a cry of admiration, "My lord is a true lover!"

The rainy season had already begun. The mountains surrounding the city, tinged with a color like pale-black ink, were wet in a misty rain and looked as if they were melting away.

Suenaga's carriage proceeded west on one of the main streets, called Shichijō.

The expansion work on the estate of the Minister of the Middle in Nishi no Ōmiya was now almost complete. The princess's rooms had already been magnificently decorated. Toshisuke behaved himself as if he were in his master's own residence. Having been fore-warned of Suenaga's visit, the princess greeted him with delight. Her light-green robe with its purple lining was particularly beautiful and went well with Suenaga's robe. The princess's mother spoke in a friendly tone and frequently looked at Suenaga's fine figure as he stood in his flaring costume.

When Suenaga and the princess were alone, they talked and de-bated with remarkable frankness. From comparing the merits of the calligraphy of Lord Sukemasa and Lord Yukinari to comparing the poetry by Lady Murasaki and Lady Izumi,[24] their opinions were in perfect agreement. Recalling the words of his uncle in Awa, Suenaga was overjoyed.

He was not aware of the approaching dusk until a maid brought

21. An ordinary costume for noblemen. (NT)

22. A divided skirt worn mainly by men for formal occasions, but also worn by some women (e.g., Shinto priestesses) performing special ceremonies. (NT)

23. The original describes the pattern as a circle in which wisteria flowers and leaves are woven. (NT)

24. Lord Fujiwara Sukemasa (944–98) and Lord Fujiwara Yukinari (972–1027) were both famous calligraphers. Lady Izumi (c. 1003) and Lady Murasaki (978?–?) both were poets. Lady Murasaki is better known for her court novel, *The Tale of Genji* (see footnote 32). (NT)

in a candlestand. When he lifted his face, he saw a small portrait hanging on a bookcase by the wall. He drew closer. In the flickering candlelight, the portrait looked alive.

"Isn't this an unusual figure? She seems to be a noble court lady of China," Suenaga remarked.

Turning her flushed face proudly toward Suenaga, the princess smiled a little and said, "You're right. I understand that in the Imperial Palace there is a folding screen depicting 'The Song of Unending Sorrow.'[25] I asked my father to have the picture copied by an artist in the Art Division of the Imperial Palace."

It is true that Suenaga had known about the screen, but he had not taken an interest in it because the picture was old. The court lady of the small portrait in the princess's room had fine presence, with abundant black hair, plump cheeks, large nose and eyes, and shiny pupils. The Yōkihi that Suenaga had pictured in his mind was exactly like this one.

"I think this Yōkihi resembles you very much. Among the flowers, you are more like a camellia than a peony."

She smiled lightly and said, "Yes, I think so, too. I am very glad that we both have the same opinion. As for the camellia trees in our front garden, I asked my father to plant them."

"It seems to me that Yōkihi was a woman of much stronger spirit than you."

"So much the better. The Emperor of China especially loved her for that."

Suenaga began to fear that a knot was being formed in the silk thread which had tied the two hearts so perfectly.

"Since I am not Emperor Gensō, I'm afraid a Yōkihi might be too great a burden," thought Suenaga to himself.

After a carefully prepared feast, Suenaga got into his carriage, and the princess and her maids saw him off. When the doors of the outer gate closed with a grating sound, he felt as if the silk thread were cut.

The rain was coming down in earnest. Amidst the noise of the wheels, mingled with the sound of raindrops bouncing against the roofs, he imagined Yōkihi on the plank-bridge of Shoku,[26] her cere-

25. "The Song of Unending Sorrow" is a long poem about Yōkihi, composed by Hakurakuten. (NT)

26. In the rebellion of A.D. 755 led by An Lu-shan (called Anrokusan in Japanese, died

monial *jūni hitoe* robe wet with a long rain; then he pictured himself, in place of Emperor Gensō, listening to the bell of the imperial carriage.[27] The effect of the *sake* wearing off, Suenaga began to feel his chilled body. He forced himself to answer his own questions and to assume a defiant attitude.

"I am not a man to be completely intoxicated by anything," said Suenaga to himself.

Toshisuke walked beside Suenaga's carriage, drops of rain falling from his low *eboshi* hat[28] and from his plain hunting custome.[29]

The following morning, as Suenaga told the story of the previous night, Toshisuke frowned a little. Two or three days later, after accompanying Suenaga's father, the *shōnagon*, to the Imperial Palace, Toshisuke went to the residence of the Minister of the Middle and asked for Emon. She came, smiling.

"What did the princess have to say about my young master?" asked Toshisuke.

"Not only the princess but the lord and lady are praising him wholeheartedly," replied Emon.

Toshisuke felt very proud and said, "That's good news. I was wondering because my lord patted my shoulder and said to me jokingly, 'What would I be getting into if I married a princess who is like the strong-willed Chinese court lady?'"

Emon looked aghast for a moment but did not break off the conversation. Politely, she said, "Your case will surely go well."

She was referring, of course, to the question of Toshisuke's would-be wife. He was hoping that in the future Emon's niece would take Emon's place and become the chief lady in waiting for the princess when she was Suenaga's wife.

Suenaga's reported jest was by no means taken as a joke but was quickly conveyed from Toshisuke to Emon, from Emon to the prin-

---

757), Emperor Gensō and Yōkihi fled to Szechwan Province. But before they reached Shu ("Shoku" in Japanese) in Szechwan Province, Yōkihi was killed by the Emperor's soldiers. Thus Yōkihi could not have been in Shoku. In his intoxicated state, Suenaga imagines fictitious situations involving both Yōkihi and the Emperor at Shoku. (NT)

27. In the original, a carriage called *ren*, a two-wheeled, covered carriage pulled by men, used exclusively by the members of the imperial family and the ministers. (NT)

28. The top of a regular cremonial *eboshi* hat folded down, worn by a man of low social status. (NT)

29. A *hoi*, worn by a man of low social status. (NT)

cess, and further to the Minister of the Middle through his wife. Toshisuke, however, was in an ecstasy at Emon's reassurance.

When the rainy season was over, bright light and humid heat hung over the city. Women peddlers, wearing short, unlined dresses, carried baskets filled with vegetables on their heads to the east market. Under the shade of tall trees, peddler men set down their goods, which they carried on their backs, and spent the noon hour judging the women peddlers.

Toshisuke, running upon his own shortened shadow, was in a great hurry to return to his lord's residence on Mate no kōji. He had rushed out of the Imperial Palace, for he had urgent business about which to see Suenaga. His *eboshi* hat and his hunting costume drooped as if beaten down by a shower.

Suenaga, enjoying what little cool breeze there was in the summerhouse over the pond,[30] was surprised to see Toshisuke appear so suddenly, with sweat streaming down his face.

"My young lord, did you know that there's a reception today to celebrate completing the enlargement of the buildings at the estate of the Minister of the Middle? I don't remember receiving any invitation for you."

Suenaga made an effort to control the strong palpitations starting up in his heart. "Oh, is that so? I haven't seen my father since yesterday. At any rate, it is good that the work is completed."

Toshisuke opened his eyes wide in astonishment, but Suenaga was looking down at a little frog sitting on a rock in the pond, and continued to meditate quietly.

In the early evening, when it had grown somewhat cooler, Suenaga casually made ready to go out, put on his unlined, blue hunting costume, and got into his carriage. For the first time, he ordered Toshisuke to ride with him. Toshisuke looked intently at his master's quiet face.

There were no longer invited guests left on the spacious premises of the Minister of the Middle. In the princess's west building, the screens of various colors had been arranged, and the candlelight was especially bright. But in the main building, which was built of

30. A small structure (called *tsuridono* in Japanese) built over a pond in the garden of an estate and connected by a covered passageway to another building. The *tsuridono* was originally used for fishing. (NT)

fine quality timber, there was no decoration or furniture which would hint at receiving a bridegroom, and there were also only a few candlestands. Humiliated for the first time in his life, Suenaga felt as if there were pain in all of his joints. The princess greeted him with a faint smile, but she looked a little tired. Her light, thin silk robe was very becoming on her today.

Their talk in the flickering light of flower-patterned candles was not quite in perfect tune. Suenaga finally made up his mind to leave, for he felt as if they were both manipulating finger puppets. Their parting words became involuntarily formal.

Suenaga said, "The work on enlarging the buildings has been completed quickly and magnificently. Every part has been given due attention, and the main building is especially majestic. Its value will become even more apparent in the future."

"However, it is of no use if it is majestic only in appearance. The value of the main building should be decided according to its harmony with the west building," replied the princess.

Was it tears that made her eyes shine? Suenaga did not know which way to look, and turned his eyes beyond the door of the middle gate, which stood open.

Just then, with a squeaking of its wheels, an ox-drawn carriage appeared in the torchlight and went past. Because of the heat, the paper screen was removed from the viewing window of the carriage. Inside was the round face of the Minister of the Middle. His two eyes filled with hatred shot a piercing glance at Suenaga. Suenaga, too, with fierce defiance, concentrated his strength in his eyes.

Suenaga and Toshisuke sat with closed mouths in their carriage once it had left the outer gate of the Minister of the Middle. Time passed. The thorn of the eyes of the Minister of the Middle still remained stuck in Suenaga's heart.

"Toshisuke, I shall never go back to that house."

Such were the heavy words Suenaga let fall from his mouth. Toshisuke repeatedly put his hand to his face. Was he pursuing even now the sadly lost vision of his would-be wife?

The full moon was in the sky. Two days before, the city had been astir with the Gion festival,[31] but tonight there was no sound. Yet as

---

31. An annual festival commemorating the Yasaka Shrine of Kyoto, celebrated on the fourteenth and fifteenth days of June of the lunar calendar. (NT)

the night wore on, Suenaga could not sleep and frequently bit the neckband of his sleeved coverlet. With his heart tormented by regret and self-hatred, he could not remain in one position in the bed. As he lay with his eyes open, it grew lighter outside.

After breakfast, Suenaga wrote a long letter to his uncle in Awa. Only after he rested his writing brush did he feel relieved. Yet a deep sense of loneliness prevented his thoughts from moving forward. He absented himself from his work at the Imperial Palace.

From that time on, Suenaga spent his days in misery. Sometimes he was angry, sometimes sad, sometimes at a loss to understand himself. Toshisuke could no longer keep up with his master's swiftly changing moods. Yet at times Suenaga showed kindness to Toshisuke.

"Toshisuke, you have grown thin lately. Take care of yourself. Talk to me about your problems," Suenaga would say.

Toshisuke, feeling helpless, smiled a grim smile, though at the same time he felt grateful for his master's kindness.

After the first day of autumn, one could at last feel freshness in the air. A letter from Awa arrived as if riding the cool breeze. Suenaga received it, his whole body tense with expectation, and read it at a stretch.

"I read your letter," it began, "and was disappointed. In truth, after your last letter, I was happy to think that a Hikaru Genji and a princess Murasaki[32] might be possible in real life. In retrospect I see that you two were too flawless from the beginning. Even the most insignificant spot would make the finest sword imperfect. Perhaps, therefore, it might have been better if both of you had looked at each other from a little distance. I am truly sorry.

"It seems that the Camellia Princess of the Minister of the Middle fancies herself to be the Yōkihi of our nation, but isn't that a little dramatic? It could be that the princess's talent and learning have inevitably created such a fate for her.

"From now on, in order to divert ourselves, let us start exchanging our poems. Poetry is indeed good for you.

"As I told you in my previous letter, I have already proceeded to

---

32. Hikaru Genji is the hero of *The Tale of Genji*, a court novel written by Lady Murasaki (born about A.D. 978). Princess Murasaki, one of the most important female characters of the novel, becomes Hikaru Genji's wife. (NT)

reclaim the swamp. I dug a pond in the middle of the arable land and built an island in the pond with the soil which had been dug out. In the future I mean to transplant the camellia trees of the island in the bay onto this island's hill and to have an image of Sarasvati carved out of the island's rock, enshrining in it a divided spirit of the island's Sarasvati. As I plan to build a simple residence nearby, I am ordering my people to cut and dry those pine trees on the beach which are not crooked.

"During my governorship, I am trying to make my administration a success, following the example of Yoshishige Yasutane. I understand that he built a shrine of Amitabha Buddha on the middle island of the pond in his garden, but wouldn't my Sarasvati's shrine be far more elegant?

"It is encouraging to hear that the retainers and servants who followed me from the capital are all planning to make their homes here. You are a man of talent who should be active in the imperial court. I hope you will take care of yourself and will try to accomplish great things."

What was Suenaga to think, having his great problem so simply disposed of with a fine sword? Although his uncle claimed that he loved the quiet place, wasn't he escaping a violently agitating reality with which he could not cope? His motives seemed both sad and ingenuous.

At that time, inside the imperial court, the friction was daily growing more serious between the *Kampaku*, who was a descendant in the direct line of the Fujiwara family, and the Minister of the Middle, an able man of the Minamoto family which had descendants in the imperial line. Those who were close to either family did their best to protect their own positions.

The current of the last days of the year was sometimes fast, sometimes slow, expanding the ring of its dark eddies until it fell into the river of the new year.

The ritual of *shihō hai*[33] on New Year's Day, the Emperor's visits to the ex-Emperor and the Empress Dowager, the banquets[34] at the

33. The New Year's religious service at court, started about A.D. 885. The Emperor would stand in the east garden of the Imperial Palace and worship the deities and the ancestral spirits, praying for the nation's peace and a good harvest in the new year. (NT)

34. Every year the ceremonial New Year's banquets were held both at the Empress's palace

Empress's and at the Crown Prince's, the investiture ceremony on the fifth day of the New Year, the imperial viewing of the white horses on the seventh day—after all of these rituals had been performed according to tradition, the ritual of appointments of provincial officials, which drew everyone's attention, was held for three days, starting on the eleventh day. Contrary to his expectations, Suenaga was appointed deputy governor of Shimotsuke. It meant a transfer to the eastern regon. He was quite surprised.

While Suenaga's present position as *shōyū* in the ministry of *Shikibu* was in the second degree of the lower Fifth Rank,[35] the deputy governor of Shimotsuke, which was one of the major provinces, was in the second degree of the lower Sixth Rank. Thus, the new appointment was far from a promotion. It was obviously due to intrigue by the Minister of the Middle. Suenaga's heart was almost shattered to pieces by the force of his indignation. He had to comfort himself with the fact that he would be closer to Awa. His gentle father, who had been sickly of late, saw him off with a sad smile at the time of his departure. His stepmother wiped away tears.

Upon his arrival, Suenaga realized that even though it was closer to Awa, Shimotsuke was a completely different world. It was true that near the provincial capital, people gathered and there was some trading; but once one left the provincial government office, one saw virgin forests stretching into the distance, while the dreary wind of early spring blew wildly between heaven and earth.

The cultivated land from the previous era was not inevitably small in acreage. The land had been devastated by the battles of the western sea, which had lasted for years, but it had later been reclaimed by the Kamakura shogunate's decision. The *Shogun* had died in the previous year, but the organization of the administrative board, the *Mandokoro*, seemed intact. Suenaga could not help recognizing with regret the ineffectiveness of the provincial government. What disturbed him most was the provincial government officials' indifference to the existing facts.

---

and at the Crown Prince's. All the ministers would go first to the Empress's banquet and then to the Crown Prince's as a part of the New Year's rites. (NT)

35. Each numerical Rank (the First being the highest) was divided into two subranks (the upper and the lower). Each subrank was divided into two degrees (the first and the second, the first being higher) or three degrees (the first, second, and third, the first being the highest). (NT)

Immediately upon his arrival in Shimotsuke, Suenaga wrote a letter to his uncle Nakanori in Awa, but no answer came. He sent two more letters with the same result.

Near the Tanabata festival, a messenger finally arrived. The messenger was one of the men whom Nakanori had taken with him from Kyoto. Putting down a square piece of luggage which he carried on his back, the man produced a letter. It was from the brother of Nakanori's deceased wife. Suenaga's hand hurriedly unfolded the envelope. To his surprise, his uncle had died.

"My brother-in-law was very happy about your appointment to Shimotsuke and devoted himself to writing poetry," the letter began. "On the day of the vernal equinox, he went to the island to view the camellia blossoms. The weather was fine in the morning, but on the return trip, his boat was caught by a sudden west wind mixed with rain and almost sank. He caught cold, which developed into consumption.

"He read your letters many times and kept saying that, as he could not tell a lie, he would answer them when he was well, until the other day he vomited a large amount of blood and died. It was a quiet ending. Please accept the books of poetry which I am sending you in accordance with my brother-in-law's will.

"I have moved into the house which my brother-in-law had started to build, modeled after *The Record of the Arbor in the Pond* by Yasutane. But neither the transplanting of the camellia trees nor the enshrining of Sarasvati had taken place before his death.

"Since I work in the provincial government office, I wish to continue to cultivate the land here until I die. I hope that my brother-in-law will be pleased.

"He was a good man and very devout. For a long, long time he had set great hopes on your future. From now on, I would like to regard you as my older brother-in-law. Please continue your favor toward me."

Suenaga repeatedly covered his eyes with his hands. He gave the messenger a number of gifts, and also handed him a bag of copper coins as the man was leaving with Suenaga's letter to his new, younger brother-in-law.

"From now on, I will ask you to be the letter carrier," said Suenaga.

That night, Suenaga opened the books of poetry given to him. At the end of the "Song of Unending Sorrow" in the book called *Ha-kushi monjū*[36] was placed a bookmark. Copied on the bookmark were those famous lines,

In heaven we wish to be twin birds flying together;
On earth we wish to be twin branches united as one.[37]

A note had been added. "Isn't this the true desire of the Camellia Princess of our nation?"

Suenaga felt as if he could hear the pounding of his heart. Was his uncle right about what was in the princess's mind? Could it be that because of his shy, gentle nature, he had not been able to reveal it? And was it that because of his youth, Suenaga had read her mind too shallowly? Alas, it was too late to mend matters now!

Suenaga's strong will rebelled but then gradually turned to resignation. It came into his mind that sometime he would build a mountain villa in a corner of his fief in the eastern suburbs of Kyoto and would name it House Number Three, following his uncle's and Yasutane's in *The Record of the Arbor on the Pond*. Therefore, when he received the report of the sudden death of the Minister of the Middle in the following year, his emotions were not particularly stirred.

Several years later, the governor of Shimotsuke completed his term of office and returned to Kyoto. He recommended Suenaga to the *Kampaku* as his successor. Thus, Suenaga was promoted to a new post as governor. He felt a fatherly affection in the good, elderly man.

Eight years later, Suenaga returned to Kyoto, leaving his achievements behind him. The spring journey on the Tōkaidō roadway made his heart light. The capital's main street, on which he stepped after many years' absence, was hard and dry. The figures of officials squirming in the cramped government office buildings of the *Dai-dairi*,[38] which surrounded the Imperial Palace, were exactly the same as eight years earlier.

---

36. The *Anthology of Po Chu-i*. See footnote 18. (NT)

37. These are from the closing lines of the poem. The "twin birds" refer to an imaginary pair of male and female birds, each with one eye and one wing and always flying together. The "twin branches" refer to an imaginary pair of tree branches which are united with one continuous grain. (NT)

38. An area 736 meters by 698 meters, or 0.45 mile by 0.43 mile, the *Daidairi* housed the Imperial Palace (*Dairi*) and all the government buildings. (NT)

About the same time as Suenaga's return to Kyoto, the ex-*Kampaku* who had received the tonsure died. Suenaga was terribly disappointed, since he had been favorably inclined toward the ex-*Kampaku*, a graceful, upright, and scholarly man. Yet it was true that, with his death, one could predict the birth of a form of government more appropriate for the new era.

In the autumn ritual of appointments of Kyoto officials, Suenaga was made *tayū*[39] in the Ministry of *Skikibu*. The light began to shine on him. Ahead, the position of *Shikibukyō*,[40] in the upper Fourth Rank, was waiting for him. Toshisuke also was made *shōzoku*[41] in the Ministry of *Shikibu*.

Suenaga, however, had missed a chance to take a wife. Ever since he had been entangled with the Camellia Princess some years back, he had come to regard marriage as something extremely troublesome. He desired a life like his deceased uncle's rather than a life bound by a worthless family. Toshisuke had submitted himself to continuing as his master's persevering though reluctant companion.

Soon the new year came, and a new world was about to open for Suenaga. In February, he and his attendant went to worship at the Ōharano Shrine in Otokuni county on the day of the shrine's annual festival. The purpose of this excursion to the shrine, which housed Suenaga's ancestral god, was to pay a visit of thanks for Suenaga's return to the capital and for his promotion.

Mt. Oshio[42] rose up, unexpectedly high, dominating the surrounding hills. The plain stretching to the south, which was mostly flat, contained the ruins of the ancient capital of Nagaoka. Only the bush warbler's song was heard. There was not a human soul.

Just before dusk, the carriage in which the two men rode crossed the Katsura Bridge. The river waves were rippling into many folds, and tiny, broken drops of light spread against the river current.

Their carriage now entered Shichijō Avenue. In less than ten years, the number of middle-class homes had increased considerably. Some of them were built in the style called *buke zukuri*,[43] equipped with a riding ground. Suenaga suddenly uttered a loud cry.

---

39. In the second degree in the upper Fifth Rank. (NT)
40. *Shikibukyō* is the title of the head of the Ministry of *Shikibu*. See also footnote 1. (NT)
41. A low-ranking official—the second degree in the upper Eighth Rank. (NT)
42. The mountain which stands prominently behind the shrine. (NT)
43. *Buke zukuri* means the style of the warrior's house, which was smaller and more aus-

"Toshisuke, wasn't it here? You must have passed by many a time."

Toshisuke also raised himself halfway. "Yes, it was here. I remember it well, although new homes have been built."

In front of their carriage there soon appeared an old, large mansion.

"Look," said Suenaga, "that is the house of the Minister of the Middle. It looks just as it did."

"Yes," replied Toshisuke. "How magnificent those camellias are!"

They stopped the carriage beside the roofed outer walls of mud and plaster, and peeked inside through an opening where plaster had fallen. The front garden and the middle island in the pond were filled with camellia trees. They had grown considerably taller since that time in the past. The gathering dusk was softly colored by the camellias' crimson and pure white. The scene was beautiful and melancholy beyond description.

The main building, the east building, and the enlarged west building were all as they had been before, but every lattice window was closed. Two women were on the wooden porch of the west building. In the face of the noble lady could be discerned the strength and loneliness of one enduring a solitary life. Suenaga's lips trembled visibly.

"Look! She is the Yōkihi!" said Suenaga.

Toshisuke's arms and legs stiffened, but a smile was on his face.

"My lord, the other woman is Emon's niece!"

Suenaga followed the Yōkihi's eyes. On the middle island stood a particularly tall camellia tree in bloom. At its foot was an image of a god about two-thirds the height of an adult. The lady's lustrous eyes were focused on this stone god.

Toshisuke straightened his back.

"My lord, please write a note. I'll take it myself."

"No, Toshisuke. Don't disturb them. Let's go." Suenaga barely managed to say that much and closed his mouth.

The wheels made a noise. The lady's face moved for a moment but was calm again.

---

tere and more practical than the earlier and more elaborate style called *shinden zukuri*, in which the large estates of wealthy noblemen had been built. (NT)

Suenaga leaned his cheek against the handle on the side of the carriage, waiting for his heart's tumult to subside.

"Is she still living in the pride of the past," he wondered, "trying to become the god in the shrine herself?"

Suenaga could not help feeling pity and awe for the woman.

"Today, I, too, have come to pay a visit of thanks to a shrine for my promotion. Even though I take pride in being a newly-appointed official, I am just like her, unable to unlock the bolt of the past."

To discover their similarity in this respect was now pleasant and ironic and would eventually lead to resignation. But it was cheerful resignation.

Toshisuke, from that time on, paid close attention to his master's behavior. A few days passed. One morning, Suenaga, with a faint smile, handed him a letter. It was written in *kana*[44] on the *kamiya*[45] paper with the pattern of flowing water and cloud.

"Deliver this letter to the lady waiting on the Yōkihi," said Suenaga.

Toshisuke's heart throbbed. He cried and laughed.

About a month later, Suenaga, accompanied by Toshisuke, directed his ox-drawn carriage to Shichijō Avenue. One could not see inside the outer walls of the mansion because, almost unnoticeably, repair work had been done. Almost all the blossoms had fallen from the camellia trees which rose above the roofs, and the thick, new leaves created a clear effect of light and shade. The two men returned home without stopping.

On the following day, a message came from the Camellia Mansion. Emon's niece came, accompanied by a young maid. The solid darkness of the princess's writing on the *torinoko* paper[46] from Echizen was the same as before, but this time, the letter was scented with aloes-wood. The content was simple.

"A small home has been made for the god of Sarasvati on the camellia mountain of the middle island in the pond. I am convinced

---

44. *Kana*, as opposed to *kanji* or Chinese characters. The written Japanese consists of *kana* and *kanji*. The *kana* writing is more gentle and elegant. (NT)

45. The paper manufactured along the Kamiya River of Kyoto. Some of the *kamiya* paper has a pattern of flowing water and cloud as described here. This pattern was symbolic of Suenaga's present feeling. (NT)

46. Smooth, lustrous paper of fine quality. (NT)

that your honored uncle of Awa was a gentle person. Please pay your respects to the shrine once on behalf of your uncle."

Standing behind Suenaga, Toshisuke looked from the flow of written characters on the paper to his master's profile, until finally, unable to restrain himself, he turned his face toward Emon's niece and smiled.

ABOUT THE TRANSLATORS

Nobuko Tsukui was born in Tokyo, Japan,
on November 12, 1938.
She received her B.A. from Tsuda College
in Tokyo in 1961. In the same year
she came to the United States to pursue graduate study in English.
She received her M.A. (1964) and Ph.D. (1967)
from the University of Nebraska.
She is now an Associate Professor of English at
George Mason University in Fairfax, Virginia.

John Gardner is the author of such novels
as *Grendel, The Sunlight Dialogues, Nickel Mountain,*
and *October Light.*

Tengu Child

Designed by Rich Hendel
with illustrations by the author
Composed by G&S Typesetters
in Linotron Zapf International
Printed by Braun-Brumfield
on Warren's 1854 Cream Regular text stock
and bound in Crown Linen
Edited by Dan Seiters
Production supervised by John DeBacher